Lake Meade

To Marion,
I hope you enjoy
your visit to Lake Meade!

Your grape picking friend,

Heather ?

Lake Meade

BY HEATHER MOSKO

Oak Tree Press   Taylorville, IL

Oak Tree Press

Oak Tree Press books may be purchased for educational, business or sales promotional purposes. Contact Publisher for quantity discounts

First Edition, September 2008

10 9 8 7 6 5 4 3 2 1

Cover by MickADesign

Cover photograph from the collection of Mary Montague Sikes

ISBN 978-1-892343-31-4

Library of Congress 2008934028

Acknowledgements

I would like to acknowledge my entire family's unfailing support (and you know who you are; Evan, Will, Dad, Blanche, Dad, Margaret, Karen, John, Stephanie, Matt, Lucille, Tommy, Lynn, Vickie, Katie, Tom, Betty, Mike, Corey, Linda, George, David, Nancy, Barry, Stephanie, Kurt, Joan, Jerry, Gail, Cherie, Bret, Ellis, Jim, Mary, Peter, Steven, Dennis W., Annie, Dennis, Mrs. Dona-Grier, Gary and anyone else in my wonderful crazy extended family that I have mistakenly overlooked, you're all wonderful), my husband Mark's ability to talk me down from the edge whenever I get discouraged, my aunt Kate's editing skills (and sensitivity when correcting my many and numerous grammatical errors), and the first readers of *Lake Meade*; Laurie P., Sue L., Denise S., Christina M., Beth M., Kim M., Karen S., Ganna M. and Sue M. for their encouragement and insight.

And for the time I spent as a child on both their farms, I would also like to acknowledge my grandparents, Tom and Eileen McAvoy, and my aunt and uncle, Patty and Butch Weidenmayer, as it is their homes that inspired the setting for *Lake Meade* – and they remain two of my very favorite places on earth. Thank you Mom for your unconditional love, you are my angel.

To my husband Mark …

and sons Evan and William

CHAPTER ONE

Maggie ran her hand up the banister as she climbed the last few steps to the front porch, the residue from the old paint leaving chalky marks on her palm. She clapped her hands together to clean them off, the sharp sound cracking the air and breaking the enveloping quiet of the woods that sheltered the honeysuckle colored cottage.

A crooked smile played on Maggie's lips as her gaze washed over the worn wooden floor and eventually rested on the weather-beaten wicker porch swing hanging from the rafters, gently swaying in the breeze as if the ghosts of her childhood still sat in it, pushing off the planks with the ends of sandy pink toes. The swing had played many roles in her youth — home base, a ship adrift on the sea or a rescue pod sent from a far off planet.

A laugh bubbled up in her chest as Maggie remembered how she and Jack had spent hours creating whole new worlds while sitting in that unraveling swing on balmy summer days. Part of her wanted to sink down onto it's faded cushion and remember, but she didn't, it would have felt too much like an intrusion on the games of two spectral children forever playing make-believe. Instead, she gave the swing a push and heard the creaking of the rusty chains.

Her eyes traveled to the other side of the porch where a carved wooden rocking chair once sat, the smile faded from her lips. How could such a small space — this tiny front porch of a lakeside vacation cottage —

hold such contrasting memories? The joys of imaginative children at play, as well as the tragedy of watching her friend's father slip from that chair onto the splintery floor, clutching his chest and staring wide-eyed into the deep blue sky overhead; his wife screaming his name, his son panting next to Maggie, desperately clinging to her arm.

She closed her eyes and then a moment latter opened them again, looking down at the now empty dusty floorboards. There is no chair, no dying man, only the barren neglected porch. Jack's family left the day after his father died. Maggie never saw him again. That was over fifteen years ago now.

Jack's mother, Christine Callahan, had come back to the bucolic Maryland town sporadically over the years to check on the house and give Maggie money for its upkeep. Christine never spent more than a day or two in Lake Meade, just long enough to air the place out and take a walk down to the dock, staring unseeing out at the rippling water. Her children would not return to this place they associated with their father's death; refusing to remember it's where they had the best of him during his life.

Maggie let out a sigh at her own memories and opened the heavy oak front door, stepping across the threshold into a brightly painted robin's-egg blue foyer. Every month Maggie walked across the old road that separated her family's property from the Callahan's and checked on the house, making sure no animals had taken up residence, no leaks appeared or pipes froze in the wintertime.

During Maggie's bittersweet pilgrimage she walked through the rooms and heard the echo of the Callahan's boisterous family, her heart harboring a faint hope that it would again someday. Before she left the house she would give the kitchen counter a reassuring pat, like she would the shoulder of a lonely old grandmother, assuring her that all would be well and someday her family would come visit her again. *Patience, old girl.*

Her inspection complete, Maggie locked the front door behind her and started walking down the dirt lane towards her own home, a rambling old farmhouse she shared with her son and her grandfather. With the lake water lapping against the shore on her left and the ancient oaks and pines standing century on her right, Maggie made her way along the rutted path without looking down at her feet. She knew this land, this path, and walked it with an unconscious ease.

Maggie wondered idly if Christine would be coming to Lake Meade again soon. It had been over a year since her last visit. *When she does come,* Maggie thought, *I won't let her wander alone around the empty house.* A smile returned to her face as she imagined bringing Christine lunch, reminiscing, maybe Christine would tell Maggie what her children were doing now —

especially Jack.

Pleased at the image, Maggie's steps lightened and her mind inevitably turned to all of the chores she had to get done before Caleb came home from school and dinner was started. Always so much to do, well, she liked it that way, didn't she? Too much time to dawdle is time to think about things better left alone. Caleb's father, Jack's father, Jack, all those memories would get neatly folded and tucked away like the antique linens in her cupboards when she began her evening routine. Busy hands were her salvation. Busy hands.

CHAPTER TWO

Water soaked through Jack Callahan's shoes and dampened his socks as he walked across the wet grass towards the white tent sheltering the open gravesite. He noticed his sister Kathy, her husband and their three children were already huddled together in front of the casket. He felt conspicuously alone when he sat down on a flimsy white plastic chair next to them. Kathy reached out and gave his hand a reassuring squeeze. He looked over at her and then up at the minister who was readying himself to speak of the eternal bliss awaiting their mother, the cloying sweet scent of gardenias from the funeral wreaths enveloped and nauseated him.

Half an hour later he was functioning on autopilot as he performed the social niceties that had been engrained in him since boyhood. Jack shook hands and thanked people for coming, accepted their condolences. He had done all this almost sixteen years ago at his father's funeral too, remembering the numbing disbelief punctuated by moments of awkward civility and blinding pain. Both his parents were gone now. The bleak reality of that slammed into him at random intervals throughout the day and filled him up with a cold and numbing sadness that threatened to choke him.

Jack had stayed with his sister and her family at their home in Summit, New Jersey for the final days of his mother's life so he could be close to her in the hospital, and then for another week after her death as all the arrangements were made and services attended. At first he had been thankful for all the noise and distraction his niece and nephews provided in those first surreal days after his mother's death, but as he opened the door to his Manhattan apartment he had to admit, he felt grateful for the silence. All he wanted now was to sink into his leather club chair with a whiskey on the rocks and stare at the spectacular view of New York from his living room window that he paid for so dearly.

With a clatter Jack dropped his bags down on the polished bedroom floor, kicked off his shoes and walked back out to the kitchen to make a drink. His answering machine light was blinking furiously, and after pressing the pulsating button, a surly sounding electronic voice informed him he had twenty-three messages. He pressed the "play" button and settled down into his favorite chair. One sip of the whiskey from the heavy cut crystal glass and the smooth warmth of the single malt radiated from his throat down into his chest, his shoulders and neck relaxed as he leaned his head back against the overstuffed leather chair, closing his eyes and listening to the messages play.

The first was from Clarissa, a woman he had taken out to dinner the night before his sister called him with the news their mother had been hospitalized after suffering a stroke. "Jack? Jack are you there? I hope you're not screening your calls? I thought we had a great time the other night, why didn't you call me back? Why do you men fucking *never* call? I'll be around the rest of the night. If I don't hear from you I will assume you have officially blown me off!" Click. Beep.

"Jack," his assistant Linda's voice, "I know you're probably still at your sister's, but I just wanted you to know we're all thinking about you here and hope you're doing OK. I guess we'll see you on Monday. Take care and call if you need anything or just want to talk. Well, OK…see ya." Click. Beep.

Jack smiled at the sound of Linda's heavily accented Brooklyn bred voice, sincere with empathy, and deep and textured from years of yelling over the loud voices of her extended family. It was in distinct contrast with the message from Clarissa, whose smooth as silk tones had been cultivated with years of finishing schools — and left him cold.

He probably would have called Clarissa again for a second date, not expecting much to come of the relationship. It was just as well it ended this way. It would have ended eventually.

The next message began… "Jack, this is Philip Peterson," the partner at the architectural firm where Jack worked, "just calling to offer my condolences." He cleared his throat and there was a pause. "Hope we see you on Monday. I know this is the wrong time to mention it, but I wanted to remind you the preliminary plans are due for the Cornwell Museum Wing next week. So...anyway...hope you're doing all right. Tough time, I know, but you'll get through it. Work's the best thing. Keep busy." Click. Beep.

Jack swished the ice around in his drink and stared at the amber liquid swirling around the chunks of ice in his glass. "Work's the best thing," he repeated in a mimicking voice and then barked out a mirthless laugh. "Don't want to miss a friggin' deadline, do we, Phil? God forbid we have some kind of life that might interfere with our billable hours."

Jack downed the rest of his drink in one swallow and walked to the answering machine. Another message had started from a woman he went out with occasionally when she was in town on business. He stabbed at the "Forward" button several times then the "Erase." He knew there were no messages from anyone who really mattered to him, or vise versa.

CHAPTER THREE

After a restless weekend of pacing his apartment, Jack was ready to get back to work Monday morning. He sat down behind his desk at exactly 7:15 AM, just as he had been doing every morning for the last eight years. At 8:00 Linda stuck her head in his office door. "Hi, stranger," she said. "Good to have you back. You holding up OK?" Jack smiled back at the middle aged petite woman with close-cropped salt and pepper hair who had assisted him for five years.

"Yeah," Jack admitted, "it feels good to be busy. Hey, I got a message from Peterson. He is not going to budge on that deadline, so I need you to set up a meeting with all the department heads. The preliminary plans are due by Friday."

"Will do." Linda spun around on her three-inch black patent leather pump and headed back out the door.

On the top of Jack's desk were several neatly stacked piles of papers Linda had labeled with pink sticky notes. He picked up the pile labeled "Preliminary Bid Forms" and sighed heavily. "I might as well have become a CPA for all the architecture I do anymore," Jack mumbled to himself as he picked up a second pile of papers labeled "Client Contracts."

Jack was back at work for two weeks when his sister called. "Jack, Marty wants to see us. He's ready to probate the will." Marty Frick had been their mother's attorney.

"I'm up to my eyeballs in this Cornwell project, Kath. Can we do it later in the week, maybe Friday late afternoon? I'll take you out to dinner afterwards."

"Friday sounds great. I'll try to set up the appointment for 4:00 o'clock at Marty's office, and I am going to take you up on that dinner. Make it some place very grown-up. I haven't been anywhere nicer than Chuck E Cheese in forever!"

Jack and Kathy arrived at Frick, Gross and Klein Associates at exactly 4:00 that Friday. Worn burgundy carpeting and black vinyl and chrome chairs adorned the small lobby and looked as if they'd been purchased when the firm opened its doors in 1972. The receptionist, with a heavily sprayed upswept hairdo and green polyester twin set, matched the decor. The faint smell of cigarettes permeated the air and Jack noticed the receptionist slip an ashtray into her top drawer and spray a can of air freshener as they approached.

Kathy reached the desk first. "Hello, I'm Kathy Burton and this is my brother Jack Callahan. We have an appointment with Marty."

"Go right in." The receptionist pressed a buzzer that released a lock to the door behind her. The halls of the firm's inner sanctum were carpeted with the same worn burgundy shag, the smell of cigarette smoke even stronger. They knocked on the first door on the left which had Marty's name printed on an etched brass plate stuck crookedly to the center of the door. Behind it they heard Marty yell out, "Come in." Jack was amused to see him also covertly stash an ashtray in his top drawer.

Marty shook Jack's hand and pecked Kathy on the cheek, then he motioned for them to sit down in the chairs opposite his desk. "First of all," he began, "I want to offer my sympathies. I really liked your mother, we worked together for years and never had a cross word between us. The world is a poorer place without Christine Callahan in it."

Jack noticed Kathy's eyes begin to well up so he turned to Marty and asked, "Well, why don't we get to it? I think we're both still pretty emotional, and we'd like to get the paperwork end of this out of the way."

"Of course, of course," Marty said. He leaned down and pulled open his desk drawer taking out a thick binder. "I don't think there is anything in here that will take you by surprise, but I do have to go over it all."

Kathy regained her composure and said, "Mom was pretty up front with everything. She told us a few years ago that she decided to leave my husband and me her house, and she left Jack her annuities and stocks."

Marty nodded his head and said, "That's about it in a nutshell, except for the house on Lake Meade, of course, she left that to both of you."

Jack and Kathy looked at each other sharply, and then back at Marty. Jack spoke first, "Marty, there must be some mistake. My mother sold that property years ago. My father passed away there and we haven't been back since. Didn't my mother revise her will only about two years ago?"

It was Marty's turn to look surprised, his bushy black eyebrows rose up on his forehead and he peered over his half moon glasses at Jack. "Yes, your mother did revise her will only last year, and I can assure you she still owns the Lake Meade house, or should I say, you two do. I have a copy of the deed right here in my file."

"I'm sorry, Marty. I just can't believe it. I guess it was just an assumption on our part that she'd sold it. We left the day after my father died and neither Kathy nor I have ever stepped foot in the house again. I didn't think my mother had either."

Marty leaned back in his chair and folded his hands over his ample belly. "I don't think she went more than a couple times in the last few years. She did tell me she was paying a woman down there to keep an eye on the place, mow the lawn and make small repairs, that kind of thing."

"Can you handle the paperwork if we sell it?"

"Yeah, no problem, but I would suggest you go take a look at it yourself. See what condition it's in, maybe get an appraisal so you know you're selling it at the right price."

Kathy laid her hand gently on Jack's arm. "I don't know if I want to sell it," she said in a tentative voice. "We really did have a lot of fun down there as children, I might like to take my kids someday."

Jack looked at her with confusion and hurt playing in his eyes. "You can have it, Kathy, but I'm not going back there."

Kathy took her hand off Jack's arm. "Well, we can talk about it later. Let's just finish up the rest of the paperwork."

"Marty," Jack asked, "do you know the name of the woman Mom was paying to keep the place up?"

"Let me see here." Marty rustled through the file some more. "There's a receipt for a check your mother sent her for the roof when it needed to be replaced. Ah, here it is, a Ms. Margaret Granger."

"Maggie," Jack whispered. *That can't be right*, he thought, *she can't still live there after all these years.*

Kathy reached over the desk. "Marty, let me see that receipt."

"Sure." Marty handed it to her. "Is there a problem?"

"No, no problem. I think we're just surprised...again." She looked over at Jack who showed no emotion, then answered Marty's questioning stare. "The Grangers lived on a farm next to our vacation house down there. Our families were pretty close. My father and Margaret's grandfather,

Griffin, were good friends. Maggie, everyone called her Maggie, and Jack were the same age, they used to play together all the time."

"Summer best friends," Jack said quietly.

"What?" Kathy asked him.

Without looking at his sister but in a louder voice Jack said, "We used to say we were 'summer best friends.' You know we were down there all summer, and Maggie and I would play everyday, swimming, fishing and running around the barn, but then we really didn't see each other during the school year, so we said we were 'summer best friends.'" Jack smiled at the memories. He hadn't said Maggie's name out loud in years, although he had thought of her often.

Jack and Kathy finished going over the paperwork, shook hands with Marty and left the office to walk two blocks down Springfield Avenue to Dominic's, a small family owned Italian restaurant. A heavily made up hostess showed them to a quiet table near the back of the restaurant. Once the elderly waiter took their orders and delivered the martinis to the table, Jack and Kathy raised their glasses to each other.

"Cheers! Glad that's over," Jack said.

"Yeah. That was a bit of a shock though, huh?" Kathy replied.

"What? About the Lake Meade house?"

"Well, yeah, and that Maggie has been taking care of it all these years." Kathy drank some more from her glass as she peered at her brother over the rim. "Don't even try to pretend that didn't surprise you. Have you thought of her in years?"

Jack avoided answering her question. "I wouldn't say hiring a gardener and making sure the roof doesn't leak is 'taking care of the house.' The place is probably a mess. Why don't we just sell it? We thought it had been sold sixteen years ago, why get sentimental about it now?"

"Because it was a great place, Jack. Because we spent so many summers there and had the time of our lives. I would love to give memories like that to my kids."

"So you can move into Mom's house, it's bigger and in the same school district as you are now, then sell your house and use the money to buy a place in Point Pleasant or Cape May or someplace. It would probably be the smartest thing to do tax wise anyway."

"Well, you have it all figured out don't you, little brother?"

"It just makes sense. Why drive three hours to a lake in Maryland when you can drive one hour and be at the ocean?"

"Because our family has a history at Lake Meade. Besides, with traffic it takes a lot longer than an hour to get to the shore anymore, and in

Maryland the kids would have a whole lake practically to themselves."

"Whatever. Whatever you want to do. I just don't really want to go there, OK? Whenever I think of that day with Dad..."

"So that's all you remember about our summers at the lake? You don't remember learning to swim there?" Kathy asked. "You don't remember learning to ride your bike on the gravel lane? You don't remember Dad and Griff playing cards till midnight while we tried to overhear the dirty jokes they would tell each other?"

Jack's mouth twitched at the memory of his sister and he lying on the hardwood floor of their bedroom above the kitchen, trying to make out the muffled voices as their father and Griff drank beer, played cards and told each other their best blue jokes. Their mother would periodically say, "Shh, I think the children are still awake, keep it down, you two." Then he and Kathy would cover their mouths with their hands and giggle.

But as always happened when Jack thought of that place, memories of John Callahan gasping for breath, his head lying in Jack's lap, tears falling from Jack's face onto his father's, came rushing back. Jack shook his head and frowned at his sister. "Enough. I told you I don't want to talk about it anymore. Keep the damn house if you want to, but I don't want any part of it."

"How do you know? You haven't been there in all these years; maybe you would be surprised. I'm not saying you won't remember what happened and have some difficult moments, but you're a man now, Jack, not a boy. There is nothing there you can't handle. And there are an awful lot of good memories that shouldn't just be thrown away. I would love to make some more together as a family, with my kids, with Mike...with you."

Jack took a deep breath and looked down at his martini glass, running his finger along the rim. "I don't know. Maybe it would be all right. I doubt if I went there I would have a mental breakdown or anything."

"Probably not." Kathy smiled wickedly at him. "But if you did, call me, that could be kind of fun to watch."

Jack's somber expression broke into a reluctant grin. "Very nice. I bet some of your favorite times at Lake Meade were when I made an ass of myself."

"Like the time you lost your swim trunks when you dove in the lake and had to run back to the house with just a handful of leaves in front of your privates?"

"Yes."

"Or when you started to fall out of the oak tree out back and your belt caught on a branch and we found you hanging there with the tree giving you the world's biggest wedgie?"

"OK, that too."

"And when…"

"Alright already!"

"So how about it?" Kathy cajoled. "Why don't you go down and check it out? See what kind of condition the place is in before I take the kids down there. You could let us know if it's even worth saving. I'd hate like hell to get the kids excited about the place, load them in the car for three hours only to find some kind of rotting shack. To tell you the truth that would make *me* feel pretty crappy too."

"So you are appealing to me as a brother and an uncle to do a reconnaissance mission to Lake Meade, is that it?" Jack began to consider the request seriously, and to his astonishment, he wasn't finding the idea totally repulsive. It would be interesting to see Maggie again too. Interesting her name was still Granger on the receipt in Marty's file. Not that that necessarily meant anything, or that he cared if it meant anything. Still.

"Alright, I have about a million hours of vacation time I haven't taken in the last eight years, and we are in a waiting mode now while the Cornwell people review the preliminary plans for the new wing on the museum we just submitted, so it wouldn't be a bad time to get away."

Kathy's face lit up, she leaned over and kissed Jack on the cheek. "Oh, this is so great! I just have a feeling the place is going to be in good shape. I can't imagine Maggie not taking care of it."

She clapped her hands together and Jack smiled at the look on her face. He was sitting across from a well-dressed thirty-six year old woman with shoulder length sandy-blond hair, but the sparkle in her eyes was that of a ten-year-old girl with sunburned cheeks, blonde pigtails and cutoff jean shorts. "Oh!" She continued in an excited voice, "I can just see my kids learning to swim in the lake, having picnics and riding their bikes down the lane!"

Then the grin on Kathy's face faded to a mellower expression. "It's been so awful these last few weeks…with Mom and everything…but this is something fun to look forward to, you know? It's like an adventure."

Jack gave an exasperated moan. "Ahh, then why don't *you* go if you're so damn excited about it? Why the hell am I going on this great adventure when I didn't want the house in the first place?" Jack tried to figure out how the conversation had begun with him being vehemently against going to Maryland and had ended with him actually using his vacation time to go himself. He put his elbows on the table and looked cynically back at his sister. "You do this to your husband too, don't you?"

"Do what?" Kathy widened her eyes innocently.

"Talk Mike in circles until he is actually suggesting what you wanted him to do all the time that he didn't want to do in the first place."

"Oh, that. Yes." Kathy laughed and motioned for the waiter who eagerly shuffled over to the table. "Another martini for me please, none for him though, my brother's driving." She handed the waiter her empty glass and gave her brother a wicked wink. Jack saw a glimpse again of the carefree young girl who used to torment her little brother at a whitewashed picnic table on the porch of a cottage on Lake Meade.

He knew at that moment he would go, if only to see if the house was fit for Kathy's family. He couldn't seem to sustain a relationship for more than a few months, but Kathy had created a warm loving family, and it would be great if they could find some of the joy he and Kathy had found there on the lake when they were kids. Still not sure how he would feel being at the lakeside cottage, he understood it was probably past time to find out.

CHAPTER FOUR

Phil Peterson quickly approved Jack's vacation time, and in fact told him to take two weeks instead of just one when he realized how much time Jack had accumulated. He wanted Jack to use up his personal time before the Cornwell project really started rolling; he was going to need him every minute of every day when that started. So the following Monday Jack found himself heading south on interstate 95 with a cup of Starbuck's coffee in one hand and a Maryland road map open on the seat beside him. The roads and countryside had changed some over the years, but he was reasonably sure he could find his way back to the lake house. After a little over two hours on the road Jack finally spotted the exit off the main highway onto Route 214.

As he continued on the secondary road for another half hour, Jack felt as if he were driving back in time. Except for the insidious beige vinyl wrapped development houses and nondescript strip malls that had sprung up in what had once been cornfields — a huge oversized crop of suburban sprawl — the farther south he drove the sparser the landscape became, and much more like it had looked in his childhood. Just too far east of the Baltimore-Washington metro area and too southwest from the ocean, Lake Meade wasn't considered commutable or chic. This had kept the area relatively unchanged over the years.

It wasn't long before a small blue sign appeared on the side of the road half covered with tree branches and read "Lake Meade" in embossed letters. Jack couldn't help but grin when he saw the sign and then took note of the first house on the outskirts of town, a large Victorian that had once been painted a deep violet color when Jack was a boy, but had since been changed to a more sophisticated shade of blue. Jack and his sister had always yelled, "Yeah we're here, we're here, there's the big purple house!" as they drove past it when they were children.

Summer cottages and prairie style homes followed the old blue Victorian, all nestled onto neatly trimmed lawns with well-tended flowerbeds. Jack scanned the road for the Lake View Diner, his next landmark that sat on the corner of the road where he would make a left-hand turn onto Granger Lane. He hoped it was still there.

Then right where, and how, he remembered it was the oblong metal and glass building with the red neon "open" sign in the window. Hungry from the trip, Jack's thoughts turned longingly to the fluffy pancakes he used to order on Sunday mornings. To assuage his rumbling stomach, he promised himself he would go to the diner for breakfast the very next morning.

Turning onto Granger Lane, Jack was surprised to find it paved. The road had been nothing more than a well-worn gravel drive when he was a boy; now several large executive style homes flanked either side of the half-mile long dead-end lane. A few minutes later Jack arrived at the end of the road, the lake in front of him only a few feet away, the water level a lot lower than he remembered. To the left, the driveway to his family's cottage, the rusted mailbox showing the shadowy remains of the name "Callahan" that had once been painted across it in bold black letters. To the right, another gravel driveway, but this one with a large shiny aluminum mailbox that read "Granger." Next to the mailbox stood a wooden sign ornately painted with old-fashioned red and gold scrawling lettering with the words "Granger House Bed and Breakfast" displayed across it.

Jack raised his eyebrows at the sign. So the Grangers had converted the old farmhouse into a bed and breakfast? He wondered if Maggie still lived there with her grandfather, maybe she helped run the B&B? He'd go over there later to say hello, but first he had to drive down the driveway to his left. He sat in the middle of the road staring at the lake in front of him, watching the water ripple in the wind and the sun play off the choppy waves.

I can do this, it's just a house. With an impatient jerking sweep of his hand Jack spun the steering wheel and turned the car down the shaded driveway. The cottage sat around a bend about two hundred yards in from the road, he couldn't see it yet, but he did notice the trees and bushes had been kept trimmed back. He knew if no one had tended to them regularly they would have consumed the entry, the forest reclaiming its own. He really did have to thank Maggie, he thought, she had kept up with the place.

As he came around the bend, Jack's breath caught in his throat and he knew he owed Maggie more than a simple thank you. The house looked exactly as it had the day he left all those years ago. The buttercup yellow paint on the wood siding appeared fresh, no fading or peeling, and the porch railings and shutters were still straight and in repair. The lawn was newly mowed, and there were even impatiens in the flower boxes on the porch. They had been Christine's favorite flowers.

A prickly feeling crawled along the back of Jack's neck. Had he just driven straight into the past? While the car idled he fought the feeling that if he shut off the engine and opened the door a spell would be broken and the vision of the yellow and blue cottage of his childhood would disappear. He looked away from the house and out toward the lake to see if the dock was still there. It was, the only thing missing from the waterfront scene was the red rowboat he had kept tied to it, two fishing poles perpetually sticking out the back. Sun dappled through the trees onto the lawn, the house and the dock. Jack's eyes became moist. It had always felt like such a magical protected place to him, the memories rushed back and swelled in his chest.

Still sitting in the car, Jack turned once again to look at the house with its slightly warped front porch and abruptly the image of that fateful day his father died came savagely back to him. The sentimental tears that had been threatening to come dried up instantly. Jack shook his head as if to clear it then finally turned off the car, got out and strode purposely towards the house. Halfway up the walk he patted his pocket and realized he didn't have any keys. He had meant to stop at his mother's house to try and find where she kept her set for the cottage, but he'd forgotten.

Staring up at the house with a question in his eyes, he thought, *the spare keys couldn't still be where we had kept them. No way.* He walked up the front porch steps and stopped in front of the door, and then he reached on top of the heavy wood trim until his finger connected with a slim piece of metal. He couldn't believe it. Jack pulled down a key that should have been rusty with age, but appeared to be brand new. He opened the screen door and noticed the lock on the front door looked new as well. He glanced back at the key in his hand, shrugged and said, "Here goes."

The key turned easily in the lock. Jack gave the door a little shove and it opened smoothly on its hinges. He stood in the threshold letting a thousand small memories of all the times he had gone bounding through that door as a boy flood through him. *God, it even smells the same,* he thought, *like warm cotton sheets.* His stomach fluttered and Kathy's words at the restaurant came back to him as if she were there whispering in his ear, "It's an adventure, Jack."

His steps felt lighter as he thought of his sister's words. He shut the door behind him and reached for the light switch, wondering if there was any electricity. *I should have called the electric company before I left.* But when he flipped the switch the lights come on bright and clear, he couldn't believe it; Maggie had even kept working light bulbs in the fixtures.

Walking into the living room, Jack expected to see the old wallpaper with the design of gold eagles holding a flag in their talons, but the wallpaper had been stripped and the room was painted an antique sage. The mustard colored drapes had been replaced with red linen valances, but the chocolate-colored leather couch and two companion chairs were still the same. Not a speck of dust or damage anywhere that he could see. Even the stone fireplace was set with logs, ready to be lit with the flick of a match. The unsettling thought crossed his mind that Maggie could be using the place as part of her Bed and Breakfast. What if someone was staying there? No, he would have seen a car. But what if they're just out?

Jack walked into the hall and turned towards the back of the house to the kitchen. If there were signs of water recently run in the sink or food in the refrigerator, he would know that someone was staying there. He wasn't necessarily angry if Maggie had used the house, he didn't know what arrangements she had made with his mother, but he would be disappointed. He didn't like the idea of anyone else staying there, especially strangers.

Jack noticed the kitchen hadn't been changed at all. The walls were still covered with white ceramic tile, and the lemon colored Formica-topped table with its four matching metal chairs still stood in the corner. Even the curtains over the sink were the same, white with little cherries and red trim. He didn't see any signs of recent use, and when he opened the refrigerator all that was there was a box of baking soda.

Jack continued his exploration upstairs to the two bedrooms, both had been given a fresh coat of white paint but the furniture in the two small rooms remained the same. He sat down on the edge of the queen-sized bed in his parent's room and ran his hand over the bumpy texture of the chenille bedspread, then he looked over at the nightstand and saw that his father's favorite antique alarm clock still sat next to his parent's wedding portrait. The tears he had felt welling up in his eyes when he pulled into the driveway threatened to come again.

Lying down on the bed and letting his arm fall over his eyes, Jack took some deep breaths in an attempt to clear his mind, willing himself to relax and absorb the quiet of the house. He thought of what his sister and had said at the restaurant, about how he would probably experience some strong emotions, but nothing he couldn't handle. She had been right — not that he would give her the satisfaction of telling her that.

Jack was just drifting off to sleep when he heard a noise, a scraping sound in the hall. About to take his arm off his eyes and sit up, a female voice said sharply, "Don't move! I have called the police and I am holding a shotgun. I do not want to use it, but I will if I have to."

He knew that voice, after all these years, he still knew that voice. "Maggie?"

After a few beats, "Oh, my God...Jack?"

"Can I move now?" Jack slowly took his arm away from his face and sat up on the bed. He had seen her target practice with a shotgun before, he had no doubt Maggie really did have one pointed at him, but it was still a shock to see the barrel only a few inches from his face. "You can put the gun down now. I promise I won't steal anything."

Maggie stood there speechless, mouth agape. She lowered the gun slowly and stood it in the corner. Jack watched her move around the room. She looked so much like she had all those years ago, just taller and somehow softer. Her hair was still a blend of shoulder length blond and red curls, her nose sprinkled with freckles. She turned her blue-gray eyes on him and he felt an electric current run through his stomach.

"I just can't believe you're here. You scared the hell out of me."

Jack laughed, "I scared the hell out of you? I was the one on the wrong end of the shotgun. Don't you think you should call off the police?"

With a sheepish grin she said, "Sorry, I lied. I did grab my shotgun but I didn't call the police. I check on the place a lot, and when I saw a car I didn't recognize in the driveway and the door unlocked..."

"...And found some strange guy sleeping on the bed."

"Exactly. Why didn't you call? I could have gotten the place ready for you. Is your mom with you? We haven't seen her in awhile."

The light left Jack eyes and Maggie instinctively knew Christine was gone. She sat down on the bed next to Jack. "I am so sorry. What happened?"

"She had a stroke. She hung on for a couple of days, but it was no good, there was too much damage. I'm sorry we didn't call you, but Kathy and I didn't even know she still owned this place or kept in touch with you until after she died."

"I wondered about that. She always came alone, just for a couple days every now and then. We would chat for a bit, but whenever I asked if you guys were going to come back to visit, she'd just change the subject."

He nodded. "I can't believe how well you have kept the place up."

"Well, Joe and Rolly really deserve the credit. They still work for us, you know. Now they do maintenance at the bed and breakfast instead of farming, and they do all the painting and mowing. Candy Stokes, our housekeeper at the B&B, comes over here once a month to clean. Your mom sent money for the upkeep and I passed it on to them."

"I can't believe Joe and Rolly are still working, they seemed old to me when we were kids."

"When we were kids anyone over thirty seemed old to us."

Jack laughed. "That's true."

"Joe is sixty-something, and Rolly probably doesn't even know how old he is himself, but he's around Gramp's age, late seventies, early eighties."

Jack remembered the farm hands as sturdy men who, along with Griffin Granger, worked from dawn to dusk keeping the cows milked and the crops tended. Joe had been a quiet man, tall and rangy with a weathered face and short cropped brown hair. In all the years Jack had known him, he had only heard Joe say a handful of sentences.

Rolly was the older and more gregarious of the two. A black man with an easy smile whose great grandparents had been slaves in Virginia and whose parents had worked on the Granger farm since before Rolly was born. As far as Jack knew, neither man had ever married or had children. They had lived in two small cottages that sat side by side toward the back of the Granger property.

"Do Joe and Rolly still live on the farm?" he asked.

Maggie nodded and grinned. "Oh, yes. Rolly tells me all the time." Maggie cocked her hip and imitated Rolly's gravely voice, "I was born on this farm and I will die on this farm and you had better not ever get any ideas, young lady, about shipping me off to some goddamned nursing home or I will kick your ass from here to Baltimore and back again."

"Oh, man," Jack was laughing heartily at Maggie's impression. "Rolly hasn't changed, I guess."

Maggie's eyes lost some of their sparkle as she answered. "Well, that's not true. He has changed, they all have. Rolly uses a cane and his eyesight isn't too great. Gramps has a hard time hearing and his arthritis in his hands is pretty bad, so they stick close and say that between the two of them they can put together a decent pair of legs, hands, eyes and ears and get along just fine."

"It's hard for me to think of your grandfather as ill in anyway," Jack said. "He stays in my mind as larger-than-life and indestructible. With those giant hands he could pick up a hay bale in one and a newborn calf in the other. I always wanted to grow up to be Griffin Granger, farming superhero."

"Don't let him hear you call him `ill.' He's just aging and fighting it every inch of the way, that's all."

"When did he decide to convert the farm to a B&B?"

Maggie bit the inside of her lip and hesitated before answering. "That was my idea actually. We decided to do it twelve years ago. We had a particularly bad growing season, and it was apparent that even with my help, three aging men and an eighteen-year-old woman weren't going to be able to keep up with the farm anymore. The barn and the house both needed major repairs. The roof was leaking and we needed to update the electrical system, and we were barely making enough money to keep up with the taxes.

"None of us would even consider moving, so we had to do something. Then I read an article in a magazine about bed and breakfasts, and I thought, hey, we have a huge house with lake front property, why not give it a try? So we subdivided some lots that had road frontage on Granger Lane and used the money to make the repairs, update the kitchen, add some more bathrooms and, *voila*, Granger House Bed and Breakfast was born."

Impressed, Jack said, "That's great. You always were resourceful, but I'm surprised you stayed here and didn't go away to college. You used to talk about how you were going to blow out of this little town the minute you graduated high school."

Maggie was quiet, again gauging what she'd say next. "Well, plans change, people change. Mostly, it was because the year the B&B was born, so was my son."

Before Jack had a chance to say anything, Maggie jumped up off the bed and moved towards the door. "I have to get back to the B&B. Why don't you come over for dinner tonight? The guys would love to see you."

"Thanks, I'd like that."

"I think you will find everything here working pretty well. We try to run the water regularly, and the electricity is on so we can keep the heat low and the pipes won't freeze in the winter. The only thing you don't have is a phone."

"I have my cell phone, so that's OK. I really do appreciate you keeping everything in such great condition. I swear it looks like it did last time I was here." The words died in Jack's throat as he once again remembered the last day he had been there.

Maggie gave him a sad smile and walked out the door. *I kept it for you, Jack. I always knew you'd find the strength to come back.*

Jack didn't move off the bed after she'd left, but sat staring at the doorway Maggie has just walked through. He felt tired again, very tired. All he wanted to do was lay back down on the bed and take a nap before dinner. He needed to gather his strength before he talked about more memories of his youth at Lake Meade with the men of Granger House. He almost got up to move to the room he had shared with Kathy as a child, and then realized he probably wouldn't fit in the single bed anymore. Jack fell back asleep on his parent's queen-sized bed. It was a sleep full of dreams and memories, mostly of Maggie.

He and Maggie are sitting on the end of the dock, their legs swinging back and forth, toes skimming the top of the water. He put his hand down close to hers. She inches hers over until their pinkies are touching and they look up into each other's eyes. They've always been summer best friends, buddies, nothing more. They played together since they were six years old.

Today feels different. They swam and fished, nothing unusual in that, but Jack feels a tightness in his stomach every time he looks at Maggie, the sun shining off her copper and blond hair. It's almost Labor Day, he will be leaving soon, and this year it seems particularly hard to say goodbye. So they sit on the dock silently, and before Jack knows what he's doing, he leans over and kisses her on the lips.

Maggie's eyes are wide when Jack pulls back and looks at her. He's scared, what has he done? Will he ever be able to look her in the eye again? Then she smiles, not just a polite little smile, but a great big sunny grin, and she leans over and kisses him right back.

When they pull away from each other they smile shyly at one another and then quickly look down at their toes. They hold each other's hand and swing their feet some more, but this time hook them around the other's.

Then it happens...his mother's scream. Both he and Maggie jump to their feet and run towards the house, reaching the front steps at the same time. Jack's father is lying on his back on the porch floor, his eyes staring blankly upwards, his breath coming in shallow rapid movements. Christine has stopped screaming when she sees Jack and Maggie running towards her. She tells Jack to hold his father's head and talk to him, she tells Maggie to run home and get her grandfather or Joe or Rolly, she's going in the house to call the ambulance.

John Callahan looks up into his son's eyes, a mixture of confusion and pain reflected in them, Jack saying "Dad, Dad" over and over again. Jack looks up to see Griff and Joe running towards them, Maggie behind the two men gasping for breath.

Jack woke up with a start, his shirt sweaty, his heart racing. Not sure where he was or what had awoken him, then he remembered the dream. He hadn't had that dream for years. Not a dream, really, but a memory.

Jack got up and walked into the bathroom, splashed cold water onto his face. He looked up into the mirror over the sink and said to his pale reflection, "This may not have been such a great idea."

CHAPTER FIVE

Maggie walked back down Jack's driveway, crossed Granger Lane and headed up her long winding gravel drive to the old farmhouse. She was glad she had walked instead of driven, it was a crisp sunny day, and she needed the cool breeze on her face to help clear her head. Jack was back.

Somehow she knew he would come back some day — it had all felt too unfinished. They had shared a very close friendship from the time she was five until she was fifteen. From Memorial Day through Labor Day for those ten years they had been inseparable and shared so much of their childhood. Jack was more than an old friend, he was part of her past woven into who she had become as a woman. And even though on that last fateful day together they had sat on the dock holding hands and sharing a kiss, she had no romantic expectations of Jack. They had been so young, and most of their relationship had been as close friends, nothing more. She was just glad to have a chance to see him again, even if it was to say good-bye properly.

They had never really gotten to do that, say good-bye. The last time she saw Jack was from a distance as he climbed into his parent's car and drove away with his mother and sister. Griff had hugged Christine and told her to call if they needed anything, but Maggie had been afraid to approach Jack. He had looked so sad, and she had no words to comfort him. She knew now she should have grabbed him and held him and told him he would be all right, but she had just stood there behind her grandfather and watched the Callahan's car drive away.

Maggie felt ashamed of that for years because she knew she could have comforted him; she had lost her mother and her grandmother. She knew about grief, she understood it. Her mother had died in a car accident when Maggie was four. That was how she had ended up at the Granger farm. Her father had been a tool salesman and when his wife died he had no idea how, nor any inclination, to raise a daughter on his own. He had dropped Maggie at the farm the day of her mother's funeral. Griffin and his wife Ann had been only too happy to take their granddaughter into their home.

The Grangers had given Maggie an ideal childhood. Her grandmother had baked cookies with her and braided her hair. Her grandfather let her drive the tractor and help milk the cows. Joe and Rolly doted on her, and she had summers filled with fishing and swimming in the lake with Jack. Her world had been a happy one until Ann had been diagnosed with breast cancer when Maggie was eleven. Ann hadn't suffered long, dying within two months of her diagnosis, but the dark cloud that came over the Granger farm hung over it for a long time.

Griffin, always a rough and tumble, happy-go-lucky man, had become quiet and sullen in the year following his wife's death, somehow diminished and smaller than his six-foot-three, robust self. Even Joe and Rolly had withdrawn, usually eating by themselves in their little cabins instead of at the main house, as was their custom when Ann was alive.

It was a difficult time, but as will happen, a year of seasons came and went and life rearranged itself, and the strength of people and love endured. Little by little Joe and Rolly started coming back to the house to eat dinner, and the three men would chat and have a beer after working all day. Maggie learned to cook her grandmother's recipes, and kept up with the housework after her schoolwork was finished. A new family was born from the old.

Maggie stopped walking, closed her eyes and took a deep breath of the musky early spring air. She tried to remember what it was her grandmother used to say, she could almost hear her raspy voice, "It's not what life hands you, Maggie girl, but what you *do* with what life hands you that counts." She felt a slight breeze on her face and smiled up at the rustling trees, she imagined her mother and grandmother smiling back down at her. She blew them each a kiss and continued her walk home.

The smell of the water from the lake, the pine needles from the trees and even a whiff of the coffee being brewed in her own kitchen quickened her steps. She loved this place to her bones. Whenever in her life she had felt the sand shifting beneath her feet, all she had to do was simply look around at this land that had been in her family for so many generations and she knew where she belonged. With just the thought of this place she was so rooted to, the ground beneath her always became solid again.

Maggie rounded the last bend in the drive and the old farmhouse came into view. The grand old Victorian had been added onto so many times over the last two-hundred-years so that it rambled with gables, round turrets and porches. The wood siding had been painted white, the shutters a deep maroon, and although the house was a large and wandering structure, it wasn't imposing. You expected someone to be waiting at the top of the porch stairs for you saying, "Hello, come on in, sit down and be comfortable."

Twelve years ago, when Maggie had proposed the idea of converting the aging farm into a lodge to her grandfather, she had been frightened of what he would say; she thought for sure he would never agree to giving up farm work, and worse still, inviting strangers into his ancestral home. She knew even if she convinced him the B&B would be a good idea, convincing him to sell the four lots with road frontage on Granger Lane to finance it would be tougher. No Granger had ever sold off part of the family's land before, but Maggie couldn't think of any other way to raise the money for the bed and breakfast. The alternative, selling the farm and moving someplace smaller in town, essentially breaking up her family and losing Griffin's birthright, was not an option.

Griff had surprised her and been open to her ideas. He had understood they weren't keeping up with the farming or repairs like they should, and the money they did bring in wasn't even paying their taxes, let alone supporting them. Still, he was hesitant about selling off the four lots — until she told him she was pregnant. Then everything changed and changed quickly.

Without another word to Maggie, Griffin had gone to the town hall and gotten the parcels of land subdivided, and then immediately went to the realtors to list them. Within three months, the lots were sold and work was being done on the farmhouse repairing and updating it to convert it into a four-star lodging. By the time Caleb had been born, Granger House Bed and Breakfast had been advertised in several tourist guides and magazines. By the time Caleb turned one, there was already a three-month waiting list to get a reservation.

Joe had become a jack-of-all-trades, keeping up with the painting and the plumbing. Rolly considered himself the head gardener; he loved using the riding mower (although with his poor eyesight guests were advised to stay well away from the lawn area when it was being mowed). Mostly Rolly and Griffin were the house's "characters," sitting on the porch for hours playing chess and telling tales to any guest that would stand still long enough to listen.

Maggie had done all of the cooking herself in the beginning, but a few years ago had been able to hire a pastry chef to make fresh pastries for breakfast and rolls and pies for the evening meal. She still enjoyed making omelets, scrambled eggs and bacon in the morning and cooking the main course for dinner, but the added help in the kitchen had given Maggie some breathing room and the guests enjoyed the fresh baked goods. Running the B&B suited them all just fine.

Opening the screen door, Maggie stepped into the kitchen to find all three men sitting around the table drinking coffee and staring at the clock. She knew they were waiting for Caleb to get home from school. Maggie chuckled to herself and then poured a cup as well. "He gets home at 3:30, fellas, you know that. Staring at the clock is not going to get him home any faster."

Griffin rolled his eyes at his granddaughter. "Don't you think we know that? We're just anxious to see if he made the baseball team. He had tryouts today."

"How long has the boy been playing baseball? How many games did the four of you play out back? How many pop flies did you make him catch?" she asked sarcastically. "I feel pretty confident he made it."

Rolly said, "You never know. Some of those boys are huge. They might have a whole bunch of big boys and Caleb will get squeezed out. They like those boys on the team gigantic now."

"Rolly, Caleb is one of the tallest boys in his class. He looks just like his great grandfather, for goodness sake. I can't imagine him being one of the smaller players."

"Well, you just never know. He'll be home in seven minutes and we'll find out then." Griffin ended the discussion. Joe just nodded his head.

"I have some news that might actually distract you for a moment from waiting on Caleb."

"I doubt it," Rolly said.

"So you don't want to hear my news?" Maggie asked.

"Now, no one said that," Griffin answered sourly.

"You are such a pack of hens, I knew you couldn't resist a little gossip. I was just over checking on the Callahan's house and guess who was there?"

"A bunch of teenagers necking, I expect," Griff said with a lascivious grin.

"No, better…I found Jack Callahan."

"No!" All three said at once and then began talking and asking questions at the same time, even Joe looked surprised.

"But I have bad news too," Maggie said, and the three men quiet down. "Christine passed away about a month ago. She had a stroke."

"Oh, now that's a real shame. That was a grand lady," Griffin said. The other men agreed.

"Jack didn't even know his mother still owned the house until they read her will."

"Really? I wonder why," Griff said.

"She probably thought the place would remind them too much of John's death."

The three men nodded their heads in agreement. "Well, I just hope they start using the place again. Kathy has kids, doesn't she?" Griff asked. "That house should be lived in and used, not kept like some kind of mausoleum."

"Yeah, it would be nice to see some life over there. Just sad seeing a pretty little place like that go to waste. Those were some nice years when the Callahan's summered over there." Rolly said.

Joe nodded his head in agreement, but didn't add anything. Then they all heard the sound of the screen door banging, and all four heads swiveled around to see Caleb come bounding through the door. He was grinning and breathing hard as if he'd run all the way down the driveway. As always, the sight of her twelve -year-old son, especially when he looked so happy and rosy cheeked, made Maggie's heart constrict with joy.

"Well, boy? How'd it go today?" asked his great grandfather.

A sly look crept across Caleb's freckled face, but he tried to act nonchalant. He let his book bag drop to the floor and went to the cabinet in search of something to eat — he was always in search of something to eat. "OK, I guess," he replied.

"Now don't be like that, boy," Rolly scolded. "What happened at tryouts today for baseball? Was there a lot of real big kids there?"

Caleb laughed and put his size ten foot up on the table. "Bigger than me, Rol?"

Maggie swatted his foot off the tabletop. "Caleb, don't torture them anymore, tell them how it went before they bust."

A smile split his face and Caleb said, "I not only got on the team, I'm the captain this year!"

All three men jumped out of their seats and started whooping and patting him on the back. "Holy sh--, I mean holy smokes, son, that's great!"

"Thanks, Gramps!"

Maggie crossed the room and gave him a big hug, kissing the top of his head, which she noticed wasn't very far from the top of her own anymore. "Oh, honey, I am so proud of you!"

"Thanks, Mom. I'm going to go out and practice pitching in the back field."

"Not until after your homework's done."

"Aw, Mom! Come on, I'm captain, I've got to be the best!"

She saw all three of the older men shift in their chairs, she knew they were itching to go out back with Caleb and throw the ball. As usual, she had to be the heavy.

"School work is first, you know that, but I'll let you off your chores tonight. Go up and get your homework done, and then you can go out and practice."

"All right." He turned to Rolly, Joe and Griff, "I don't have much homework. I'll be back down in an hour." He ran out of the room. They could hear him bounding up the stairs two at a time.

Joe said, "I'll go do his chores quick, he deserves a night to celebrate." A rare smile lit across his face as he got up from the table and headed into the living room to empty the wastebaskets. Maggie heard him say quietly to himself, "Captain! Hot dang, what about that."

Dinner was served at Granger House at 6:45 every night in both the dining room and the kitchen. Jack tapped lightly on the screen door and called out, "Hello," at 6:40. No one replied, so he opened the door a crack and stuck his head farther in the room. "Anybody here?"

Just then a tall boy with sandy blond hair came through the doorway from the dining room. He carried a big silver tray, and when he saw Jack he asked, "Can I help you, mister?"

"Hi, you must be Maggie's son."

Maggie burst through the dining room door. "Caleb, I need the butter from the fridge, honey, the guests are going to be down in a minute. Oh, Jack? I'm sorry. You just caught us at rush time. Come on in and sit down at the kitchen table, we'll be right with you, let me just get everything settled." Then she realized Jack and Caleb were staring at each other. "Oh, sorry, Caleb, this is a friend of mine from years ago, Jack Callahan. His family used to spend the summers next door. You remember Gramps and me talking about them?"

The boy relaxed and nodded at Jack. "Oh, yeah. Hey, how are you?" Then he rushed over to the refrigerator and took out two glass butter dishes and hurried out the swinging door back to the dining room.

"Can I help at all?" Jack asked.

Maggie ladled stew into a big white Wedgwood tureen. "No, no, we do this every night, we kind of have a routine. Gramps and the guys will be in in a minute, they're just finishing putting the silverware out on the table and setting up the coffee service on the sideboard. Once we get the food out and everything set up we're pretty much done, it's a family style service." She noticed his questioning look. "It means the guests serve themselves, you know, pass the food around like they were at dinner in their own home."

"Oh. But, I thought this was a bed and breakfast, not bed, breakfast and dinner?" Jack cocked his eyebrow at her.

Maggie blew a curl off her forehead and finished piling rolls in a hand woven basket. "It *is*, smarty pants, but there are only a few places to eat in town, so for an extra charge guests can eat dinner here as well. Since I'm cooking for my family anyway, I just triple the recipes and serve the guests too. Truth is, I make almost as much with the dinners as I do with the lodging."

Maggie loaded up her tray and backed out the swinging door into the dining room. Jack caught a glimpse of the three older men and Caleb bustling around setting the table and arranging the steaming bowls of food around the table. A minute later a bell rang, the door banged open and the men of Granger House ambled into the kitchen.

They were so busy talking and laughing amongst themselves they didn't see Jack at first. Waiting for them to notice him, Jack realized he was holding his breath. He was a little nervous to see this trio, who in his childhood memories were almost mythical in their height and strength. They looked a little shorter and older than he remembered, but there was no mistaking them. He would recognize any of these three men even after all these years.

Griff was the first to see him. "Oh Lord, if it isn't Jack Callahan all grown up." Jack stood up and Griff walked over to him and shook his hand. He may have been grayer and more stooped than Jack remembered, but Griffin Granger's voice and handshake were just as powerful as ever.

"Well, well, well, you grew up tall, didn't you, son? Good to see you. So sorry to hear about your mother's passing, we were all real fond of Miss Christine," Rolly said as he shook Jack's hand as well.

Joe muttered his agreement with Rolly and shook Jack's hand in turn.

Caleb was already sitting at the table piling food in large mounds on his plate. "Mind you wait for your mother before you start shoveling that food in your face," Griff reminded him.

"Don't I always? I wish she'd hurry up though before I starve to death."

Rolly chuckled, "Not much chance of that."

Everyone sat down at the table and started passing food and filling their plates. Jack noticed Griff add some to the plate next to his as the food came around. Maggie came through the door a moment later and sat down at the place where Griff had been filling the plate.

"Thanks, Gramps, but you always give me too much." She patted her grandfather's hand and then placed her two hands together. Jack realized everyone else had as well. He hurriedly did the same and they all offered thanks before digging into the food piled high on their plates.

It was a simple meal, beef stew, homemade rolls and potato puffs, and so different from what Jack would have been eating for dinner in New York, probably an order of Sushi barely tasted as he hunched over his desk working until well past 8:00 o'clock. The meal was delicious and Jack found himself accepting more when Maggie motioned if he'd like seconds from the large pot in the center of the table. He noticed Caleb was almost through his seconds and reaching for another roll in the basket.

"This is fantastic, Maggie," Jack said between mouthfuls.

"It's just stew, Jack, nothing special, but thank you."

Griff sat up straighter in his chair and said, "Maggie is the best cook around. We got a four-star rating in *Bed & Breakfast Magazine* last month, and they did a big write-up on how her cooking was one of the best parts of staying here."

Jack saw Maggie blush and give her grandfather a look. "Just eat your stew, Gramps."

"And did you hear my boy Caleb here is the new team captain for his junior high's baseball team?"

Now Caleb blushed. "Gramps!"

"What? Can't a man be proud of his family?"

"That's great, Caleb, congratulations," Jack said to the boy. The rest of the dinner was spent catching up. Maggie asked about Kathy and her family, Griff wanted to know what Jack did for a living, and Rolly told stories about some of the more notable guests that had stayed at Granger House.

Once the pie and coffee had been eaten, Caleb asked to be excused to get a few more minutes of practice in before it was totally dark. The other men followed him out the door in a shuffling parade. Maggie smiled at their retreating backs. "They are all so excited about him being captain, it's so funny."

"I think it's great," Jack said, "They are obviously proud of him. He's a wonderful kid, Maggie."

"Thank you, I think so too." She took another sip of coffee and got up to clear the dishes. Jack stood up to help her. "You don't have to do that," she said, "you're a guest."

Jack felt a pang of saddness. "I was never considered a guest in the Granger house before, and I'd hate to be thought of one now."

Maggie looked over at him thoughtfully for a moment, and then threw a dishtowel at his head. "You're right, get to work, Callahan." Jack laughed and Maggie's stomach did a small flip-flop. What was that about? She wondered. It had been a long time since a man made her feel that way. Hell, she thought, it'd been a long time since a man made her feel much of anything.

Once the kitchen was cleaned up, Jack followed Maggie into the dining room. The guests had finished eating and left the room. When Jack was a boy, the dining room had been painted completely in bright turquoise, Ann Granger's favorite color. Now it was a light gray with turquoise trees stenciled around the upper half of the walls.

Maggie saw Jack looking around, noticing the changes in the room. "I had to keep some of Gram's color in here, but we needed to lighten it up a little for the guests."

"It looks great."

"I'll give you a tour once I get these dishes loaded in the washer."

An hour later, Jack and Maggie sat down in two rocking chairs on the front porch. After cleaning up the dining room, Maggie had given Jack a tour of the house, except for the occupied guest's rooms. He was impressed with how she'd decorated the B&B. The rooms were all painted in bright, yet calming colors. Most of the furniture was original to the house, and what wasn't were obviously authentic antiques.

"You really have something special here, Maggie."

She closed her eyes, leaned her head back against the whicker rocker and moved lazily back and forth in the old chair. "I couldn't do it without Gramps, the guys, and Caleb too. They all make this place work."

An affluent looking middle-aged couple walked out the front door hand in hand and started down the steps. Noticing Maggie, the woman said, "That was a great dinner as always, Maggie."

"Thank you, Mrs. Walters. Are you two going for your evening walk around the lake?"

The silver haired man spoke, "Yes, what a great night for it. But I've never seen the water level so low, Maggie."

"I know, we're having the worst drought in the county's history. We need to pray for a rainy spring."

The couple nodded in agreement, waved and turned to continue their walk. Maggie explained to Jack that the couple had been coming every year to celebrate their anniversary since the first year the B&B opened. "We have a lot of guests like that, they come back every year for a special occasions."

"So you're happy here? You don't regret not having left like you planned?" Jack surprised himself with how intimate a question he had just asked. It wasn't like him to pry. Yet, it felt so normal with Maggie. It was strange, but five minutes into dinner he'd felt like his friendship with her was still as easy and solid as it had been as children. All those years in between had dissolved.

Maggie didn't show any surprise at his question and answered frankly. "No, not at all. What's the expression? `We plan and God laughs.' I wouldn't change a thing. What about you? You always wanted to be an architect, is it what you thought it would be?"

Jack paused a moment before answering, "It was in the beginning. I tried every type of architecture. I did houses and schools, office buildings and municipal buildings. Then I got good at managing the bigger projects, and somewhere along the way I stopped being an architect and started being a manager."

Maggie opened her eyes and looked over at Jack. "You don't sound very happy about that."

"I'm not. But it's hard to go back, you know? You go too far down that road and it's hard to turn around. I haven't even touched a drafting tool in two years."

Jack sounded so disappointed Maggie stopped rocking and studied his face more closely. She said after a time, "So go back. Just figure out where you made a wrong turn and start from there."

Jack gave her a sad smile. "You make it sound so easy, so simple. `Just go back.' If I go back to sitting at a drafting table, I don't get to keep my nice apartment in Manhattan, or my gym membership."

"Or that nice car I saw in the driveway next door? I know. But I also know you don't sound very happy now and you have all those things, so...?"

"So I should give it all up and open a little firm and design houses and municipal buildings again?"

Maggie's expression didn't change. "Why not? Would that be so terrible? You just said that's when you were happy, when you were doing those things."

"Yeah."

"So what's the big mystery, Jack?"

Maggie's rocking chair creaked regularly against the old wood floor. "What's the point of having all that stuff if you're miserable? I'm not saying you need to give up all your worldly possessions and move to a Buddhist colony, I just mean if your life is not working, not making you happy, adjust it. Life's too short not to try and be happy."

"You've been living in Lake Meade all your life, Maggie, and you've always had this place. You don't know what it's like in the `real world.' It's not that easy." Jack sounded defensive even to his own ears, but he couldn't seem to stop himself. "The choices are tougher out there, Maggie."

She didn't open her eyes, but a fleeting smile ran across her face and disappeared. "It's tough everywhere, Jack. I don't live in damn Disneyland; I live where I *choose*. You're right, I have had this place all my life and I am grateful for it, but this life didn't happen by accident or because tough choices weren't made."

The tone in her voice had Jack remembering. He was talking to a woman who he had watched take over most of the adult responsibilities her grandmother had left her when she was only twelve. Since then she had become a single parent at eighteen and then turned an aging penniless farm into a thriving business. He knew she was right; she'd made some tough choices in her life too.

"I'm sorry. I don't know what I'm saying," he said with a sigh, "I don't even know how we got into this conversation. I've never told anyone I'm unhappy at work, now I'm with you for a couple hours and I'm spilling my guts."

"Jack, you just lost your mother, your only living parent, which tends to make us all take a long hard look at our own mortality and where life's going. It's only natural." She looked into his eyes. "I'm sorry if I made it seem like making that kind of change in your career and lifestyle wouldn't be difficult. I'm sure it would be."

Jack met her stare and Maggie spontaneously reached out for his hand. "Oh, I missed you, Jack Callahan."

"I missed you too, Mags. I don't think I realized how much till right now."

Without a word they stood up and hugged each other. Jack could smell the apple scent of her shampoo, and Maggie felt the strong broad shoulders of the man Jack had become. Then they took a step apart from each other, still holding hands, and Jack said, "I don't think I've had such a deep conversation since we were nine and sat on the dock contemplating where babies came from."

Maggie tossed her head back, her curls floating around her shoulders. She laughed and said, "Oh, man, I remember that!"

From the bottom of the porch steps a man's voice called up, "Hey you two, can you share the joke?"

Jack turned from Maggie to see a tall handsome brown-haired man dressed in a shirt and tie standing at the bottom of the steps. He appeared to be roughly the same age as Jack and Maggie and was looking up at them questioningly. Maggie dropped Jack's hands and skipped down the steps to greet him.

She gave him a smacking kiss. "Greg! I didn't know you were coming out tonight." Maggie turned to include Jack in the conversation. "Greg, this is an old friend of mine, Jack Callahan. You probably remembered me talking about the Callahans — they used to spend the summers next door when we were growing up."

The man extended his hand and Jack walked down the stairs to take it. Greg said, "Oh, yes. I remember you and Griff talking about the Callahans. Been a long time since you've been back, hasn't it?"

Jack felt put off by the comment, even though the truth was he *hadn't* been back in a long time. "Yeah, almost sixteen years."

"It's so funny though," Maggie said, "we just caught up over dinner and it feels like all that time just went away." She smiled up at Jack and he noticed Greg looking at him appraisingly.

"Well," Greg said, "I hear we have a new captain on the junior high baseball team. I had to come out and congratulate him in person."

"Oh, of course." Maggie explained to Jack, "Greg is the high school's vice-principal, he probably knew Caleb was going to be captain before Caleb did."

"I had a little heads up from the coach. Caleb's got a great swing and a good arm, you know that's one thing he got from his—"

Greg abruptly stopped talking and looked back at Maggie with wide apologetic eyes, it was only for a second, but Jack noticed. "I mean he was born with that arm. Remember even as a baby he could throw his toys clear across the room."

A strained smile came over Maggie's face. She said to Greg, "Caleb's out back with the guys. Go on back, then come in for some coffee, we have some left from dinner."

Greg looked from her to Jack "No, thanks. I've got an early meeting tomorrow. I'll just go say hi and then I have to head out. See you on Saturday night?"

"Of course." She gave Greg's arm a squeeze and he walked towards the back of the house.

"Oh, nice meeting you, Jack. Are you staying for a long visit?"

"About two weeks."

"Well, I'm sure we'll run into you again then." Greg waved and disappeared around the corner of the house. Jack couldn't put his finger on it, but somehow the way he had said, "*we'll* run into you and *visit*" had put his teeth on edge.

Maggie crouched down and started to pull some weeds from the flowerbeds. Jack bent down to help her. "Boyfriend?" he asked.

Maggie cocked an eyebrow, but she kept weeding. "Old friend. We went to school together. He's been a good friend for years and good to Caleb."

"Standing Saturday night date? Sounds like more than just friends to me."

Maggie stopped pulling at a dandelion and turned her full attention to Jack. "And what would that be to you?" she asked.

"Nothing, nothing," Jack held up his hands in mock surrender. "Just still trying to catch up, wondering what's going on with you?"

Maggie gave him a mischievous grin, "'What's going on with me?' is that what you just said?"

"Yes." Jack wore a rueful grin. "Lame, I know. I was just wondering, that's all." More seriously he said, "I'm sorry, you're right, it's none of my business."

Maggie shook her head. "It's OK. I have to admit I'm curious about you too. Why you don't have a wedding ring on that finger, mister big shot architect? I can't believe someone hasn't caught you yet."

"You spoiled me for other women."

Maggie chuckled, "Oh yeah, that one kiss we had on the dock was so good it ruined you for life, did it?"

"You have no idea." Jack looked in her eyes and realized that he wasn't completely joking. Maggie had been his first love, he had admitted that to himself already, but he also knew there was some validity to the fact that he had measured all other woman against her. In his mind no one had made him feel the way she had, and no one's character had compared to her resilience, sense of humor and compassion. He was afraid no one ever would.

Maggie was uncomfortable with the way the conversation had turned. "OK, hotshot. I've got to go in and play hostess to any guests who might like a night cap, so you go on back to your side of the road now."

"That was subtle."

"Subtly has never been my strong suit."

Jack leaned over and kissed Maggie on the cheek. "Thanks for dinner. It was great to see you all. I hope I get to see you again while I'm here."

"We're right next door, and you know the door's always open to you."

"Same goes at my place. And if I haven't said thank you for taking such great care of the house, let me say it again, thank you."

"You're welcome." Maggie walked up the porch steps and through the front door. Jack felt a mix of both elation and longing as he heard the slam of the spring loaded screen door shut. He didn't want to go. He wanted to follow her up the stairs into the warm glow of the house, but he was happy too, like he'd found a missing piece of himself that had been lost so many years ago. He'd come home.

Jack's cell phone rang in his pocket just as he was walking through the door of the cottage. He looked at the digital screen on the front of the phone, clicked the "talk" button and said, "Hey Kathy."

"So tell me! I have been waiting all day to hear about the house. Is it a mess? Do you have electricity? Did you see Maggie yet?"

"No. Yes. Yes. Ok, goodbye."

"Very funny. Tell me, tell me."

So Jack told her about the house, how it was kept in perfect condition, and about Maggie, the B&B and her son.

"Her son? Is she married?"

"No, but I think she has a boyfriend. I met him tonight."

"Is he the boy's father?"

"I don't think so. We really didn't get into it."

"Why not?"

Jack rolled his eyes and in a mocking voice says, "Oh, hi, Maggie, haven't seen you since I was sixteen. How are things? Oh, you have a son? Who's the father? Did you ever marry him? Please, my nosey-ass sister wants to know."

"Alright, alright. I'll find out myself when I come down."

Jack cringed. "Kathy that was sarcasm, meant to demonstrate that you should *not* ask highly personal questions of someone you have not seen in many many years."

"Whatever. You want to hear my theory on you and her?" She didn't wait for him to answer. "I think you had a crush on her when you were kids, and I think it would be great if you could pick up where you left off. So, you need to find out these things, Jack."

Jack paused, knowing she was closer to the mark than he would ever admit. "And I think you have been watching way too many soap operas and need to get a hobby, do needle point or something and stay out of my love life."

"Ha," she barked. "What love life? You have a social life and a sex life, but I haven't seen any sign of a *love* life."

"You know what? I've been analyzed by women enough for one day. I'm hanging up now. Goodbye."

"Jack." Beep.

CHAPTER SIX

That night at Granger House, Maggie went through her usual routine of taking a last walk through the house turning off the lights and checking that all the doors were locked. When the house was settled, she got ready for bed. She took the back service stairs from the kitchen to her bedroom on the second floor, passing Caleb's room and hearing the sounds of music coming from behind the door. She knew he was still wound up from his big day and would probably have trouble getting to sleep.

She tapped on his door and asked, "Can I come in to say goodnight?"

"Sure, Mom."

Lying on his bed staring at the ceiling, Caleb was tossing a ball up in the air and catching it. The room was dim, only his bedside light was on, and his favorite CD playing low. Maggie sat down on the edge of his bed and pushed his silky hair back from his forehead. He smiled up at her, and she saw a pensive look in his blue eyes she hadn't expected.

"You've got to get some sleep, honey, you've got school and practice tomorrow. Everything alright?"

"Yeah. I'm OK," he sighed.

"Come on, tell me. What's bothering you? You know I'll keep bugging you until you tell me, so you might as well give it up now."

Caleb looked up at his mother. "Oh, I know you will."

"So give."

"It's just...it would be cool to...I mean I know I have Gramps and Rolly and Joe and Greg."

Maggie realized in that moment what was bothering him. This was the type of day you shared with your father. He had felt like this before. Even on happy days like his birthday, there was always a little part of Caleb that missed a father he had never known. And he was right, he did have his great grandfather, Rolly, Joe and Greg, who all doted on him and gave him the type of love and support a father would, but they weren't his father.

Maggie understood. She hadn't ever lacked for love after her mother had died. Her grandmother and the guys had given her more love than anyone could ask for, but there had always been a missing spot in her heart that only her mother could fill. She wanted to give Caleb everything in this world she could, but this was the one thing she could not.

"I'm sorry, honey. I know you wish you had a dad to share all this with."

"Yeah, well. It was cool Greg came over, huh?"

"Yes, it was." His mood lightened. She stroked his head some more.

"They all took turns pitching the ball to me, and I hit five of them way out past the willow tree in the back field."

"Holy smokes. I can't wait to come watch your first game. We are going to fill a whole row in the bleachers."

Caleb laughed. "Oh, man, Gramps and Rolly better not wear those big foam fingers that say `Caleb is #1' on them."

"I'd like to see you try and stop them."

Caleb groaned and rolled over.

"OK, captain. Twenty minutes and lights out." She kissed the top of his head, gave him a pat on his back and got up off the bed.

"Alright, Mom. Goodnight."

"Goodnight, honey." Maggie walked into her own room and closed the door.

Once she was ready for bed, Maggie sat in front of the mirror at her antique mahogany vanity, the one that had been her mother's, and stared at her reflection. She hadn't really looked at herself in a while. Oh, she'd passed the mirror to check if her hair was staying put or her earrings were straight, but now she really stopped to take stock in her appearance.

As she leaned a little closer to the mirror, she imagined how she looked today through Jack's eyes. She wondered what he saw; how he thought she had changed after all these years. She pulled her hair back away from her face and turned her head each way. Not so bad for the mother of a junior high school kid, she thought to herself.

Turning thirty-one last month, she had acknowledged there were the beginnings of fine lines around her eyes, and her first gray hair was at her temple. But for the most part, she felt she had earned both and didn't fret too much about growing older.

"Why am I worrying about what Jack Callahan thinks anyway?" she said to her reflection. She hadn't seen him in years, and he was only going to stay in town for two weeks before he headed back to his big-time apartment and job, and probably multiple sophisticated Manhattan girlfriends. She'd barely thought of him in years anyway. She looked back at her reflection and into her own eyes and knew you couldn't lie to yourself so easily. Of course she's thought of him — a lot.

Jack had been her first best friend and then her first kiss, her first love. She'd missed him terribly the summer the Callahans hadn't come back, and to a certain extent, she'd missed him right up until she found him lying on his parent's bed that day. But life had gone on fifteen years ago, and life would go on again when he was back in New York.

She blew a stray strawberry colored curl off her forehead and started to rub moisturizer into her skin. How her life and dreams changed in those years since she'd seen him. Jack had reminded her that she had wanted nothing more as a young girl than to leave Lake Meade the day after she graduated high school and never look back at the small rural town. College, the Peace Corps, she'd have done anything to get away. That had all changed in one horrible night.

But she couldn't and wouldn't dwell on that night. When she thought of it, she consciously turned her mind to thoughts of her son instead. She wouldn't have Caleb if it wasn't for that night, and she would have endured a lot worse than that to have him.

Maggie pushed the pump down on the moisturizer bottle again and started to rub her elbows. She had a life she had grown to love, didn't she? She wouldn't change a thing about it, and she really hadn't thought anything was missing; she had a wonderful family, a business she enjoyed and great friends like Greg. What more could anyone ask for? And then Jack Callahan had come back and reminded her.

Jack opened his eyes to sun streaming in through the windows across his bed. At first he was disoriented. He was used to being up before the sun, encased in cream-colored Egyptian cotton sheets and a designer comforter, not in a room with lace curtains and a chenille bedspread. Then he remembered where he was and his next thought was the pancakes at the Lake View Diner.

Jack actually clapped his hands, rubbed them together and said out loud, "Hot damn! Tall stack with bacon, here I come!" He was dressed and out of the house in ten minutes. It was a beautiful morning and he decided to walk the half-mile down the lane to the diner. In his childhood, his family had performed this ritual at least once a week during the summer. He actually wished Kathy and her kids were there now to take the walk with him.

As he headed down the lane, Jack breathed in the sweet early spring air mixed with the scents of the trees and the lake, but he also noticed something was different. He knew the four big houses on the road were new, but there was something else. Suddenly he stopped and realized what it was, no crunching. When he was a child Granger Lane was a gravel road and whether you walked it or rode your bike on it, there was always the loud crunching sound of the stones against your sneakers or tires. Now there was just the light tap of his boots on the pavement.

The parking lot of the Lake View Diner was packed. Filled mostly with pick-up trucks and work vans as the local contractors ate a big breakfast and had their fill of coffee and gossip before beginning their workday. Jack saw a blue Ford pick-up with the words "Granger House B&B" painted on the side in stenciled red lettering.

The boisterous voices of the diners and steamy syrup flavored air assaulted him as he pulled open the heavy glass door. Everyone in the restaurant seemed to be talking at once. It was only 7:30 in the morning, but on the weekdays, that was the morning rush. Jack noticed Joe sitting with Maggie at a booth towards the back of the diner, sipping coffee and listening to the waitress as she leaned over talking to them and popping her gum.

"Good morning. Can I join you?" he asked them.

The waitress looked him over and then moved away. Joe and Maggie looked up at him and Maggie said, "Of course." Jack slid into the red vinyl covered booth next to Maggie. Joe looked across at Jack and didn't say anything.

They were both finished their breakfast, sipping the last of their coffee. Jack said to Maggie, "I'm surprised to see you here. I would think the proprietor of a bed and breakfast would actually need to be there at breakfast time."

Maggie pulled an exaggerated look of surprise. "Oh, my goodness! Is that what the second 'B' is for in B&B?" She turned to Joe who had a small grin playing on his lips. "Well, gracious, Joe, we've been forgetting that all these years. It's a good thing Jack here came back all the way from the big city to tell us."

Maggie's face went blank and she picked up her coffee cup for a sip, looking at Jack over the rim. "Very funny," he said.

She explained, "Griff and Rolly set up the dining room and put out the breakfast pastries while Joe and I drive Caleb to the end of the lane to catch the bus. Then we have a quiet breakfast here before we go back and I start making omelets and sausage for the guests."

"A 'quiet' breakfast? It's loud in here."

Maggie laughed. "I swear, nobody can gossip like a bunch of grown men." Joe cleared his throat and Maggie looked at him apologetically. "Except for Joe here, he doesn't participate in the local gossip. But I can tell you his ears pick up every word that's being said in this place."

Joe raised his eyebrows at her.

"Come on, Joe. You may not say much, but you hear every word."

Joe shrugged his shoulders and turned his attention back to his coffee.

The waitress came back to take Jack's order, when he was done, she looked at him appraisingly. After she'd gone Maggie said, "Oh, boy, you are going to be the hot topic in here this morning."

"Why? All I did was order a tall stack and sausage."

"Because no one knows who you are and here you are sitting with us. By the end of the day it will be all around town that you are a long lost Granger cousin, a new employee or—"

"Caleb's father," Joe said this so quietly Jack wasn't sure if he'd heard him right.

Joe looked up with soulful eyes at Maggie, who'd gone very pale. The solemn look on his face hadn't changed, but he had a wary stare. Maggie's cup rattled when she put it back down on the saucer. "Well, let them wonder," she said with iron in her voice. "It sure as hell won't be the first time they gossiped about that topic and I am sure it won't be the last."

Jack sat very still watching the two of them, Maggie suddenly all nervous energy as she started gathering her purse and keys. Joe threw fifteen dollars on the table and slid out of the booth while Jack stood up to let Maggie get out.

With more bravado than her jittery countenance suggested, Maggie said to Jack, "Sorry we can't stay, it's time to feed the paying customers." On their way out, Maggie and Joe waved to several of the other diners who were finishing their breakfast. Shouts of, "See ya, Maggie, see ya, Joe," followed them out the door. Jack watched through the window as they walked to the blue truck, Maggie with a grim look on her face while Joe's expression was unreadable. Jack saw them sit in the cab of the truck and talk for a few minutes before Joe started the engine and pulled out of the parking lot.

Jack wondered about their conversation. Why did the town gossip about who Caleb's father was? Was it just the fact that she had been a young, probably unwed, mother? He didn't have to wait too long that day to find out.

Jack finished his breakfast, paid at the counter and decided to stretch his legs and walk into what was considered downtown Lake Meade. As he walked along Main Street, Jack admired the neatly kept yards of the houses tucked up next to each other on each side of the street and the well-kept brick and stone buildings that housed the town's few businesses.

Majestic old trees had grown on the narrow strips of grass that ran between the sidewalk and buildings. He tripped a few times on the tree roots that had pushed up through the concrete slabs of the sidewalk. There were only about four blocks between the diner and the primarily commercial section of Lake Meade and soon Jack found himself looking into a bookstore window, then a jewelry store's. A few minutes later he was standing in front of a large open parking lot filled with new cars. In the center of the parking lot was a two-story brick building with a prominant illuminated sign across the front that read "Harding Prestige Motors."

Jack had been thinking of trading in his Audi convertible for something that could seat more than two people, so he decided to wander around. He wasn't in the lot more than two minutes when a rail-thin woman with unnaturally black hair cut into a short, straight bob walked briskly towards him. She held out a well-manicured hand for Jack and he took it.

"Hello, I'm Cynthia Harding. Can I answer any questions for you today?" she asked.

Jack was looking at a small-sized SUV and asked her if he could see the specifications on it. "Certainly," she said, "why don't you come into my office and I'll get you a brochure."

They walked through a small showroom where the latest model truck was displayed in the center of the room. Scattered around the edges of the open space were tan vinyl chairs and Formica topped tables. Framed posters hung on the walls showing the dealership's full line of vehicles.

Cynthia's office was more feminine than the other décor in the building. Her walls were done in pink flowered print wallpaper and the chairs were imitation French provincial.

Jack watched her as she searched her shelf for the brochure. Her skin had a tanned and weathered appearance. She was older than Jack had first thought. *Middle fifties maybe?* He thought.

Her credenza was crowded with awards from the car manufacturer and a heavy glass trophy from the local Rotary Club shaped like their gear shaped symbol, a little gold plaque reading "Member of the Year – 1986" faced out for visitors to read. Cynthia turned around and smiled at Jack. "Ah, here we are." She handed him a thick glossy pamphlet. "This gives you the engine size, gas mileage and color selection. You can take that with you if you'd like."

"Thanks."

"I don't remember seeing you around her before, Mr..."

"Callahan. Jack Callahan. And no, I haven't been back here in a long time. My family has a summer place on the lake, right next to the Granger's. We spent a lot of time here when I was younger, but this is the first time I've been back in years."

Something in Cynthia's expression shifted. The practiced smile frozen in position on her face and she lowered herself slowly in her seat, her eyes sharper, but her voice still even and pleasant. "Do you know the Grangers then?"

Jack was looking at the brochure, but the curious tone in her voice made him look up. "Yes, Maggie Granger and I were friends, we played together as children."

"How old were you the last time you were here?" Cynthia leaned forward ever so slightly in her chair as if the answer to this question was more important to her than her casualness would imply.

Jack had the impression she was fishing for information. He decided to play along. "I was sixteen the last time I was here."

Cynthia's smile remained fixed on her face. "So it's been over twelve, is it, years since you've been back?"

"Well, now you're flattering me," Jack said with false good humor. "I'm thirty-two, it's been over fifteen years since I've been back to Lake Meade."

Cynthia's posture relaxed and she sat back in her chair, then, as if something else had suddenly occurred to her, she asked, "I assume you went to college up north as well?"

"Yes, actually, I went to Columbia University in New York."

Jack was sure he detected a look of disappointment flicker briefly across her face, but before he could say anything else, the practiced salesman's smile was back in place. "That is a fine university," she said, "What did you study?"

"Architecture. I'm an architect in a firm in New York now."

"Oh, your mother must be so proud." She glanced over at a framed picture of a smiling youth in a high school football uniform.

"Yes, she was." Jack decided he'd had enough small talk in the stifling tiny pink office. He couldn't say exactly why, but he didn't particularly care for this woman, and her office was growing claustrophobic. He stood to leave and said, "Well, I'll let you know if I decide to change vehicles."

"You do that, Mr. Callahan. I consider you a local since your family owns property here in Lake Meade. I'll do right by you."

Yeah, right. Jack was halfway out the door when she asked, "So what do you think of the Granger's bed and breakfast, Mr. Callahan?"

"I think they did a great job. The place looks beautiful and seems to be doing well."

Jack saw the plastic smile definitely slip this time. "Yes, I suppose. Of course, *I* wouldn't have strangers traipsing through my house, but I guess you have to do what you have to do to make a living."

Jack really didn't care for this woman. "I guess so," he answered noncommittally as he left the office. He would have to ask Maggie about Cynthia Harding, and what she ever did to Cynthia to deserve her snide little comments.

CHAPTER SEVEN

Jack returned to the lake house to find a dusty Chevy Nova parked in the driveway. The front door of the cottage was unlocked; he opened it and yelled, "Hello." A stout middle-aged woman with sandy blonde hair walked out of the living room only a few feet from him. Jack jumped with surprise.

"Oh, I am so sorry, Mr. Callahan. I didn't mean to startle you." The woman wiped her hands off on a flowered apron. "My name's Candy Stokes. I've been cleaning the place for your mom. This is my regular day to do it and Maggie told me to come on over as your mom had paid me through next month."

"That's fine, Candy, and call me Jack. Just let me know what my mother paid you. I'd like to continue with the arrangement if that's all right. You've kept the place looking great."

"Well, it's not too much trouble, no one's here to mess anything up. I just try and keep the dust from settling. It was nice to see a pair of shoes next to the bed and a toothbrush on the side of the sink. A house should be lived in."

Jack smiled at her. She had warm blue eyes and an easy smile. "I think so too, Candy. It's good to be back." And at that moment, he knew he meant it.

Candy noticed the brochure in his hand. "Were you over at the Harding's place?"

"Yes, looking at a new car, why?"

Candy grimaced, two parallel frown lines forming between her eyes. "Did you talk to Cynthia Harding?"

"Yes."

"Did she know you were a friend of Maggie's?"

Jack was intrigued now. "Yes. Although I got the distinct impression that she was not."

"You got that right."

Candy walked towards the kitchen. Jack followed, watching as she turned on the burner under the kettle on the stove. She said to him, "I usually have some tea around now, would you like some?"

Jack didn't particularly care for tea, but he sensed she wanted to talk and he wanted to know what she had to say, so he answered, "Sure."

Candy pulled two tea bags out of another pocket in her apron. How many pockets does she have in that thing, Jack wondered. She opened a cabinet and pulled out two mugs and plopped a tea bag in each one, then she pulled a metal chair out from the kitchen table and sat down heavily with a satisfying grunt. Jack joined her at the table.

Before speaking, Candy looked down at her dry calloused hands and then back up at Jack. "Do you mind me asking what Cynthia said to you to give you that impression?"

"Not much, just a comment she made about the B&B. It was more her tone than what she said that made me think she didn't care for the Grangers very much, and Maggie in particular."

Candy pursed her lips and glared at the wall. "Oh, she's such a bit— oh, excuse me."

"No need to excuse yourself, that was my impression as well."

Her eyes softened, and then she hauled herself up from the table and went over to the stove to get the whistling kettle and pour hot water into their mugs. After she had set a mug in front of each of them and settled back down in her chair, Candy contemplated what to say next.

After a few moments she said, "I know you're only going to be in town a short while, Jack, but be careful what you say around that woman, especially about Maggie."

"Why?"

"You like Maggie, don't you? You guys were friends when you were kids?"

"Yes."

"Well, that woman is *not* a friend of Maggie's and if she can get even a little dirt on her, she will, and she'll twist it and spread it around this town as fast as she can."

Jack asked again, "Why?"

Candy took a sip of her tea, and then said, "I do not like to gossip, especially about people I care for and I care very much for the Grangers."

"I understand that and appreciate that, I don't want to gossip about Maggie either. I just want to understand what this woman has against her. I don't want to stir anything up here just because I don't know what's going on."

Candy put her mug down on the table, looked into his eyes and seemed to decide something. She said, "Maggie and Cynthia's son Scott dated their junior and senior years in high school. Scott was the town's shining son and star football player, and the apple of his mama's eye."

"OK?"

"Well, let me think how to explain this. Maggie is a sweetheart, but she's different. She walks to her own drummer, and Cynthia never liked her much or thought she was good enough for her golden boy. She had groomed Scott to take over her business one day and had hopes of him becoming mayor of Lake Meade. Hell, she probably had him becoming a congressman or senator too in her warped little mind. Cynthia didn't see Maggie as the type that would become the proper wife of a high-powered man."

"Alright, I get that. Maggie is never going to be a 'Stepford wife,' but it doesn't look like they got married, so what's the problem?"

Candy paused again to gather her thoughts. "Scott and Greg Detrick, he's our high school vice-principal now, they were best friends."

"I just met him at Maggie's yesterday."

"Well, Greg, Scott and Maggie were all friends in high school and hung out together." She stopped to take a breath. "I'm not sure what is the truth with the rest of the story, but it's what Cynthia believes and it's why she hates Maggie so much." Candy took a fortifying sip of her tea and then continued, "Maggie and Scott were going to their senior prom together, of course, and Scott had told some of his friends that he planned to propose to Maggie that night.

"Scott was going to Penn State to study business and Maggie was going to Baltimore to the Maryland Institute of Art. Scott was going to ask Maggie to marry him so they would be promised to each other through their separation at college. The night of the prom Scott showed up at the Granger farm to pick Maggie up and ask her to marry him, but instead he found her and Greg together."

"Together?" Jack asked.

"You know...together," Candy looked at Jack knowingly. "So Scott freaked out at finding Maggie with his best friend and went home, packed his bags and left Lake Meade. He left his mother a note saying he couldn't stand to be in the same town as Maggie and Greg and he would never come back."

"Never?"

"Nope. Cynthia says he rarely even writes anymore. She says since both Maggie and Greg are still here, he won't ever come back."

"That seems a little extreme. We've all have our heart broken one time or another, especially when we're young, it doesn't usually take a decade or more to get over."

Candy raised her eyebrows and said, "I'm not so sure about that, but I agree with you that it does seem a little extreme. Like I said, this is all speculation and appears to be what Cynthia believes. She couldn't tell enough people around town what a slut she thought Maggie was and that she had been right all along about her not being good enough for Scott. Cynthia was *so* pissed off. All her dreams for her little Harding dynasty were gone. And when Maggie came home pregnant from college, well, everyone thought maybe Cynthia might have been right about the `slut' part. She sure as hell pointed it out to anyone who would stand still long enough to listen."

Jack went very still. The thought of anyone thinking that about Maggie made his stomach churn. When he found his voice he said, "I didn't think Maggie even went to college."

"Just for the first semester, then she came home pregnant and the Grangers started turning the old farm into a B&B."

Jack looked out the window at the trees swaying in the light breeze. He imagined Maggie coming home to Lake Meade a pregnant unwed teenager, to this town where she was already being judged harshly for her supposed betrayal of Scott Harding, the prodigal son. His heart ached for that young girl. And where had he been? Back in New Jersey being mad at something he couldn't even describe instead of being there for his friend.

Jack traced his finger around the rim of his cup. "Can I ask? Could Greg be Caleb's father?"

"Hon, she has never told *anyone* who Caleb's father is, I don't even think Griff knows for sure. People mostly assume it's Greg, but it could just as easily been someone at college."

Candy stood up and put her empty mug next to the sink, and then turned back and looked down at Jack. "Look, I don't want to give you the impression Maggie's walking around this town with a big scarlet letter on her shirt or anything. The truth is, except for that hag Harding and her clique, you won't hear a bad word about Maggie Granger in Lake Meade. She's good people and Caleb is a great kid.

"When my husband died last year, Maggie made sure I made enough money to get by and keep my mortgage paid. That's the kind of person she is. And if you tried to shake a stick at how many people around this town were born on the wrong side of the blanket, well, your arm would get mighty tired.

"But you've got to understand, Cynthia will never let this thing go, and she is a prominent person in this community. She's on the town board of directors and she's got one of the most lucrative businesses around, so sure as shit she will churn up any trouble she can for Maggie any chance she gets. That's why when I heard you say you'd been talking to Cynthia Harding…well…I didn't think you'd want to become friendly with someone that felt that way about our Maggie."

"I appreciate you telling me, Candy."

"Don't tell Maggie I told you all that, she'd be pissed. She hates it when anyone brings up Scott or, God forbid, she hears anybody speculating on who Caleb's father is. Can't say I blame her, but you know, rumors like that cast long shadows."

CHAPTER EIGHT

Jack decided to take a walk outside to let Candy finish her work in peace. He spent some time puttering around the yard and the property, reacquainting himself with the little cottage by the lake. Once he'd satisfied himself that everything in and around the house was in working order, he walked down toward the lake and the woods surrounding it. The trees were budding and shoots of green were making their way up through the blanket of dried leaves and pine needles.

Jack had never seen the property this time of the year. The Callahans hadn't come to the lake until Memorial Day weekend, when everything was already green and starting to blossom. It seemed to Jack that he was witnessing a secret, a whisper of what was to come. He knew in only a few weeks the shoots he saw peeking their heads up would be daffodils and tulips, the lawn a moss-green and the trees thick with leaves.

As he stood at the edge of the tree line, about 50 yards from the lake, a hint of color mixed with the mostly brown background caught his eye. He walked towards it. *It can't be! Oh, man, it is!*

Jack jogged to the swatch of color until it became a faded red and the nondescript form the bottom of his old rowboat. He brushed the leaves and debris off the overturned dingy, checking for any damage, but it was just like the house had been, no sign of rot or aging, as if it had been waiting for him to return.

Jack took a deep breath and pushed on the side of the boat until it turned over. On the ground beneath the boat were his oars and two mildewed orange life vests. He took a step back and surveyed the rowboat that had once been his pride and joy, a gift from his parents on his eleventh birthday.

What had once been bright red paint was now faded to pink, and the metal oar holders rusted, but the hull appeared solid. Jack contemplated how far the lake was from where he was standing next to the boat. There was a gentle downward slope and no trees between him and the water, he pushed the boat down towards the dock without too much difficulty.

After about fifteen minutes of pushing, pulling and grunting, Jack reached the edge of the water. Because of the drought, the water level was much farther down on the dock's pilings than he remembered. The bottom of the wooden ladder that extended from the dock into the water had once been several feet under the surface, now stuck out of the lake a yard or more.

By the time he got the boat turned the right way around and floating on the water, Jack was so excited he didn't even notice his two hundred-dollar Nike sneakers were covered to the laces in mud. With a running leap, he jumped into the boat, pushing off the muddy shore with an oar. Jack steadied himself and settled on the middle seat, grabbing the oars and setting them in their rusty holders, rowing farther out into deeper water.

Once Jack got the rhythm of pulling the oars back in the water smoothly and evenly, he started to take a look around him. Except for a few more houses on the other side of the lake and the severely lowered water level, the landscape looked much the same as it had when he was a boy.

The air is so sweet here, he thought, nothing like the air in the city — not that Jack minded the smell of New York City, actually he liked it, the unique mix of hot dog vendors, car exhaust and too many people — but the lake air was remarkable, as if there were twice as much oxygen. The amount of open space and sky was a change for him too. He was used to being surrounded at all times by high walls, traffic and other people. Just sitting alone on the quiet lake with nothing but water around him and a huge blue sky above made him feel smaller somehow.

He decided to row halfway around the lake and then head back to his own dock. About ten minutes into rowing he found himself adjacent to the Granger's property. He could see the top of the old barn roof over the trees, and that the Grangers had built a much more substantial dock than what was there when he was a boy. There were two paddle boats and a canoe tied up to it, he assumed for guest use.

It was so quiet that all he heard was the splashing sound his oars made when they hit the water, he stopped rowing for a minute to coast along and watch the Granger's place drift past. There were suddenly voices mixed in with the sounds of the water and Jack looked over at the dock, but he didn't see anyone, then he noticed two people were standing in the tree line. He thought one of them was Maggie; he could see her bright strawberry blond hair. The other figure looked like a man, but he wasn't sure who. Jack was about to shout and wave to get Maggie's attention, but the voices suddenly rose as if in anger and Jack stopped.

He rowed away from shore then, feeling as if he was intruding, but as fast as he rowed the shoreline seemed to stay in the same place. Then he heard Maggie's voice. "You can't do that!"

The other voice was quieter. Jack could only hear a few words. "I have to...lying...time..."

Maggie's voice was pleading and louder. "No! I understand it doesn't feel right, but think of Caleb. And what if you had to go away?"

Again Jack heard the other voice, but only a few words come across the lake clearly. "When? I won't...forever...It's no use...Scott."

Jack finally started to move farther away from shore, the voices becoming fainter. He was relieved when he finally made it to the other side of the Granger's dock. Jack was pretty sure the other voice was a man's, and he wondered what it was that man was lying about.

CHAPTER NINE

Men! She didn't understand them...she was surrounded by them...she loved them...but sometimes she wanted to kick them square in the ass. Maggie stomped her way through the woods with no particular destination in mind; she just needed to clear her head.

All these years...all these years everything has been fine! Now he wants to change it all! And for what? Everything is going along just fine! He has the job he has always wanted, and I have a great life too. What the hell is he thinking? Why would he want to throw everything away? If he could just stay strong a little while longer then...then what?

Suddenly, Maggie felt like a popped balloon. *Then what? Then what?* She let out a heavy sigh. She knew she was being unreasonable, even irrational, but she had felt like ranting and fuming, even though in her heart she knew Greg was right. Life was changing and they had to change with it.

The last few weeks she had felt anxious, restless, and couldn't put her finger on why, like just before a storm moved in and you could feel it in the change in the air and the strength of the wind, but you couldn't see it yet. She'd been ignoring her feelings and she should know better than to discount her own instincts.

Her pulse calmed and her breathing slowed. Maggie stopped stomping through the woods, closed her eyes and took a deep breath. What was she really so afraid of? There was nothing that could hurt her now. She listened to the sounds of the lake, the sounds of the birds in the trees. The ground steadied again beneath her feet.

Once she'd regained her composure, she looked around to take note of where she had ended up. She knew these woods and most of the people who lived on the lake, so she wasn't concerned that she was lost or trespassing, but it was getting close to when Caleb would be coming home from school and she should head back. A moment later Maggie spotted Jack, a goofy grin on his face as he rowed in smooth easy strokes in his old dingy, as if he'd been on the lake only yesterday. Oh, Jack.

Maggie watched him for a few moments, watched the muscles on his arms stand out with each stroke of the oar, how strong his back looked and how the sun reflected off his chestnut brown hair. His pleasant boyhood features had matured into a strong chin and almost hawkish nose, just like his father's. She had to admit, Jack Callahan had grown into one good-looking man.

On impulse, Maggie walked to the edge of the lake and shouted out, "Hey sailor! Can a girl get a ride?"

Jack had been having such a good time rowing around the lake he'd startled at the sound of Maggie's voice, especially since it was so far from where he had last seen her. She was practically on the other side of the lake now. Maybe it hadn't been her he'd heard after all. Maybe it had been one of her guests. Jack cupped his hand around his mouth and yelled back, "Hey! Stay there! I'll row over to you."

Jack maneuvered the little boat into a turn and headed back towards Maggie. She'd taken off her sneakers and socks and rolled up her pants, wading in to her knees. Jack pulled up next to her. She jumped into the boat and he pushed off the bottom with his oar.

As Maggie settled herself on the seat closest to the bow, Jack glanced at her face for any signs of stress from the argument he thought he had overheard between her and a man. Maybe Greg? He didn't notice any tension and wondered again if he had been mistaken. He wondered too if he should admit what he overheard. His next thought — which crowded out all other thoughts — was that she looked awfully pretty with her hair pulled back in a ponytail and her bare feet propped up on the side of the boat. Eyes squinting against the sun and an easy smile hovering around her lips.

"So you found her, huh?" Maggie patted the side of the boat.

Jack gave himself a mental shake. "Yep. And look at her, not so much as a single leak after all these years."

"There shouldn't be. You primed, painted and waxed this thing every summer. It would have been preserved another sixteen years."

"Well, I'm glad I didn't wait to find out."

Me too.

He watched silently as Maggie tilted her head up to the sun. "I really am sorry it took me so long to come back."

She lowered her head back down and looked him in the eye. "Sorry? You don't need to be sorry. Your father died here, Jack. He died in *your arms* here for goodness sake, that's going to change a place for a person. I'm just glad you found your way back. I hope you and Kathy come and use the place again."

"Yeah. I think we will. But what I really meant was that I'm sorry I walked away from our friendship. You and I were good friends and I should have kept in touch. I should have been here when you needed me."

Maggie looked over at his profile suspiciously as he stared out into the distance. "When I needed you? Oh, now I get it. Are you feeling sorry for me, Jack? You were at the diner this morning; you got all caught up on the local gossip, or did you run into Candy at the house? Hope you got your fill." She couldn't keep the anger out of her voice. Abruptly she said, "Can you take me back to the dock now? I have to go, Caleb will be home soon."

Jack leaned forward and reached out to touch her arm. "Maggie, wait, don't be angry. I did hear about all the gossip that went on about you, especially when you were pregnant with Caleb. I just wish I could have been here for you, that's all. It must have been a difficult time."

Maggie leaned her head back again with a tired sigh and closed her eyes, letting the sun dry up any tears that threatened to come, but none did. Her tears over that time in her life had dried up years ago. Without looking at him she asked, "Do you know what Caleb's middle name is, Jack?"

Jack was momentarily stumped by the abrupt change in the conversation. "No, I don't."

"It's Phoenix. Caleb Phoenix Granger. Do you know why?"

"No."

"Because from the ashes of one of the worst periods of my life came the best of my life...Caleb, the bed and breakfast, keeping my family together. After that night when Scott left, I couldn't walk down the street or go anywhere around town without people staring and whispering." Maggie spoke in a voice with a heavy southern drawl, "Did ya hear what happened on prom night? Scott found Maggie f--ing Greg. Scott left town for good, can't blame 'im. His best friend and his girlfriend stabbed him in the back, poor guy. Cynthia was right, she said Maggie was loose. Brought up strange in that house with all those old men."

Jack watched her imitate the town's people; her eyes still closed as she shifted position so she was lying down with her arms draped across the sides of the boat. He wanted to tell her to stop talking if it hurt her to remember, but he also wanted to know what happened. He needed to know about this period of her life, all that he had missed. He wanted to know her again, all of her.

Jack stopped rowing and they just drifted for a while in silence. Jack had also shifted his position so that he too was halfway lying down opposite Maggie, his arms propped on the end of the boat and his legs resting on the seat he had been sitting on. He wouldn't rush her.

Without warning Maggie let out a mirthless laugh that echoed off the lake and said bitterly, "And then when I came back from college pregnant...ooh, didn't I just prove them all right. Couldn't walk into the store or the post office without everyone turning to stare and click their tongues at me."

She was quiet again for a few moments, and then said, "So I was a scared unwed pregnant eighteen--year-old living with three old men on a penniless and decaying farm and dodging gossiping old bitches every five minutes." She shook her head. "No, sir, that was not the most fun I've ever had."

When she opened her eyes and sat up straighter, she stared directly into Jack's eyes. "But I wouldn't change a minute of it, because when I got done being scared and feeling sorry for myself, I got angry. I mean really pissed off. And if I hadn't been so pissed off I may never have tried anything so drastic as starting the bed and breakfast. And having Caleb has been my greatest joy, not even the old gossiping hens in this town could take away a split second of the shear bliss that boy has given me. Caleb and running the B&B and keeping all my old men fed and together on this land are the greatest gifts I could have asked for. I swear I am the most blessed woman on this planet. Don't you *dare* feel sorry for me, Jack Callahan."

Jack stared back at her into her clear gray-blue eyes and smiled at his old friend. "Phoenix," he repeated.

"God damn right, Phoenix." Maggie's clear voice rang with laughter.

After a while of drifting around they bumped into a log floating in the lake and Jack sat back up in the seat and started to row towards the Granger's dock. Maggie watched him and once again admired his muscular arms and shoulders as he pulled back on the oars. Jack caught her watching him and they both grinned at each other. "You grew up all right, Callahan," she said.

Jack barked out a laugh, "You too, Granger."

"So who filled you in on my misguided youth anyway? Candy?"

Jack shook his head. "Promised I wouldn't tell."

"Oh, I know it was Candy. That's all right. If I was going to be gossiped about, I'm glad it was a friend telling the story. Candy has always stuck by me through everything. After my grandmother died, Candy was the one who took me shopping for 'girl things,' like make-up and my first bra. Griff would give her money and we'd drive over to the mall in Dover." Maggie smiled at the memory.

"Just so you know, she only told me because I ran into Cynthia Harding at her dealership today. Candy just wanted me to know she was not a friend to you and why I should steer clear of her."

Blotches of red instantly appeared on Maggie's face and neck at the mention of Cynthia Harding. "Oh, she is such a bitch."

"That was my observation."

"Ah well, what can you do. I learned a long time ago I was never going to win that one over and I gave up giving a damn. She wants to think I drove her son away, I'll never convince her otherwise."

Jack wanted to ask her, "Then what did happen?" But he didn't. If Maggie wanted to tell him what happened on that prom night all those years ago, she would in her own time and in her own way.

He rowed up to the Granger dock and Maggie stood up gingerly in the small boat, grabbing hold of the ladder. Jack didn't like seeing her leave; he didn't want to go back to his house alone, which was an unfamiliar and unsettling thought for a man who had lived happily by himself for many years.

As if reading his mind, Maggie looked down at him when she reached the top of the dock and asked, "Would you like to come over again for dinner tonight?"

Jack nodded his head vigorously 'yes' but said in a mockingly formal voice, "Oh, I couldn't possibly impose on you again."

Maggie laughed at him. "Uh huh, I get the message, Callahan. Be back here at six-forty-five on the dot."

"Yes, Ma'am." Jack stood briefly and saluted her, then sat back down and rowed towards his own dock. He was tying up the little rowboat when a man in a slightly larger metal flat-bottomed boat with a small outboard motor and a fishing pole puttered past him. The man waved his hand in greeting and Jack waved back. *People are just friendlier around here*, Jack thought to himself.

The man was heading towards the western part of the lake where he'd heard the fishing was particularly good, but more than fish would end up on his line — a boy's bones and Maggie's secrets.

CHAPTER TEN

After a shower, Jack was changing into a fresh pair of jeans and a cotton t-shirt when his cell phone rang. He looked at the tiny screen and saw it was Kathy.

"Hello, sister dear."

"You sound happy."

"I am. Guess what I did all afternoon?"

"This is a perfect opening for me to say `Maggie?' but I won't be so crude. So what did you do?"

Jack shook his head at the phone and then said, "When did your mind get so far in the gutter? And yes, I did see Maggie today and we *talked*, but the best part was I found my old boat and it's in great shape. The paint's a little faded but it's as tight as a drum. I rowed all around the lake this afternoon."

On her end Kathy had to smile, she couldn't remember the last time her brother had sounded so carefree and happy, but of course she had to tease him, she was his big sister and teasing him unmercifully was her God-given right. "Your little rowboat? That's what has you so excited? Oh, come on, Jack, you're killing me. I want to hear what you and Maggie talked about, not about your damn dinghy."

"That little boat still looks the same as it did sixteen years ago. Can you say the same thing?"

"Ha! When that *dinghy* can give birth, deal with a husband, three kids, a dog and a wayward brother, then you can tell me how great it looks."

"Wayward brother? Ha. I am a model brother, a pillar of respectability, a scion of—"

"Yeah, yeah. So what did you and Maggie do?"

"Not that it is any of your business, but we went for a ride in my 'dinghy,' as you call it, and *she* appreciated it."

"I never said she wasn't a little off herself, that's what makes you two perfect for each other. She always liked going out fishing in that thing with you. I could never figure that out. Worms and fish and mud. Yuk!"

"You're such a girl."

"Come on. You're stalling, what did you guys talk about?"

"All right, if you want to know the whole story I better start at the beginning." Jack told her about meeting Cynthia Harding, what Candy let him know about Maggie's past, and then what Maggie had talked about in the boat that afternoon. When he was finished, Kathy was unusually quiet.

Jack looked at the second hand on his watch. "I think this is a record for how long you have ever gone without saying anything. It's been a whole ten seconds."

Kathy's voice held a note of sadness. "I guess we've all had things to deal with. I'm just sorry I didn't know what was happening to Maggie, that I didn't keep in touch."

"Yeah, that's how I felt too, but I have to tell you, the last thing Maggie wants or needs is our pity. She's really doing great." Jack changed the subject. "The best news is that the pancakes at the diner are just as good as ever."

With enthusiasm Kathy said, "Oh, man, I am so excited to bring the kids down! I can't wait to take them there for breakfast and out in your boat on the lake."

"Hey, hey, a minute ago you were maligning my boat!"

"Yeah, but I know the kids will love it. So what are you doing tonight for dinner?"

Jack hesitated, then said, "I'm going over to the Granger's again."

"Ooh! Listen, after dinner ask Maggie to take a moonlit stroll around the lake. Oh wait, better yet, ask her to..." Beep

Maggie was hustling around the kitchen trying to time her brussel sprouts to be done at the same time her rolls were finished warming and her turkey was done roasting. She had prepared this same meal a hundred times before, but it was always a challenge to get everything on the table simultaneously and still warm.

Joe and Rolly were in the dining room setting the table. She could hear Rolly complaining to Joe that they should use the pink linens because it was spring. She had to cover her mouth to keep them from hearing her laugh out loud, Rolly caring about pink linens of all things. This was a man that used to birth calves, bail hay and hunt deer.

"What are you grinning about over there?" Griff caught her smiling to herself. He was sitting at the kitchen table shelling peas that would be used in the next evenings dinner.

"Just amazed at how things change, Rolly getting himself worked up about what color the napkins and tablecloths are, and fighting for the pink ones of all things. Can you imagine him worrying about anything like that twenty years ago?"

Griff chuckled heartily. "No, I guess not."

Just then, Caleb came running in and slammed through the screen door letting it bang shut behind him. He was breathless and wide-eyed.

"Caleb, what have I told you about wiping your feet before you come in this kitchen and don't slam the door."

Caleb was still trying to catch his breath and Griff asked him in a quieter voice than his mother's, "What is it, boy? What's going on?"

"Police," was all he could get out.

"Police?" Maggie asked, "Where?"

Caleb gulped in a few more breathes of air and said, "Down at the other end of the lake. I was in the back field hitting walnuts out toward the water—"

"When you should have been in here helping get ready for dinner."

"Yes, ma'am…when I saw a helicopter fly by and it looked like it was going to land. So I ran over to the dock and leaned out as far as I could. I could see some lights flashing way down by the Olson's place at the west end of the lake."

Maggie and Caleb looked toward Griff who had picked up the phone and was holding it at arms length so he could read the numbers — he'd use his glasses to read them if he could find the darned things. Griff hit some buttons while Caleb gave his mother a questioning look. She shrugged her shoulders and looked back at her grandfather.

Abruptly, Griff said into the phone, "Hello, Mattie? Hey, it's Griffin Granger. My boy Caleb here tells me he saw police lights over at your end of the lake. Everything alright?"

He was quiet for a few minutes listening and then he replied, "Really? Holy smokes! He used your phone to call, huh? Do they know who it is? Oh, all wrapped up. All right, I expect we'll find out more in time. Just wanted to make sure you were OK over there. I know you've got that heart condition, and Butch's not getting around like he used to. Alright then, talk to you later."

By the time Griff had hung up, Rolly and Joe were in the kitchen listening as well. Griff was just about to tell them what he had learned when there was a tap at the door and Jack walked into the kitchen. Sensing something was amiss; he looked from one to the other of the Granger's as they stared back at Griff with anticipation.

"Everything alright here?" Jack asked. Then he smelled something burning and pointed to the stove. "Maggie is that pot suppose to be smoking?"

Maggie turned back to the stove. "Oh hell, the gravy's burning!"

Rolly was impatient. "Griffin, what's going on? Why'd you call Mattie Olson?"

Griff answered, "Caleb told me he saw police lights down their way, and I wanted to know if there was something wrong and if they needed any help."

"What did they say?" Rolly asked.

"They said that a fisherman found a dead body, or at least human bones, all wrapped up in a bag or something. Said the fisherman came tearing up to their house yelling that he needed to use the phone to call the police. They've got local and state police crawling all over their place, they're at the Olson's dock to put divers into the lake."

"Holy sh—!" Maggie glanced over at her son and stopped herself. "I mean, wow, that's something."

As there wasn't much more to say at that point and hungry people were waiting in both rooms, Maggie pushed food into people's hands and sent them out to the dining room. She enlisted Jack to put food around the kitchen table for their own meal. The dinner conversation in the kitchen that night was consumed with speculation on whose body it could be in the lake, a tourist, a drifter? Only Joe didn't say anything, but then there was nothing unusual in that.

The men of the household volunteered to clean up the dinner dishes and shushed Maggie and Jack out onto the porch. Maggie suspected Rolly and Griff harbored some latent matchmaking inclination towards her and had their eyes on Jack. She was just happy not to have to clean up.

Jack and Maggie sat down in the same rocking chairs they had the night before. There were several guests sitting around the porch, it was one of the first mild evenings of the season. Maggie and some of the guests exchanged pleasantries and Jack felt content just to rock back and forth in the old wooden chair. The flashing lights on the top of a police cruiser coming down the driveway interrupted the otherwise quiet evening. Maggie and Jack both stood up as the cars approached, as did most of the guests. They were murmuring amongst themselves when a stout middle-aged man in a blue uniform got out of the car and walked towards the porch.

"Hey, Tom," Maggie called to him as she walked down the front steps.

Tom raised his hand up in a kind of general greeting and said, "Nothing to worry about folks, just came to give Ms. Granger here some information." Maggie stepped down off the porch and stood next to him. Jack started to walk behind her, but then paused, not sure if he would be intruding.

Maggie motioned Jack to come stand next to her. She introduced the two men, "Tom Snyder, this is Jack Callahan. His family owns the place next door."

The two men nodded to each other. Tom said, "Nice to meet you. I guess you should hear this too as we're talking to everyone who has lake front property." He addressed them both. "Jim Tomlinson took his boat out to go fishing today and got his line caught on something. When he pulled it in he found it was attached to what he thought was a bundle of rags, till he saw a hand bone sticking out of it. Turns out it was the skeletal remains of someone who'd been weighted down with stones and wrapped in a burlap bag."

"Oh, my goodness. Gramps heard from Mattie Olson they found a body, but it's still shocking hearing it officially from you," Maggie said.

"Well," Tom scratched his head and continued, "We think the body had been lying on a submerged rock ledge for years, but with the drought and all, it was a lot closer to the surface than it was before. Darndest thing too, if that body had been dropped a few feet farther out, it would have been another forty feet down and probably no one would have ever known it was there.

"We sent the remains down to the coroner's office, but seeing as how nobody generally wraps themselves up in burlap with a bunch of heavy rocks and jumps into the lake, I think it's safe to assume we've got ourselves a homicide investigation. And as that is the case, I want to inform everyone here on the lake we will be diving for evidence and walking around along the edge and such."

"Of course, Tom, whatever you need to do."

"Thanks, Maggie. Everyone on the lake has said the same thing. Makes my life easier as I don't have to do the paperwork for all those warrants."

"You can have full access to my property too," Jack said.

"Appreciate it. Well, I've got a lot of stops to make. I'll see ya'll around."

"Tom," Maggie stopped him as he was lowering himself back into his police cruiser. "What kind of a burlap bag was the body wrapped in?"

"I expect a grain bag of some kind. You know, something you'd have animal feed in." Tom got in the car and pulled away and Jack turned back to look at Maggie, who had grown pale and pensive.

It was dusk as the three men stood on the end of the dock staring out towards the western end of the lake. They could still see the flashing lights from the police vehicles reflected in the darkening sky.

Rolly was leaning heavily on his cane squinting out at the scene, although all he saw were misty colored images edged with flashing blue and red. Griff was stooped over his pipe as he packed it with tobacco, an indulgence he allowed himself every great while. His arthritis made the simple task more difficult, but he took his time and finally the pipe was filled.

As Griff patted his pockets and searched for the lighter he could have sworn he remembered to bring, but didn't, Joe wordlessly pulled one from his own pocket and held it up to the pipe. Griff pulled on it until the tobacco glowed red and Joe closed the top of the heavy metal lighter and slid it back into his pocket.

They didn't talk. They didn't need to. The three men had worked, laughed, grieved and raised children together for decades. They were comfortable in their own skins and in their silence with each other.

Smoke billowed from Griff's pipe and drifted out into the night air, mingling with the mist hanging over the lake. Rolly shifted position and leaned against a piling to get the weight off his aching leg.

Joe just continued to stare in the direction of the lights. Then he said quietly, "Trouble's coming." The other two men nodded silently.

CHAPTER ELEVEN

"I'm sorry, Cynthia, it looks like the body we found might be Scott's." Tom Snyder hated this part of his job, even when the news was thirteen years too late; there was still no good way to tell parents their child was dead.

Cynthia Harding gave the sheriff a dead-eyed stare and he asked her if she'd heard him.

"Cynthia? Cynthia, do you want me to call someone to come be with you? Maybe drive you home? You shouldn't be alone right now."

She remained unnaturally still in the heavy metal chair for a few more moments, then said in a cold flat voice, "You are mistaken, Tom, I have had several letters from Scott over the years from different places around the country. You said the body you found was estimated to have been in that lake for at least a decade."

"Cynthia, the body was of a young male approximately sixteen to twenty years old wearing a Lake Meade High class of '92 ring, and his left collarbone had been broken at one time in two places and then healed."

Cynthia looked up sharply at him then, there was real fear in her eyes, they both remembered the football game Scott's junior year in high school when he was sacked and his left collarbone had been broken in two places. Scott also wore a Lake Meade ring for his graduating year of 1992. Tears started to swim in her eyes. "No! No, there must be some mistake.

The last letter said he was living in New Mexico. My boy is fine, he's living in New Mexico, dammit!" Cynthia practically screamed out the last words.

Tom reached over the desk and patted her hand, which was twisted around a tissue. "We are going to run a DNA test to make sure, but I thought I had better let you know now what we found. I'll need a DNA sample from you for the test, and I would like you to bring me all the letters you received that said they were from Scott."

Tom watched as Cynthia's expression shifted. He could practically see her mind clicking, putting together all the information he had just given her. Her voice was calm but strained when she said, "Tom, I need to get this straight and say it out loud. You are telling me you think that yesterday afternoon you found the body of my son. The son I thought was alive and well and living in New Mexico, but was really murdered thirteen years ago and thrown into Lake Meade."

Tom answered gently, "That's correct."

Cynthia lowered her head into her hands and Tom got up, rested his hand on her back for a moment. "I'll give you a few minutes alone." He left the room and went to get them both some coffee. By the time he returned and handed Cynthia the steaming mug, there was a grim set to her mouth and a look of steely determination in her eyes. Tom sat back down in his chair across from her, he looked up and what he saw was a depth of anger that seemed bottomless. There was a foreboding in the air that had him reflexively reaching for his Tums.

Cynthia's voice was strong, calm and steady when she said to him, "Well, it's obvious that Granger slut is a murderer, probably along with her boyfriend Greg Detrick. I want you to get your ass down to the courthouse and get a search warrant for that whore house she loosely calls a bed and breakfast. Immediately."

"Wait a minute, slow down, Cynthia. We haven't even officially confirmed it's Scott yet."

Cynthia leaned over the scarred wooden desk. "Listen to me, Tom, you and I both know it's going to be Scott that they found, and we also know the last people to see him alive were Maggie and Greg on prom night. I want every inch of that farm searched and everyone that lives there questioned. Margaret Granger, Greg Detrick or one of those filthy old men murdered my child. Hell, maybe they're all in on it. All I know is my boy is dead and someone, or all of them, are going to pay." She leaned back in her chair and looked up at the ceiling. "They will pay." Tom reached for the Tums again.

Tom assured Cynthia that he was going to do everything in his power, with the help of the state police and their forensic labs, to bring the murderer, or murderers, to justice. He finally convinced her to let his deputy drive her home.

As he sat staring at the dregs at the bottom of his coffee cup, his uneasiness mounting, he started to grasp nature of the investigation he was about to embark on. He had to deal with Cynthia from time to time on official business, she was heavily involved in the local politics of Lake Meade, and he had to admit he had never found that to be a pleasant experience. And now he not only had a murder investigation — something that didn't come up too often in Lake Meade — but it was the murder of Cynthia Harding's son. "Holy shit and back again," he muttered under his breath as he ran his hand through his thinning crew cut.

Cynthia is going to be on me like white on rice until I figured this out, he thought. The fact that he was going to have to look at the Grangers for the murder didn't make him any happier. Tom had never had any trouble with the Grangers before; in fact, personally, he liked the lot of them. But his feelings had no place in this, and it was his duty to find out what happened all those years ago to Scott Harding, and he was going to have to accept help from the state police to do it.

To say that the trail had gone cold was an understatement. He was going to need all the new fangled forensic equipment the state police had to offer to help analyze the body and any evidence they might find. The state would help with the evidence, but the people were his. He'd lived in Lake Meade his entire life, as did his parents and their parents. He had gone to school with Maggie Granger's mother, even had a crush on her in the third grade, but he had to put all that aside, to look at the situation without bias. He didn't like where that was taking him.

Unfortunately, Cynthia was right. Tom did have to start with questioning the Granger's and probably search their property. The last known sighting of Scott Harding was when he left home en route to the Granger Farm to pick up Maggie for their senior prom thirteen years ago. When you added that to the facts that the body had been found in the lake that the Granger property bordered and it had been wrapped in burlap used frequently on their farm, there was no avoiding it, he had to get a search warrant.

There was a tap on the doorframe and Tom looked up to see the detective assigned by the state police to assist him in the investigation. The detective said, "We've finished up for now at the site, not much there really. We sent divers down to comb the area below the body, but they came up empty. The remains have been transported to our lab in Annapolis. I'll get you the report on that as soon as it's in. Have you identified any other location you need my forensic team for?"

Tom sighed heavily. "Yes, I'm going to need you all to come with me to the last place the victim was assumed to be alive."

The detective raised an eyebrow at him. "You think you know whose body it is already and where he was last seen?"

"Yes. I'm almost positive you will be able to identify the victim as one Scott Harding, age eighteen. His mother is going to provide DNA for you to compare."

"Alright, do you have a search warrant for the site?"

"I was just about to call the judge." Tom picked up the phone and punched in the numbers for the courthouse.

CHAPTER TWELVE

The next day there was a chill in the air, reminding everyone that spring was still just beginning and the weather could change to cold and damp as easy as it could to warm and sunny. Maggie finished cleaning up the kitchen after making breakfast for her guests and put on a sweater to go outside to sweep the porch.

She nodded a greeting to two guests who had come out the front door and walked down the steps towards the dock. It was their first time at the B&B and Maggie hoped they were enjoying themselves, they seemed to be and she expected a return visit. After all these years running the bed and breakfast she had developed a good sense of which customers would become returning regulars, and she was proud of the fact that the majority of her guests did come again.

Once the porch floor was swept of leaves and dried mud from people's shoes, Maggie raised the broom over her head and started sweeping off any cobwebs making their home in the porch rafters. From the corner of her eye she noticed Joe walking out to the woods with an axe in one hand and a spike in the other, Griff and Rolly trailed behind him. *Going to chop some wood for a fire tonight*, she thought.

Just as she reached the last of the cobwebs, Maggie heard the sound of a car coming down the drive. It was Greg's Saab and she wondered why he'd left the school office in the middle of the day, very unlike him. Greg parked in front of the house and walked up the porch steps to Maggie. When he reached the top of the steps, he held out his arms and Maggie stepped into them naturally and comfortably.

There was nothing unusual in this gesture, they had been close friends for more years than she can remember, but there was an urgency in his embrace that day that had her pulling away and looking at him curiously. "What's the matter? Why are you here in the middle of the day?" Then her eyes widened and her hand went up to her mouth. "Oh, my God, is it Caleb? Did something happen?"

Greg shushed her and pulled her down to sit on the top porch step next to him. "No, no. Caleb is fine." He rubbed her icy hands between his.

"Then why are you here?"

Greg stopped rubbing her hands but kept holding them. "You know my assistant, Claire? Her sister is the secretary over at the sheriff's office, and she overheard one of the state officers say they had officially identified the body that was found in the lake."

"So soon? Tom was here last night and said there were only skeletal remains. I assumed they'd been there for a long time. I'm surprised they were able to identify the person so quickly."

Greg looked strained and Maggie pulled her hands from his and placed them on his arm. "What's the matter, Greg? You look like you've seen a ghost. Who is it they found? Is it someone we know?"

He took a deep breath and said, "Maggie…it's Scott's body."

Before Maggie even knew what she was doing, she sprung to her feet in one fluid motion. "No! No it can't be."

Greg got up and guided her to a rocking chair and made her sit down, he sat in the one next to her and spoke quietly and slowly. "It is, Maggie. Cynthia gave them a DNA sample. Claire told me the body was wearing a Lake Meade High class of '92 ring and the left collarbone had been broken in two places at one time."

Maggie stared at him in disbelief, as if she didn't understand the words he was saying. Leaning forward, her hands clasped together, she said, "But Cynthia has gotten letters, letters from Scott."

"I know, baby, I know. But someone else must have sent them so Cynthia would think Scott was still alive."

Maggie's eyes darted around and she stood up out of the rocker and paced around the porch. Greg had known her long enough to let her go, she needed to move and think. Abruptly Maggie stopped at the porch railing and looked out toward the woods where her grandfather, Rolly and Joe had walked off a few minutes before. "We were so careful, Greg, weren't we? They didn't know anything? Tell me they never knew anything."

The shrillness of her voice had Greg jumping out of his chair and putting his arm around her shoulders. "No, Mags, no. They never knew anything. Remember, we made sure. We cleaned everything up."

She sought his eyes with her own, eyes she had trusted and loved for so long. Greg had always protected her, always done what she'd asked, even when he didn't wanted to. "What if they found out somehow? Oh, my God, Greg, you know what they would have done."

"Shh, it's alright. Let's just take this one step at a time." Greg enfolded her in his arms again and rocked her back and forth, feeling every muscle in her body taught, as if ready to spring. He had the image of a lioness poised in the brush, ready to leap out at anything that threatened her family.

Jack decided to walk over to the Grangers instead of drive. He was curious to see if they had heard anything more about the remains the police had found in the lake. That morning he had stood on the end of his dock with a cup of coffee looking across the lake at the Olson farm and wondering what, if anything more, the police had found. As he rounded the bend in the driveway, he saw the green Saab that Greg Detrick had driven over the other night, then he noticed Greg and Maggie standing on the porch in each other's arms.

Maggie had her head on Greg's shoulder and he was gently rocking her back and forth. The sight of Maggie in Greg's arms made him irrationally and instantly tense, he felt as if a rock has just dropped into his stomach. Jack was honest enough with himself to know that what he was feeling was jealousy, and rational enough to know he had no right to the emotion — but there it was anyway.

Rooted to the spot, not sure of what to do next, Jack heard a rustling sound to his right. Griff and Rolly were coming out of the woods, Griff holding a couple of logs in his arms and Rolly ambling along beside him with his cane in one hand and an axe in the other. Joe followed behind them, his arms full of split wood.

At the sight of him, Griff yelled out, "Hey, Jack!" and motioned with his head towards the house. "Come on up to the house. We're just getting some wood for the fire tonight. It feels a little chilly, thought we'd get one more good fire in before it warms up again."

"Alright, let me take some of those for you." Jack took a few logs off of Joe's pile and followed the men to the back of the house. He noticed Maggie had pulled away from Greg and was staring intently at her grandfather and the other men as they all walked through the kitchen door. Her face appeared red and puffy as if she'd been crying.

Following the other men's lead, Jack stacked the logs in a neat pile next to the fireplace. While the older men were busy with setting up the kindling and wood to get the fire ready to light during the evening's meal, Jack wandered to the front of the house. Maggie was no longer on the porch, but Jack saw that Greg was sitting on the top porch step staring into the distance. About to turn back towards the dining room, Jack heard Greg say, "Jack?"

Jack looked back around and walked onto the porch. "Oh, hi, Greg. Just helping the guys bring some wood in for a fire tonight."

"Ah," Greg said distractedly. He turned back around and stared out into the distance. Jack was beginning to feel uncomfortable in the silence when Greg said, "Maggie will be out again in a minute if you want to wait."

Jack shrugged, although the other man's back was towards him and couldn't see his movements. He said in an offhand tone, "I just stopped over to say hi and get some local gossip. Wondering if there was any more information on whose body that was they found in the lake. I figured Maggie and Joe were at the diner this morning and the place was probably buzzing about it."

Greg's back went stiff. He didn't turn around when he said, "Yes, they know whose body it is."

Jack hadn't heard Griff come up behind him. "They do?" Griff said. "Joe told me everyone was talking about it down at the Lake View, but no one really knew anything. How'd you find out?"

Greg fully turned around to talk to the older man. "Claire," he answered simply.

Griff nodded his head and yelled to Rolly and Joe. "Get out here, Greg knows whose body they found in the lake and I don't want the boy to have to tell it three times."

In a few moments Joe and Rolly joined Griff, Greg and Jack on the porch, then Maggie walked back out as well. She gave Jack a half smile and then asked Greg, "Did you tell them yet?"

"No, not yet."

Taking a deep breath she exhaled slowly. "OK. Go ahead."

Greg looked at the group of men that were eagerly waiting for his news. "It's Scott Harding."

The group that had looked expectant, almost eager for some juicy gossip, deflated in front of Jack's eyes. Griff and Rolly both found rocking chairs and sat down heavily, while Joe leaned his weight up against the porch railing.

All the faces on the porch look somber and thoughtful, except for Jack's, who just looked curious. "Isn't that the guy you went out with in high school?" he asked Maggie.

Maggie nodded in response. Greg walked over to Maggie, putting his arm around her shoulders. She leaned into him. Jack wished with an intensity that surprised him that she was leaning on him instead. A moment later they all heard the sound of tires on gravel as two police vehicles pulled up behind Greg's car.

For the second time in two days, Tom pulled himself out of his Lake Meade police cruiser in the Granger's driveway. Two men and a woman got out of a Chevy Blazer with the words Maryland State Police on the door that had pulled in behind him. The woman and one of the men each carried a black bag with the word "Forensics" in white lettering on it. Tom nodded to the group on the porch and walked up to Griff Granger, he handed him a sheet of paper. Griff said, "Tom, just tell me what this is about. I don't need some damn piece of paper."

Maggie took the document out of her grandfather's hand and read it. Tom said to Griff, "That is what's called a search warrant, and it gives these people here the right to go through your house and outbuildings."

"What the hell do you want to go and do that for?"

All morning Tom had rehearsed how he would word what he needed to say next. This was not what he wanted to be doing this morning, but it had to be done. "Griff, they positively identified the remains we found in the lake as belonging to Scott Harding."

"We just heard that."

Tom rolled his eyes and looked at Greg. "Claire?" he asked.

Greg nodded.

"Anyway," he continued, "this farm is the last known destination of Scott Harding before he died. No one saw him after he left his mother's house on prom night headed here to pick up Maggie. That, and the fact that the body was found relatively close to your home and wrapped in an item common to your farm at the time, the judge felt there was just cause to search the premises."

There was a stunned silence as everyone on the porch absorbed this information. Tom took advantage of the silence to go on, "Griff, I have got to start somewhere, and this is the last place I know that boy was heading. My hope is that I don't find anything and I can go ahead and leave you folks alone and look elsewhere. What I'd like to do is interview each of you all here in the kitchen, instead of taking you downtown, while these folks from the state go do their thing in the house and barn. I tried to get here early enough so we can try to be out of here by the time Caleb gets home from school."

Maggie rallied herself and said, "I appreciate that, Tom. Let me just speak to the guests who are still here and then I'll meet you in the kitchen."

Jack was at a loss. He had no idea what to do or what to make of all this. The policeman told him he was free to go, but he refused, not sure what he could do, but knowing he damn well he wasn't going to leave Maggie or Griff in the middle of all this. Tom informed them all that he would interview them one by one, everyone waiting in the dining room until he called them into the kitchen. Jack sat at the dining room table with Joe, Rolly and Greg while Griff was called first. No one in the room spoke.

Maggie came down the main staircase and into the dining room a few minutes later. She said, "I told the guests that there are some police here doing routine checks because of what they had found yesterday in the lake."

Pouring herself a glass of water from the pitcher on the banquet, Maggie took a sip as the policewoman with the black forensic bag came into the room. The woman asked her, "Have these walls and floors been refinished in the last thirteen years?

"The walls have been repainted, but the floors are the same. They've never needed to be stripped, so they've only been polished with Murphy's Oil Soap."

The woman nodded and left the room. She was holding what looked like a flashlight with a screen attached to the top of it, she walked off looking through the screen at the beam of light coming from the flashlight. Everyone looked over at the door to the kitchen when it opened and Griff came out with Tom right behind him. "OK," Tom said, "Rolly, your next. Come in here please?"

Rolly hoisted himself out of the straight-back chair and disappeared behind the swinging door. The others in the room all waited for Griff to tell them what had happened. Maggie asked, "What did he ask you?"

Griff shrugged. "He just wanted to know where I was the night of the prom and if I saw Scott at all."

"What did you tell him?" Maggie asked anxiously.

Griff looked at her curiously. "Darlin', I just told him the simple truth. You had tricked the three of us into thinking the prom was the next night 'cause you thought we'd embarrass the hell out of you and make a big fuss, which of course we would have. So the three of us went to the Lutheran Church over in Kennedyville as usual for Friday night bingo.

"We all got home around eleven from there and you were already up in bed. Greg was waiting for us and told us you and Scott had had a big fight and broken up, and that you had never even gotten to go to the prom. We left you be that night and all went to bed shortly after. I never saw Scott Harding at all that night, or ever again for that matter."

Maggie was clutching the back of the dining room chair as she listened to Griff, her knuckles white with the pressure. Griff walked over and put his hand on his granddaughter's. "It's all right Maggie, my love. They have to do this. They'll ask their questions and look around and then that will be that. They'll leave and everything will go back to normal."

Fifteen minutes later Rolly came out of the kitchen, he told Joe that Tom wanted to see him next. Joe walked into the kitchen, and Rolly turned to Maggie and told her basically the same thing Griff had. After a few more silent minutes, they all watched the woman with the flashlight come back into the room. She didn't look at any of them as she walked briskly through the door and into the kitchen. They could hear her voice as the door swung shut behind her. "Chief, Detective, we found some blood in the wood flooring under the living room rug."

Tom and the state police detective followed the woman through the dining room back into the living room. Maggie looked fearfully at Jack and they both jumped out of their seats and followed. The corner of the oriental carpet had been folded over, the state police detective shining the flashlight devise around on the floor. The detective confered with the woman and then he handed the flashlight to Tom. Curious, Tom crouched down and stared through the little screen for a few minutes, then stood up with a resigned grunt.

Tom asked Maggie, "There was a considerable amount of blood here at one time, Maggie, we can see it in the grooves between the floor planks. Can you explain that?"

Maggie was suddenly so pale Jack instinctively put his arm under her elbow, he was afraid she was going to pass out. Greg walked up behind her and took her other arm. He leaned down and murmured something into her ear. She nodded and Greg said to the police, "Let's go into the kitchen, detectives, please. We'll explain about the blood."

"Whose is it?" Tom asked.

"Mine," Maggie whispered.

CHAPTER FOURTEEN

When Jack hesitated, not sure if he should follow Maggie into the kitchen, she grabbed his hand and pleaded with her eyes. Jack looked to Tom who said it was all right to stay with her, but that Jack was not to say anything. Coldness settled into his bones, he couldn't ever remember seeing Maggie so scared. He had no idea what he was going to hear in that kitchen, but he knew it wasn't going to be good.

Greg was right behind them both, heading for the kitchen too, when the state police detective put his hand on his arm to stop him. "Mr. Detrick, I think we'd like to take your statement separately. Why don't you follow me into the den?"

Maggie and Greg stared across the room at each other for a long moment, then Greg gave her a weak smile and mouthed the words, "It's going to be OK." Her expression didn't change. She walked resolutely into the kitchen and sat down across from Tom. There was a tape recorder on the table and a deputy sat unobtrusively with a note pad in the corner of the room.

Tom hit the record button on the tape recorder and had Maggie acknowledge verbally that she knew she was being recorded. "OK, Maggie," he said, "Just tell me what happened on your senior prom night, the last night anyone saw Scott Harding alive, and why your blood was on the living room floor."

Letting her breathing slow and her mind calm, Maggie let herself go back to that night. She squeezed Jack's hand and began in a quiet voice, which gained strength the longer she spoke. "I had been thinking of breaking up with Scott for a while. We were both going away to separate colleges, and I thought it would be a good time for us to make a fresh start. I knew we didn't want the same things out of life. He was going to come right back here after college and take over his mother's dealership and get into local politics. I didn't know what I wanted beyond art school, but I knew it wasn't that.

"I decided I had to tell him before we went to the prom. It would have felt like a lie to go with him thinking we were still going to be together later. I guess I hoped he would understand and we could still go as friends. We'd been together a long time and it felt right that we'd do this one last thing together."

Her stare became distant. Jack knew she was reliving that night. She continued, "I had lied to Gramps and the guys. Later I told them it was because I didn't want them making a fuss about me in my prom dress and everything, but it was really because I wanted to be alone with Scott to talk. You can't really tell a guy you want to break-up with him with your family around, so I convinced them all that the prom was Saturday night instead of Friday. They went to their usual bingo night at the Lutheran Church."

Tom studied her closely. He hadn't said anything or moved at all since she'd started talking. Maggie paused and Tom prompted, "So you have the house to yourself and Scott arrived to pick you up. Did you invite him in the house to have this break-up talk?"

"Yes," she answered, "I asked him to come in to the living room for a moment and he said he would like that. I told him no one was around and we could have a few minutes alone before we went out."

Maggie stopped again and Tom said, "So you told him what was on your mind?"

Maggie nodded without saying anything.

"And then what happened?"

Maggie's voice caught in her throat. Jack rubbed her hand and she looked at him for a moment, seemed to focus and gather strength. Then she whispered, "He was so angry. In all the years I had known him I had never seen him so mad. I told him it was for the best. That he should be with someone that wanted the same things he did. I told him it didn't change the last two years, I was glad he had been my boyfriend, but it was time to start the next part of our lives, separately.

"It was as if I had opened some box and let this stranger out. He screamed at me. He told me he should have listened to his mother all along. He couldn't believe he had wasted all that time on me and fought with his mother about me." She took a gulp of air and said, "And then he got this horrible look in his eyes and came at me. He grabbed my arms and told me that if I thought he had waited two years to fuck me for nothing that I was sadly mistaken. That's when I really got scared."

Maggie took another shaky breath and continued, "I guess when he was yelling I was stunned, but then when he got quiet and looked at me like that, I saw how truly angry he was, and I got scared. He was such a big guy, and I realized I was all alone in the house. I tried to run out of the room towards the front door, but he grabbed me."

Jack held on to Maggie's hand and willed his strength to go through him into her. He knew what he was going to hear next and he wasn't sure he could bare it. For now he would sit there with her and try to be strong for her, but later, when he was alone, he would kick the shit out of something.

Tom prompted her again, "He grabbed you and…"

"He threw me down on the floor in front of the fireplace, there wasn't a carpet there then, and he held me down and he raped me." Maggie choked out the last few words. Jack wondered if she had ever said them out loud before.

"I think because I was a…a virgin and because he was so…rough with me…I bled a lot. It seemed like there was blood everywhere."

Her voice trailed off. Tom sat very still; he needed to hear it all. He needed to know everything that had happened, but the part of him that had known and liked Maggie Granger all her life was fighting with the cop part of him that told him he had to remain impartial and unemotional. But if Maggie was lying, he thought, it was the most convincing performance he had ever seen.

He said, "Then what happened, Maggie?"

Maggie wasn't crying, but her voice was disconnected and distant. "He got up and looked at me lying on the ground and said, 'Great. Now look what you've made me do. You'll probably tell everyone you didn't want that to happen, won't you?' I just looked up at him. I couldn't speak. Truthfully, I think I was in shock. It was like I was watching this all happen to someone else, like it was a movie. I guess after a while, I must have called out my grandfather's name because Scott went white.

"He looked at me for the first time like he was actually frightened himself. He said, 'Oh shit, Griff! He'll kill me. Oh god, oh god, oh god, Rolly and Joe will help him.' He looked around as if Griff were behind him already. He grabbed his coat and ran out of the house and that was the last time I saw Scott Harding."

The worst of the story was over. Maggie took a long drink from the glass of water Tom put in front of her. Her hand shook badly, and Jack took the glass from her and set it back down on the table.

Tom said, "If that happened, why didn't you tell anyone? Or did you end up telling Griff?"

Maggie almost jumped out of her seat as her voice rose up, "No! No, I never told Griff or Rolly or Joe. The only one that's ever known is Greg. I called him that night after Scott left. I was crying and I hurt so badly, but I dragged myself over to the phone and called him. He's my closest friend. Everyone thought because he, Scott and I hung out that Scott and Greg were best friends, but really it was Greg and me that were close. He and Scott just tolerated each other because of me.

"I knew Greg wasn't going to the prom, so I called his house and luckily he answered instead of his mom. I asked him to come over. He could tell I was upset and he came right away. When he saw me he started to freak out, especially when I told him what happened. He looked at all the blood, and he wanted to go after Scott, but I wouldn't let him."

"Why?" Tom asked.

"Because Scott had been right about one thing...Griff would have *killed* him."

Jack could tell she was deadly serious. She and Tom stared at each other. Tom nodded his head, acknowledging what she had said. "Griff, Rolly and Joe are very protective of me, if they knew what Scott had done, I don't think they would have thought twice about taking him out to the barn and beating the crap out of him at the very least, or stringing him up from the rafters and killing him at the worst. Even in the state I was in, or maybe because of it, I knew that as clearly as anything I've ever known."

Maggie continued to look directly at Tom. "Those three men were the only family I had in this world and I couldn't lose them. If they touched a hair on Scott's head, Cynthia wouldn't have rested until they were in jail. I couldn't let that happen."

Tom didn't answer but nodded his head again.

"Greg didn't want to go along with it at first, but I think he knew Griff well enough to know I could be right, and even if I wasn't, at that moment, covered in blood and shaking like a leaf, he would have done anything I asked." Maggie twisted a tissue through her fingers. "So he helped me clean the blood off the floor, obviously not with bleach though, or you wouldn't have found it all these years later, then he helped me clean myself up and put me to bed. I asked him to wait up for the guys and tell them when they got home that Scott and I had just broken up and I was upset and had gone to bed. He did that for me and then went home."

Maggie sat back in her chair and scrubbed her hand over her face. She was still pale but looked better than she had before she'd started talking. The secret of that night had been trapped in her a long time, like an infected splinter — it was long overdue to come out.

Tom tapped his fingers on the table. "I have a few questions."

"OK."

"What did you think the next day when you found out Scott had left his mother a note that said he'd found you and Greg cheating on him and then left town?"

Maggie shrugged, "I figured he wanted to get out of here in case I told Griff, or the police, so he made up that lie as a good way to get out of town and discredit me at the same time. Truthfully, I was relieved. As long as he was out of my sight, I figured it was over. I thought I could just pretend it never happen and go on with my life."

"As long as Greg never told."

"He wouldn't. He didn't."

"Why are you so sure? Maybe he decided to tell Griff that night after you went to bed. Maybe he, Griff, Rolly and Joe went out after you went to bed and found Scott. Maybe they even did what you were most afraid of and took him out to the barn and beat him to death, then grabbed some rocks and old feed bags and threw him in the lake."

Maggie stared at Tom wide-eyed with her mouth hanging open. "That's ridiculous, Tom. Greg would never break a promise to me. He swore to me that night he would do as I asked, and I know he didn't break his word."

Tom leaned back in his chair and crossed his arms. "If he was as good a friend as you say, Maggie, he would have wanted to kick Scott's ass, and he would have loved some help doing it. What makes you so sure he kept his promise to you and didn't tell your grandfather?"

"Because Greg and I keep our promises to each other."

"And your secrets?"

Maggie sat back in her seat and was quiet. She crossed her arms and she and Tom stared at each other. "I've told you everything about that night, Tom, there's nothing else to say."

Tom was thoughtful for a moment and said, "I doubt that. I doubt that very much, but for now I think we will just take a look at everyone's separate stories and see if they all add up, or if there are some holes that may need more questions and more answers. We'll also need some of your DNA to compare with the traces of blood we found on the floor to make sure it is, in fact, your blood and not Scott's. Do I need to get a warrant for that or would you like to volunteer a sample?"

"I have no problem giving you my DNA."

"Thank you. I'll send the forensics person in to take it. We'll be out of here soon, but we'll be in touch tomorrow. Do not leave this county, Maggie."

Maggie pushed the swinging door open and walked into the dining room with Jack right behind her. Griff, Rolly and Joe all stood and moved towards her. She was drawn and tired, but resigned to what she had to do next.

She said to Jack, "I'd like to talk to these guys on my own right now." She reached out for Jack's hand and squeezed it briefly before letting it go. "But I want to thank you for being in there with me." She motioned with her head towards the kitchen, "That was...difficult...I was glad you were there."

Jack squeezed her hand back and leaned down to kiss her on the forehead. "I'm glad you let me." He paused, unsure how to tell her what he was feeling. "I wish I had been there for you thirteen years ago."

Maggie gave him a sad smile and ran her hand down his cheek. She shook her head at him and said, "Don't waste your wishes, Jack. We can't go back. I'm just glad you're here now."

Griff growled, "Dammit, Maggie! What's going on?"

Maggie turned her full attention to the three older men and asked them to sit down. Just then Greg walked back into the room, followed by the police detective. The detective continued to walk past them to join Tom in the kitchen. Greg looked over at Maggie questioningly.

She said to him, "I'm going to tell these guys everything."

Greg took her gently and quietly into his arms and held her there for a long moment, then he kissed her on the top of her head, looked her in the eyes and said, "It's time."

It was then Jack realized it had been Greg's voice he heard talking to Maggie at the edge of the lake. *It's time.*

Greg held her away from him and gave her a reassuring smile. "It's all right now, you know. It was a long time ago, Maggie. Scott can't hurt you now."

With a voice full of irony Maggie said, "Since they found his body yesterday, it feels like he can hurt me in ways I never expected."

Greg and Jack left the room and walked onto the porch. Both men felt numb. Greg said, "I could use a drink about now, how about you?"

Jack nodded. He didn't have the energy to summon up any jealousy towards this man and his relationship with Maggie. "I wouldn't turn one down."

"I know where there is a great wine cellar, you can choose whatever you want."

"Really, around here? Where?"

"My place."

It only took a few minutes for Greg to drive them to the other side of town and pull up in front of a craftsman-style cottage. "We're here," he said as he pulled on the emergency brake and opened his car door.

Jack followed Greg up the walk and the three steps to the stone-pillared front porch, and watched as Greg took his keys out of his jacket pocket and unlocked the heavy oak front door with a leaded glass window with the design of lilies in the center. There were several mismatched antique rockers on the porch along with colorful clay pots filled with thriving ferns. The effect was pleasant and Jack grimaced internally as he thought of the austerity of the blank white walls and stainless steel of his New York apartment compared with the character and hominess of Greg's house.

Inside, Greg had furnished the rooms with mission-style furniture and more antiques. Jack commented on a massive mahogany highboy that stood in the corner of the living room.

Greg said, "Yeah, that's one of my favorite pieces. Maggie and I do a lot of antiquing on Saturdays and scout out any promising looking garage or yard sales. Believe it or not, Maggie and I found that highboy at a house right outside of Chestertown. The house and contents were being auctioned off and I got it for a song.

It made Jack itchy when Greg talked about what he and Maggie did together. Jack was aware his was an unjustified jealously, but that didn't make him feel it any less keenly.

"I made a great wine cellar in the basement out of an old canning pantry," Greg said, motioning to a door next to the kitchen. "Come down and let me show it off to you."

Jack followed Greg down the narrow staircase towards the back of the basement, brushing his hands along the stone of the foundation wall. The house was old and the basement ceiling low, but it was dry and clean. They came to an old door fashioned with heavy black hammered hinges and door latch. Greg turned towards Jack and waggled his eyebrows. "This is where I keep the good stuff." He gave the door a push, it opened smoothly on its hinges. The first thing Jack saw were rows and rows of neat little wood squares, each one holding a corked bottle. The second was an old butcher block table that held nothing but a temperature controlled humidor.

"This is impressive," Jack said, pulling out a bottle to read the label. "You've got some nice stuff here."

Greg was pleased by the compliment. "Yeah, I have a thing for wine, and this cellar stays the perfect temperature all year long. This is like my little secret room. I figure if we ever have a hurricane or bomb scare, I'll just come down here and lock myself in and have a good old time."

Jack pointed at a bottle and said, "Call me, I'll join you, and that Merlot is mine."

Greg smiled and grabbed the Merlot Jack had pointed to and a Riesling. "These ought to do it."

"A bottle for each of us?"

Greg gave Jack a sardonic look. "After that afternoon? You bet your ass."

Following Greg back up the stairs, Jack couldn't help but acknowledge that he was begrudgingly beginning to like this man. Greg poured the wine as Jack wandered around the living room looking at the pictures scattered around in silver frames. Some were old black-and-white photos Jack assumed were of Greg's family, there were also several pictures of Maggie, Caleb and Greg, or a combination of them, and still more of exotic looking locations around the world.

Greg handed Jack his glass and noticed he was looking at the photographs. "Besides antiques and wine, travel is my other passion." He picked up a picture of himself in shorts and a t-shirt smiling at the camera in front of an adobe styled chapel. "This was my last trip two years ago out to Santa Fe, incredible place. I'd like to go to Ireland next, maybe in a year or so."

"I helped design a small airport out there. Beautiful country."

Both men sat down in matching wing-backed chairs in front of the fireplace, remaining in silence for a few moments, sipping the wine and letting their thoughts settle after an unsettling afternoon. Greg spoke first, "How was Maggie when she was talking to Tom in the kitchen?"

Jack stared into his wineglass and then looked back up at Greg. "She was Maggie. Strong. Honest."

Greg nodded and half smiled. "Yes, that's our Maggie." He took a sip of wine and then continued, "I'm glad that you were in there with her. I should have known they would want a separate statement from me. I would have hated to think of her reliving that night without any support."

Jack swirled the wine around in his half empty glass. "Yeah, but you were there for her that night, and all these years since…I wish I'd been."

Greg cocked his head to one side and studied Jack. Then he said, "You really do care about her, don't you?"

Jack wasn't sure where this conversation was going, he hoped not into anything confrontational, but he decided to be honest. "Yes, yes I do. I always have. Even though I couldn't come back here — or wouldn't come back — I never forgot about Maggie."

With an appraising stare Greg finally said, "Good," as if deciding something.

Jack raised his eyebrow at Greg. "Good? That's it?"

Greg chuckled. "Yeah. I think Maggie's going to need all the friends she can get until they figure out what happened to Scott. The more support she has the better."

Jack was halfway through his second glass of wine when he asked Greg, "Tell me about Maggie in high school, and Caleb when he was little. Fill me in on some of the stuff I missed."

The fading light played on Greg's wineglass; he turned the glass around and around and then finally said, "Where to start? Well, I guess you knew Maggie up to junior high or there abouts, and I came into her life when we entered high school. My parents had just divorced, and my mom and I had moved here from Washington, D.C. I didn't know a soul and I felt out of place here in the country. Everything about me felt wrong, felt 'city.' My clothes, the way I talked."

A grin spontaneously lit across Greg's face as he said, "And then I sat down next to this gangly girl in my English class who wore pink high top sneakers and plaid skirts with her long curly hair in a ponytail on top of her head, and I thought, if this girl can fit in here, I sure as hell can too."

Both men laughed out loud. Jack asked, "Maggie?"

Greg was still chuckling at the memory of the first time he saw her. "She had been living so long on the farm with just the guys that she was completely out of touch with how most girls were acting and dressing." He continued more quietly, "Yet she was really mature, you know? I guess from taking over so much of her grandmother's responsibilities at the farmhouse, she just didn't seem to really care about fashion or trends, or what other people thought really."

Jack took another sip of wine and tried to picture Maggie as an awkward teenager. He did remember that during the summers his sister Kathy usually had her nose in a Teen Beat magazine or was trying to imitate the hairstyles she saw on other girls, but Maggie was always more interested in climbing trees and swimming in the lake, so he had no difficulty imagining that she wasn't a fashion plate in high school.

Greg said, "Maggie and I became friends quickly. We started talking that first day in English class, and it was like picking up in the middle of a conversation we had been having some time before." He looked at Jack over his wineglass. "You'll think I'm crazy, but it felt like we had known each other in another life, it was just so natural and easy between us from the first moment we met."

Jack shook his head. "I don't think that sounds crazy at all." Another twinge of jealousy licked at his stomach, he quelled it with more wine.

"Anyway, I thought Maggie was fine the way she was, but sometimes she would feel awkward or left out because she didn't really fit in with the other girls, so I gave her some pointers on what the girls had worn back in Washington, and eventually, I got her out of those high tops and into sandals, and then convinced her to get her hair professionally cut instead of going to her grandfather's barber, and well, people started noticing her."

Jack lifted his eyebrows. "People? You mean guy people, don't you?"

"Oh, yeah. By junior year she had grown nicely into those gangly legs and arms, and she had a self-confidence about her, like she knew who she was, and that made her stand out." Greg was thoughtful as the memories flashed in his mind of moments in their teenage years together, his eyes clouding over as he said in a lower tone, "Then she caught the attention of our star quarterback."

"Scott Harding?"

"Scott Harding." Greg took a long drink of his wine, then reached over to the coffee table and picked up the half empty bottle he had set there and refilled his glass. "Scott Harding was handsome and popular, and Maggie was absolutely dazzled by him. She had never had anyone like Scott pay that much attention to her."

"He sounds like the kind of guy that should have been dating the head cheerleader."

Greg grunted. "No, that would have been what Scott's *mother* would have wanted, and Scott took every opportunity he could to piss off his mommy. At least I think that's why he asked Maggie out to begin with, his mother would have thought she was beneath him, and it would have really gotten under her skin if she knew they were dating."

Jack cocked his head and asked, "You said `that's how it started?' You think Scott's feelings changed?"

Greg nodded. "Yes, actually I do. I think he ended up falling in love with Maggie, probably as much to his surprise as anyone else's. They dated for almost two years. You don't do that if you don't care for someone, even if you are a teenager and it's making your mother crazy."

Jack said, "You sound like you liked Scott, or at least thought he genuinely cared for Maggie." Jack suddenly realized he was talking about the man who raped Maggie. He stammered, "Well, at least he did…before…"

"Before that night," Greg finished the sentence for Jack, his face unreadable.

"Yeah…before that night."

"Actually no…I didn't like him at all. In fact I hated the bastard."

Greg's voice was filled with an intensity Jack hadn't heard from him before. He looked up sharply at Greg. "You hated him?"

"Oh, yes. Yes, I did. Scott was the most two-faced bastard I have ever met in my life. I don't think I've ever known anyone before or after Scott that could so completely be two different people at one time."

He saw Jack's confusion and contemplated for a moment how to explain what he meant. "I saw Scott when it was just the guys, in gym or football practice, and he was 'Mr. Big Shot,' telling everyone about how he and Maggie 'did it' every weekend in her grandfather's barn and crap like that. I knew it was all bullshit, but I didn't say anything. Then I'd see him with Maggie, and he was like a completely different guy, considerate and kind. He had her convinced for a long time that he was Prince Charming come to life."

"But you knew differently?"

"Yeah, but I couldn't say much to Maggie. She was in love with him and I didn't want to burst her bubble. I knew she'd figure it out eventually and I didn't want to be the one that she thought would say 'I told you so.'"

"I guess she figured it out for herself, if she was going to break up with him that night."

"I think she started seeing him for what he was around the middle of senior year. They had a really big fight about Rolly."

"About Rolly?"

"Rolly gave Scott a hard time one night when he brought Maggie home after curfew. Scott told Rolly to shut the hell up and mind his own business. Maggie told Scott never to speak to Rolly like that again, and Scott told her he didn't have to listen to some old *nigger* tell him what to do."

"I can't believe Maggie didn't break up with him right on the spot."

Greg shrugged. "You have to remember, we were naïve, only seventeen years old, and Scott was very good at sweet talking his way out of things. He told Maggie he was sorry, and he had been drinking, yada yada yada, but it was never the same between them after that. I think that was when she started noticing more and more things about him that didn't seem right to her."

"Did Rolly ever say anything about it?"

"I don't think he ever said anything to her, but I know he wasn't heartbroken that prom night when I told him, Griff and Joe that Maggie and Scott had broken up."

"Did he say something to you?"

Greg nodded and stared into the distance as if he could see that night long past. "After I told them Maggie and Scott had broken up and she had gone up to bed, all Rolly said was, 'Good riddance to bad rubbish' and walked out the back door. I can't say Griff or Joe seemed too sorry at the news either. I mean, they felt bad for Maggie that she was upset and all, but neither of them seemed too sorry about not having Scott Harding in Maggie's life anymore."

Greg quietly drank his wine for a while and Jack thought about everything he had learned about Scott Harding. The mood was heavy in the room and Jack remembered that all Greg had wanted to do was relax and forget about the day's events, so he changed the subject and asked Greg to tell him about what it was like when Caleb was a baby. As soon as Jack said Caleb's name, a soft smile spread over Greg's face, and he willingly told Jack about the night Caleb was born. Through more wine and over the next hour, Greg regaled him with more stories about Maggie and Caleb. Jack fell in love all over again with the woman Maggie had grown into, and he found himself compelled to know the child she had raised as well.

Reluctantly and despite himself, the more Jack talked to Greg the more he liked him. The jealousy of the man who had shared so much of Maggie's life in the years Jack had missed was dissolving and being replaced by a feeling of kinship at caring so deeply for the same woman at such different times in her life — although Jack still wished he understood the nature of Greg and Maggie's relationship better.

By ten o'clock both men were tired from the wine and the tension of the day. Greg picked up the phone and called a man named Smitty to come pick Jack up and drive him back to the cottage. Smitty turned out to be Lake Meade's one-man cab company, and Jack was grateful for the ride. Back at the lake-house, Jack sat on the front porch and let the cool night air coming off the lake wash over him and clear some of the wine out of his head. He looked at his watch, twenty minutes after ten. He knew it was late to be calling, but he had an urge to talk to his sister.

"Hello?"

"Hey, Kath, is it too late to talk?"

"No, I was just reading. The kids are all in bed and it's my only time in the day to have some quiet. What's up? You sound funny."

Jack took a deep breath and then told her everything that had happened that day, starting with the police showing up at the B&B and ending with his evening with Greg.

"Holy shit," was all she could find to say.

"I know."

"Holy shit."

"Kathleen Marie, say something else."

"I'm not sure what else *to* say."

"You know, I thought I was going to come back here and deal with some peeling paint, maybe a few difficult memories about Dad but, man, there's a whole lot more going on here in Lake Meade."

"Are you up for it?" she asked.

The question surprised him. "What do you mean?"

"I mean you haven't exactly…how should I say this…*invested* yourself in anyone…ever. Are you going to really stick this out with Maggie?"

"What do you mean, I haven't `invested' myself?"

"You know what I mean, beyond dinner and a roll and a tickle."

"A roll and a tickle?"

"You heard me." Kathy paused, and then continued in a more serious tone, "Listen, Maggie is going through something very real here, and very messy and very emotional. You *hate* messy and emotional. I just want you to think about that before you get close to her, and then you freak out and say `sorry, too much, too messy, not my thing' and run back to New York."

Jack knew she was right, he did tend to keep people at arm's length, but when it came to Maggie he couldn't imagine not doing whatever he could for her. More surprisingly, that thought didn't scare him at all. It felt right and it felt natural.

"Kath, I'm just going to wing it. Who knows what's going to happen? The police will probably be able to confirm her story and everyone else's at the farm too, and they'll go look somewhere else for the murderer. I can't imagine Maggie or anyone at Granger House killing someone."

"I can't either, but Jack we haven't seen any of these people since we were kids. Things change, people change, how well do we really know them anymore or what they're capable of?"

Jack became defensive and his voice rose, "Kathy, we *do* know these people. Nobody changes that much."

"Just be careful, that's all I'm saying, Jack. Be careful for your sake, and be careful with Maggie."

CHAPTER FIFTEEN

Tom stood contemplating the evidence that had been assembled from the Granger's property. It was all laid out on a brown folding table in the conference room. Several tools wrapped in plastic and small-labeled bags filled with soil samples were spread out in neat little rows. A handwritten sign that read "Evidence-Scott Harding Murder Case" was taped to the front of the table.

The state police detective walked up behind Tom and asked, "What are you thinking, Sheriff?"

"Nothing good, Harvey, nothing good. Since you told me about the DNA test coming back positive for Maggie's blood, I haven't liked where my mind is taking me."

"I know you've known these people a long time, Sheriff, but you can't let that sway you."

Tom turned to glare at the younger man. "Don't you think I know that? I'm not going to look at the evidence any differently than I would for anyone else, but that doesn't mean I'm going to like it."

The other man nodded. Satisfied. "All right, so where are we? We spoke to everyone separately, and all their stories match up. And we know the bloodstain is Maggie Granger's, so there is some substantiation of her story. But since there were no witnesses to the alleged event, we can never be one-hundred-percent certain Maggie is telling the truth."

"Yeah, but why make that story up? When we went out to the Granger place I really thought we'd look around, find nothing and be able to scratch them off the list. I couldn't see any motive for why any of them would murder Scott Harding.

"But if her story is true..."

"She just handed us one hell of a motive. Maggie Granger wasn't kidding when she said Griff or the others would kill that boy if they knew what he'd done. I've known Griffin, Joe and Rolly my whole life. They are good men, but they live by their own rules.

"When they need to burn some tree branches, they make a bonfire and burn them; it wouldn't even occur to them you're supposed to get a burning permit. When they've got a dog that's too old and in pain, they don't take it to the vet to 'put it to sleep' — Joe goes in the shed, gets the shot gun, and puts it out of its misery."

"You're making an awfully big leap from illegal burning and putting down a dog to murdering an eighteen-year-old boy."

Tom rubbed his chin and stared at the tools they had taken from the Granger's barn. "I don't know. It's the nature of these people to take care of things on their own, to take care *of* their own. Those three men raised Maggie, and they are *very* protective of her. If they found out Scott had done damn near the worst thing a man could do to a woman...I don't know if they'd think at all or just act on instinct."

The detective said, "All I know is we've got a dead eighteen-year old-boy whose body was found near the Granger's house, which is also the last place we know he was alive. And if Scott did rape her, all the people living on the farm, and Greg Detrick, had a motive to kill him and no alibi."

The detective scanned his notes in a black spiral bound notebook. "Maggie says she went up to bed, but no one saw her after Greg helped her to her room around 10:00. Same with Griff, Rolly and Joe, they all said they went to bed after they spoke to Greg. That was 11:00, but they all sleep in separate places, so they can't even vouch for each other. And Greg Detrick's mom was the only one at his home that night, and she's since passed away, so he doesn't have anyone to vouch for his whereabouts after 11:00 either."

"Shit." Tom scratched his head and looked over at the detective. "Alright, when are you going to get that imprint of Scott's head wound from the coroner?"

"They're sending someone down with it by late this afternoon."

"Good. Maybe we'll be able to match it with something here." Tom motioned to the tools on the evidence table that had been taken from the Grangers.

"I wouldn't count on it, Sheriff. The coroner said the blow to the head was most likely what killed him and I can't imagine whoever did it kept the weapon around for thirteen years."

"You never know. What is strange to me is that there is no trace material left at all on the skull or in the wounds. You would think that if it were a farm tool that hit that deep into the bone it would leave some kind of metallic or organic residue."

"Well, that skull has been in the water a long time, not too surprising there isn't much to get from it other than the general shape of the object that did the damage."

Off the evidence table Tom picked up a heavy hammer with a round nose and a sharp claw side for taking out nails. He felt the weight of it in his hand. "The coroner said there were several indentations on the skull that seemed rounded, but there was also a sharp straight edge component to the wound as well."

"Yes. He said whatever it was, it was an unusual shape, which will be helpful if we ever find something to match it."

Tom kept staring at the hammer with the evidence tag that read "Property of Joe Tripp" hanging off the neck. "Maybe it was multiple blows?"

The detective shrugged, "Maybe, but the coroner thinks that the way the skull cracked indicates one single blunt force trauma."

Tom sighed and put the hammer back on the evidence table. "Well, why don't I send out Pete to get us some sandwiches from the diner. I don't remember the last time we stopped to eat, and I can't think on an empty stomach."

A half-hour later, Tom and the detective had spread their sandwiches out on napkins on Tom's desk. They both looked up as the door to the office crashed open and a high-pitched voice said, "So here you sit stuffing your faces while the people that murdered my baby are still free? What the hell's the matter with you, Tom Snyder?"

Tom sighed and lowered the sandwich from his mouth. "Cynthia, we're doing everything we can."

She snorted at him and sat down in the only other empty chair in the small room. She crossed her thin legs and then her arms and stared at him.

Tom almost decided to give up eating his sandwich, as it was awkward eating with Cynthia glaring at him. Then he thought, the hell with it. I haven't slept or eaten in almost eighteen hours. He took a big bite of his grilled ham and cheese.

Cynthia squirmed in her seat watching him with a look of distaste on her face. "I don't know how you can eat that greasy food. That's from the diner, isn't it? I wouldn't eat in that place on a bet."

Tom didn't say anything but enjoyed the last bites of the crunchy greasy crust and took a long drink of his ice tea. He wiped his mouth with a paper napkin and said, "OK, Cynthia, I have a few questions for you. I want to piece together as much of the last night Scott was seen alive as I can."

Cynthia practically jumped out of her seat. "Me? You have questions for me? I am the one who came here to see what *you* have done so far. It's the people over at the Granger farm that need to answer questions, not me."

"We'll get to that in a minute. I just need to fill in a few blanks so I can try and account for all Scott's movements that night."

"Fine," Cynthia answered crossly. "What do you want to know?"

Tom and the detective both rolled up the paper plates their sandwiches had been on and threw them away, and then got out their note pads. Tom began, "You said you were working late at the dealership that night and you got home around 11:30 to find Scott's note. His suitcase and car were gone."

She sighed heavily. "That's right, that's what I told you. I gave you the note already."

Tom got up and went into the evidence room, then returned with the note in a sealed baggie. "This was the note you found?"

"Yes! Tom, why are we going over all this again?"

Tom read the note out loud:

> Mom,
> I went to pick up Maggie for the prom and found her fucking Greg right on the living room floor! My best friend and my fucking girlfriend, I can't believe it. I can't believe I was going to ask her to marry me.
> You were right all along about her. I can't face anyone in this town right now. I am too hurt and humiliated. I need to get away for a while. I'll let you know where I am soon.
> Love, Scott

Tom stared at his notes for a moment, frowned at them and then asked her, "Didn't you think it was strange that Maggie and Greg would pick that time to, ah...consummate their affair...right there on the living room floor when they *knew* Scott would be coming to pick Maggie up for Prom?"

Cynthia leaned forward in her chair. "Who the hell knows why Maggie Granger does anything? She was a strange child and has grown into a strange woman. For God's sake, three old men, one of them colored, raised her. She got herself knocked up about two seconds after she got to college, and now she allows total strangers to traipse in and out of her house as long as they throw her a few bucks.

"You want to know what I *really* found strange? Why my Scott, a smart handsome, athletic boy who had his pick of any girl in that high school, would date Maggie Granger. Of course when I read the note, and later when she came back from Baltimore pregnant, well, I knew right then exactly what it was that had kept my boy seeing that…girl."

The detective noticed Tom's face had colored slightly and a red blotch had sprung out on his neck. He decided he would ask the next few questions to give Tom a chance to cool down. "And why was that, ma'am?"

Cynthia turned to look at the detective like he had lost his mind. "Have you been listening to me, boy? Because she's a slut! Because a young man of Scott's age was sowing his oats, hormones flying every which way, he wasn't thinking seriously about his future or who would be a good wife for him one day. She obviously was opening her legs for anyone that walked by, and I guess that night Greg Detrick walked by!"

Tom took a breath and said, "OK, *if* Scott wrote that note, he would have been home between 10:00 and 11:00, packed his clothes and driven off. You said his car was missing too?"

"Yes, the car I had given him on his seventeenth birthday." Cynthia's face softened at the memory. "The morning of his seventeenth birthday I let him walk out onto the lot and pick any new car he wanted. He was so excited. He must have sat in half the cars I had out there. He finally picked a cherry red Camaro, the Berlanetta model."

"You never saw the car again?"

Cynthia's frown returned. "Tom, you know I never saw my son or that car again after that night."

"It's just surprising we never found it abandoned or anything."

"Tom, that was a beautiful car. The killer could have driven it to any street in Washington or Baltimore, left it for five minutes, and it would have been gone. That car was easy to break into because it had a removable sunroof. It was a high theft car and it doesn't surprise me a bit that we never saw it again. Obviously, I never reported it stolen because I thought Scott had it."

Tom and the detective were both making notes, and the room was quiet for a few minutes. Cynthia tapped her red nails impatiently on the battered desktop. "Well, are you done interrogating me?"

Tom finished writing and looked at the detective who shrugged at him, then he turned back to Cynthia and said, "I think that's all for now."

"Not for me it's not. What happened when you questioned Maggie?"

"Cynthia," Tom said, "this is an open investigation. Just because the victim was your son doesn't mean I have to, or should, share every detail with you immediately. We are still trying to figure out Scott's movements that night. I will let you know when we have anything concrete."

Cynthia looked like she was going to explode. "You listen to me, Tom, that was my baby that got murdered, and I want to know what that bitch said happened!"

The detective said, "Mrs. Harding, we can tell you that we did interview Margaret and Griffin Granger, Greg Detrick, Rolly Beaumont and Joseph Tripp. We also got a search warrant for the Granger's home and currently have several items bagged and tagged in the evidence room from that search. We have just received back some lab reports on evidence gathered there and are waiting for some more information from the coroner.

"We are also waiting for a report back from the handwriting analyst who is examining the letter you found the night Scott disappeared and the subsequent letters you received over the years, supposedly from Scott. She is comparing them to a sample of writing we *know* is Scott's that we got from the school's archives."

Cynthia sat back a little in her chair and looked somewhat placated. "Alright," She conceded, "so you've done a little more than just eat greasy food from the diner." She fiddled with the sleeves on her blouse and then looked from Tom to the detective. "What I want to know is what she said. What did Maggie Granger say happened that night?"

Tom hesitated. He looked to the detective for direction. The detective gave a small shake of his head and Tom answered, "We can't give you details yet, but I can tell you that her story was very different than the one in that note, and there is some evidence to substantiate it."

Cynthia tried to get more out of Tom and the detective, but neither would give her any more information. She didn't know what Maggie had told the police happened that night, but she knew in her heart it had to be a lie. Finally, and to Tom's great relief, she put on her jacket and got ready to leave.

On the way out she said, "Oh, your new police cruiser will be in tomorrow. You can pick it up Friday." Then she pulled out a handwritten invoice from Harding Prestige Motors for the police car and handed it to Tom.

Tom took the invoice from her. "OK. Thanks, Cynthia."

"I don't want your thanks, I want you to prove that Granger woman killed my son, or knows who did."

"We're doing everything we can to investigate this murder, Cynthia."

She rolled her eyes, made a huffing noise and marched out of the office.

When they heard the front door of the station firmly shut behind her, the detective said, "Wow, that woman's a piece of work."

"Yeah, well, you have to cut her some slack. She just found out her only child she thought had been living in New Mexico has really been dead for the last thirteen years. That can't be easy."

"No, I guess not. It's not going to be any easier for her to hear the story Maggie Granger told us either."

"Cynthia will never believe it," Tom said. "She'll just think Maggie made it up."

"Probably. And since there were no eyewitnesses, just proof that at one time Maggie Granger bled on her living room floor, she could be right."

"Maybe, but I don't think so. There would be no reason for Maggie to make up a story like that, all it does is give her and every one of those men a motive and no alibi. That wouldn't be too smart. And no matter what you think about Maggie Granger, she ain't dumb."

"Still early days, we've got a lot more evidence to go through and another round of questions for the Granger crew." With a lighter tone the detective asked, "So you're getting a new cruiser?"

"Yeah, we finally got one approved in the budget, been waiting years to get a third car. Cynthia's dealership has the contract for the town on all municipal vehicles."

"Isn't she on the town's Board of Directors?" Tom nodded and the detective rolled his eyes and said with sarcasm, "Boy, I wonder how she got that contract?"

Tom chuckled. "I never said Cynthia was dumb either."

Cynthia drove out of the police station parking lot and headed back to the dealership. She couldn't believe Tom wouldn't tell her everything about their official visit to the Grangers.

I am a respected businesswoman in this community. I am a chairwoman on the Board of Directors of this town, and my son was the victim, for God's sake. I should be told everything that goes on in the investigation immediately, everything. I'll deal with Tom Snyder at the next election.

That Granger bitch might have everyone believing she's as innocent as fucking Snow White, but I know different. I'll make sure she pays for Scott's death one way or the other.

CHAPTER SIXTEEN

The next morning, after Maggie had served her guests their breakfast and assured them that the police presence the day before was purely routine, she decided to take a walk outside to clear her head. Yesterday had been difficult, looking her grandfather in the eye and telling him what had happened to her all those years ago had been painful.

Joe and Rolly had sat on either side of Griff when she told them. All three men remaining quiet long after she had finished telling them the same story she had just told Tom Snyder. Her grandfather had looked up at her with tears swimming in his eyes and said, "I can't believe you never told me, told us. We could have helped you."

The other men had nodded and looked at Maggie with intense sorrow in their eyes. She realized it was there as much for the fact that they hadn't been able to protect her and that she hadn't relied on them or trusted them, as it was for what had happened to her. She reached out for her grandfather's hand and took it in hers. "I was so scared something else would happen if I told you. Something bad. I couldn't take anything else happening, especially that night."

Rolly understood what she was saying. "You thought we would have gone after Scott and hurt him bad, didn't you?" he said gruffly.

Maggie had bowed her head and replied quietly, "Yes. I couldn't let you all get in trouble over me, over *him*. I needed you here on the farm with me, not in jail. Even though I didn't tell you what happened, you *were* all here for me, you have always been here for me. That's all I've ever needed."

Her grandfather opened his arms and Maggie fell gratefully into them. The other men put their hands on her shoulders. They stayed sitting close together until the police finally packed up their things and left.

Maggie thought she would have trouble getting to sleep after such an emotionally charged day, but to her surprise, she slept better than she had in years. Feeling drained, and without the terrible secret of that long ago night weighing on her, she had drifted off into a deep and restful sleep. She woke up feeling hopeful. It was a new day, a day without dark secrets hidden away in the corners of her heart.

Sunny, and with a warm breeze that stirred the tree branches, Maggie listened to the rustle of the leaves as she walked briskly down the lane heading in the direction of the Callahan's house. She wanted to talk to Jack. They hadn't seen each other since he had sat with her during her interview with the sheriff.

Maggie was a little scared about how Jack would react to her today. He had only been back in her life a few days, and he had learned so much about her yesterday, things even the people closest to her hadn't known. She wondered if it would be awkward between them. Like it was between people who were intimate with each other too quickly, and then had trouble looking each other in the eye the next morning. Well, there was only one way to find out.

She found him sitting on the end of the dock, his legs dangling over the edge and a steaming mug of coffee in his hand. He heard her walking down the wooden boards towards him; he didn't need to turn around to see who it was. When she stood next to him, Jack gave her a warm smile and patted the wooden decking next to him. The fear that things would be awkward between them vanished.

Maggie sat down and noticed Jack's eyes seemed only half open and there were dark circles under them. "What's the matter with you, Callahan? I swear you look hung over."

Jack grimaced and said, "That would be because I am. I went to your friend Greg's house and sucked down a whole bottle of wine."

Maggie put her hand over her mouth and chuckled. "Ah, you got to see the wine cellar?"

"Yes. Yes, I did."

"Poor baby." She rubbed her hand on his back and looked out at the water.

They sat silently for a while until finally Jack asked, "How did it go after we left?"

"About as good as it could, I guess. It's funny, I could have told them so many times, you know?"

"Why didn't you? Later, after Scott had been gone awhile."

"I really thought Scott would eventually come back, so I never really felt comfortable telling anyone. Then the years went by and Scott still didn't come home, and the guys got older, so I thought maybe I could tell them, but...it just never seemed like the right time."

"Probably not something that would come up in dinner conversation."

Maggie gave a dry short laugh. "No, not in the normal day do I find myself saying, 'Oh, by the way, Gramps, remember prom night? I lied, Scott and I didn't break up, actually he raped me on the living room floor.'" Maggie's smile faded. "It's so weird to be talking about it now. Talking to someone other than Greg, out in the open like this."

Jack took her hand in his. "Freeing?"

She looked back at him. "Yes, it is. I guess because it served me just as well for everyone to think the rumors about Greg and me that night were true, part of me started believing them too. Like I really *had* done something wrong."

"Didn't your grandfather ever ask you about that? He had to have heard those rumors too, about you and Greg being...together...that night."

Maggie shook her head. "No, he never did. The morning after the prom Gramps, Rolly and Joe were all up before me and had made this big breakfast. They fussed over me, but we never really talked about anything. You could tell they thought I had broken up with my boyfriend and was feeling down about that, that was all, and I didn't tell them any different."

"Well, it's all over now."

Maggie looked thoughtful for a moment. "I wish I could believe that. I have a feeling it's just beginning. Tom Snyder and the investigation into who killed Scott aren't going to go away. And Cynthia isn't going to rest until someone pays for Scott's murder."

"Do you have any theories about how he ended up in the lake?"

Maggie chewed thoughtfully on her lower lip. "I really don't. Truthfully, I haven't thought about it much yet. I'm still getting over the shock of finding out he's dead. You know, I don't like Cynthia, but I have to feel sorry for her. If it's a shock to me, I can't imagine what *she's* feeling."

"I was thinking about that. Scott's been dead all these years, and yet his mother just accepted that a few letters meant he was alive and well. I mean, how do you go almost thirteen years without a visit, or even a return address to write back to, without thinking something's wrong?"

Maggie shrugged her shoulders. "I don't know. I can't imagine not seeing Caleb that long, even when he's grown, but Scott and Cynthia had a very different relationship."

She cocked her head to one side and thought how to explain it to Jack. "It was almost adversarial. Looking back, I think one of the main reasons Scott dated me was because it pissed his mother off so much. Scott could have dated anyone in that school he wanted to, and I'm not saying I was a pariah or anything, but there certainly were girls a lot prettier and a lot more suited to dating the star quarterback than me."

Jack gave her a playful punch in the arm and said in a mocking tone, "Aw, get out of here, I bet you could out fish and out shoot any of those girls."

Maggie laughed at him and punched him back. "Shut up! I was pretty damn cute in high school, I'll have you know!"

"I would argue that you're pretty damn cute right now."

Maggie stopped laughing and saw something more serious in Jack's eyes. He said, "Does any of this seem familiar?"

Maggie looked around her and then back at him. "Uh, yeah, I'm pretty sure this is Lake Meade."

"No. I mean this." Jack held up their hands that were clasped tightly together and motioned with his other hand to the dock and the view.

"Oh, you mean us sitting here like this?"

"Yeah, but we're missing something."

"What?"

"The kiss." Jack leaned over and kissed her gently on the lips. He pulled back and felt the same feeling of apprehension he had when he was sixteen. But just as she had all those years ago, Maggie smiled at him and then leaned over and kissed him right back. Unlike all those years ago, they didn't pull away from each other. This time they let the kiss deepen.

Jack put his hands on either side of Maggie's head and buried them deep in her strawberry-colored curls, his mouth firmly kissing hers, running his tongue gently around hers. Exploring, tasting. Maggie put her arms around Jack's neck and let the warm sensations slide down and through her body.

Maggie felt as if she were sinking, down, down into a dream. She realized Jack had lowered her so that they were both lying on the dock. Their arms were wrapped around each other, the kissing becoming more urgent. Jack slid this hand along her body up toward her breast. Something in Maggie froze.

In one motion she pushed Jack away and was sitting with her arms wrapped protectively around her knees. She hadn't even remembered moving. Jack reached out to her.

She said, "Oh, my God, I'm sorry. I...I don't know...you didn't...oh, shit!" Maggie lowered her head onto her knees, not sure if she were more confused, embarrassed or disappointed.

Jack sat up next to her and put his arm around her shoulders. "I'm sorry, I was moving a little fast. I've only been back for a couple days, after all these years, and you've had a lot going on...I shouldn't have...I'm sorry."

Jack started to stand up and Maggie grabbed his arm and pulled him back down next to her. "No. No, don't go. You didn't do anything wrong." She looked up at him, her eyes glistening with unshed tears. "Trust me, I have been hoping for a follow up on that first kiss for sixteen years, and I was not disappointed. It's just...I'm not sure how to explain this."

"What? Is it Greg?"

A puzzled expression crossed Maggie's face, then she realized what he was asking. "Oh, no. Greg and I are just friends. In fact he's been telling me for years I should get out there and...well, you know."

Jack cocked an eyebrow. "What...kiss someone on an old wooden dock?"

"Yeah, something like that."

"I knew I liked Greg."

She laughed as she searched Jack's eyes, her face becoming more serious as she reached up and brushed back some of the hair that had fallen into his eyes. She ran her hand down his cheek. He felt so good, so warm and solid.

Jack reached up and took her hand away from his face and kissed it. "Hey, it's me remember? It's your 'summer best friend.' What's wrong? I'm sorry if I went too fast...it's just...I've thought about you a lot over the years. I guess I started kissing you and I got carried away." He shrugged and asked, "Forgive me?"

A tear slid down her face. "Forgive you? There's nothing to forgive. We're both adults. Adults that have probably wanted each other bad since we were teenagers." She paused and took her hand from his. "No, it's me. Before we go any farther, I need to tell you something."

"OK."

Maggie looked uncomfortable. "I don't really know how to say this, or if I even should...ah, dammit." Maggie jumped up and stomped off toward the driveway.

Jack jumped up after her and grabbed her arm. "Hey, what's going on? Maggie?" He turned her around and lifted her chin up until she had no choice but to look into his eyes. She stared at him with both defiance and uneasiness. He hugged her to him and after a few moments she relaxed and put her arms around him and returned his embrace.

Loosening his grip, Jack led them over to sit on the porch steps. "Come on, Mags. Look, I'm not going to pressure you to say or do anything you don't want to, but I do want you to remember it's *me*. It's Jack. I may be all grown up and an architect, but inside I'm the same guy you spent your summers with digging up worms, talking about life and sharing your first kiss." He gave her a cockeyed grin.

Something in Maggie shifted, loosened. She wanted to kiss him again, and feel those strong arms around her. She took a deep breath and made a decision. "OK. Since this seems to be my week for telling all...here goes."

Jack waited, an expectant look on his face. Maggie looked like she was going to say something several times and then stopped. Then she started again, "I don't have a lot of experience with...this," and she motioned her hand back and forth between them.

Jack frowned. He didn't understand. "You mean this?" And now Jack repeated the same motion between them.

"Yeah. I, um, I haven't really wanted to be...intimate...with anyone since that night with Scott. Truthfully, I haven't had a lot of time or opportunity. I've been pregnant, had a son, started a business." She looked at Jack as her words trailed off. Then she gathered her thoughts again and said, "I guess I've just kept myself so busy that I have been content with my life. I've been raising Caleb, taking care of the guys, running the B&B and I've had Greg in my life for companionship. I just haven't wanted to get any closer to anyone. I'm sure that night with Scott had a lot to do with it too. It's just been fairly easy *not* to get that close to anyone that way. But now..."

Jack's eyes widened as he fully understood what she was saying. "You mean you haven't been with anyone intimately since Scott?" And then he rushed to say, "And I don't mean that night, prom night, that wasn't intimacy, that was an attack."

Maggie nodded her head in agreement.

Jack sat with a stunned look on his face, and when Maggie almost stood up, his arms reached out reflexively and pulled her back down and closer to him. "Just give me a second, don't go running off anywhere."

"I'm not running off...I just...oh, hell, I don't know what I'm doing."

"Wait a minute," Jack said, "if it was only Scott...then Caleb?"

Maggie nodded her head again.

"Does Caleb know?"

"Not yet. I told him that his father and I were young when we conceived him and that we didn't want to stay together, so I decided to raise him on my own, which is all true. I told him when he got older I would tell him all about his father. I've been able to put it off until now, but I think with everything else coming out that I had better tell him sooner rather than later."

Jack hugged her to him and she said, "I have no idea what to say to him."

Jack kissed her on her forehead and asked, "Does anyone else know Scott is Caleb's father?"

"Only Greg, but I told Gramps, Joe and Rolly when I told them everything else last night. They deserved to know."

She shifted position so she could look at Jack's face. "You know, none of them ever asked me in all those years who Caleb's father was. When I came to them at eighteen and said, `I'm not going back to college because I'm pregnant, and the father's not in the picture so I'm going to raise this baby without him,' they didn't bat an eye. Actually, they seemed happy I was coming home. And all three of them have loved and cared for Caleb like he was their own since the day he was born."

Tears slid down her face and Jack rocked her back and forth. He rested his chin on the top of her head and felt her weight resting against his body. He was enjoying the feel of her leaning on him, but he had to wonder if there were any more revelations coming.

After a few minutes of sitting in silence and staring at the lake, Jack took Maggie's hand and led her into the house. Candy had left a box of tea bags in the cupboard, and Jack put the kettle on to make them some. While the water was heating, Maggie wandered around the house looking at all the family photographs and touching the knickknacks on the shelves.

Jack stood in the living room doorway and watched her. The sun was streaming in through the window, and with the bright light all around her Maggie looked like she could have been fifteen again. Then she turned and walked towards him, her image becoming clearer as she walked out of the bright sunlight, and once again she looked like the strong mature woman he had met a few days ago. "What are you grinning at?" she asked.

"Who knew you'd grow up to be such a `girl,' Granger?"

She moved toward him. "I was always a `girl,' Callahan. It just took you a long time to notice."

"I guess so, and I have to tell you, I'm really noticing right now." He leaned down and kissed her. She let the kiss deepen, tongues touching, Jack's hands moving to hold her face, the heat spreading between them again. When they finally pulled away from each other, Jack said breathlessly, "I know you want to take it slow, so just tell me if I'm making you uncomfortable."

Blowing out her breath, Maggie looked up at him with desire in her eyes. "You know what? Now that I finally said everything out loud. Now that you know it all, I feel freer than I have felt in years. I feel like I did the last time we were out on that dock sixteen years ago."

A slow smile spread on both their lips. "And how was that, Granger?" Jack asked.

"Like I wanted to make out with you and hoped I'd find out what all the fuss was about at second base."

"Oh, my," Jack said with false shock in his voice. He kissed her again, then took her hand and led her to the couch. In a mocking tone he asked, "What if your grandfather stops by? We could get caught."

They both plopped down on the couch. Maggie curled up in Jack's arms, her face tilted up to his. "It's a chance I'm willing to take."

Jack ran his fingers up and down her cheek and looked into her eyes. "Me too." And he bent down and kissed her until her toes curled.

CHAPTER SEVENTEEN

"Sheriff? We got the report back from the handwriting analyst." The detective handed the manila envelope to Tom.

"Have you looked at this yet, Harvey?"

"No, it just got here."

Tom took a deep breath and opened the envelope. "Let's see what we've got." He was silent for a few minutes as he read the report, then handed the first page to the detective and continued reading the second.

When both men were finished reading, they sat down across from each other in Tom's office. Tom said, "Well, that clinches it, doesn't it. Officially the last place Scott Harding is known to have been alive was the Granger's farm."

"Looks like it. The handwriting is conclusively not his on the note left for his mother, so there is no evidence that he ever went back to his house that night."

"The analyst says the writing is a good copy, so it was most likely someone who was close to the victim, someone that was familiar with the way he wrote."

Tom looked up from the pages of the report. "Good enough that his own mother didn't know the difference."

"The handwriting expert also concludes that the handwriting *is* a match between that letter and the ones that followed from different locations over the next ten years."

"So whoever our killer is, he or she has traveled around the country periodically sending letters to Cynthia just to keep up the pretense that Scott Harding was alive and well."

"I find it almost unbelievable that it worked so well for so long."

Tom rubbed the stubble on his chin. "What do you mean, Harvey?"

"I mean, if my mother didn't *see* me, actually *see* me for years on end, without even a way of contacting me, she would have been hounding every policeman, FBI agent and private investigator she could find to get a hold of my sorry ass.

"But here, Mrs. Harding just seems to take it for granted that her son is going to write her once a year or so and never come home, and all because he found his girlfriend and his best friend doing the nasty. It just doesn't ring true."

Tom had been listening with his chin resting in his hand. He looked up at the younger man. "You know, you have a point. Although, I doubt your momma and Cynthia Harding are anything alike."

The detective gave a snort. "*Nothing* alike."

"I have known Cynthia as long as anyone in this town, and she has never come across to me as overly maternal. However, she is *very* possessive of what is *hers*, and she definitely perceived Scott as belonging to *her*. It does surprise me too that she didn't wonder about him never coming home, even if it was just on the principle that someone may have stolen what was hers."

"Let's read the first few letters again with that perspective and see if they're that convincing."

"OK." Tom shook out the copies of the subsequent letters supposedly written by Scott to his mother from the manila envelope. The accompanying envelopes to the letters had postmarks from different locations. The envelopes and letters had been sent to the print lab technicians, who had turned up nothing but Cynthia Harding's prints from opening the letters.

The first one read:

> Dear Mom,
> I just couldn't stop driving that night after I found Maggie and Greg. Every time I stopped driving the image of them came back to me like I was watching a movie or something, so I just kept going.
> Well, the next thing I knew I was in Maine. Do you believe it? I couldn't. The only time I've even been out of Kent County was for football games.
> Anyway, I stopped at a coffee shop and there were a bunch of fishermen there. One of them commented on how big I was and wanted to know what boat I worked on. When I told him I didn't

work on a boat he asked if he could hire me for his, to pull in nets and stuff.

I really don't feel ready to come back yet, so I figured why not. I need to make some money anyway and he's going to let me sleep in the back room of his house, so I won't even have to pay rent.

I'll write again soon and let you know how I'm doing. Don't worry about me, Mom. I just need a little time and space right now.

Love,
Scott

The postmark on the envelope was from Little Cliffs, Maine, dated twelve years ago.

When Tom had finished reading the letter again he handed it to the detective. Tom turned his attention to the next one in the pile. It had been dated several months after the first.

Dear Mom,

Sorry it's been so long since I wrote you last time. The fishing was hard work, we were out on the boat for days at a time, and when I was finally on dry land, all I wanted to do was eat and sleep!

I decided I had had enough of fishing so I pointed the car west and I am now in Chicago. This place is wild! And I always thought Baltimore was big! I took a class on bartending and I found a job real quick at a club here. The tips are great and I have my own place now. It's only a studio apartment, but I like it.

I know you are probably really pissed I didn't come back to see you or go to college, but I really don't ever want to have to face Maggie or Greg or that town again. I can't imagine ever moving back there and seeing them day after day.

I'm starting over here and I like it. I'm meeting interesting people, some cute girls and I'm doing it on my own. It feels good.

Just know I love you and I miss you and I'm fine. I'll write to you again soon.

Love,
Scott

Tom handed over the second letter to the detective and sat back in his chair. When the other man had finished reading they looked at each other. Tom said, "They are pretty well-thought-out. Detailed."

"Yeah, I suppose. If you are not the overly maternal type, this might ease your mind enough that you wouldn't call out the National Guard."

"She had no reason to suspect that he didn't leave Lake Meade, just like the first note said, so she had no reason to be suspicious."

"No, I guess not. And all the letters run along the same line." Tom flipped through a dozen or more pages of letters. "Moved on to a new place, making a decent living, meeting nice people, don't worry about me, I don't want to come home, love Scott."

"That seems to be the gist of them, and they've been working all these years keeping Cynthia's suspicions at bay. I wonder…*if* there hadn't been that cliff of rocks underwater that stopped the body from sinking all the way to the bottom of the lake, and *if* we didn't have that drought which brought the remains so close to the surface, how long would the killer have gone on writing letters to Cynthia? How long before she would have gotten suspicious and finally tried to find him?"

Tom shrugged his shoulders. "Doubt we'll ever know the answer to that." He heaved himself out of the chair with a sigh and said, "I have to go back out to the Granger's. I need them all to come in and give a handwriting sample. I'm hoping they come in voluntarily, but I don't think I'll have a problem getting a warrant if I need one."

"No, I wouldn't think so," the detective said.

Tom put his hat on and turned to walk out the office door. "I don't think we've got enough to arrest anyone yet, everything is circumstantial, but if any of the handwriting matches up or any of the tools on that table look like they match the head wound, we're going to have a solid suspect real quick."

Tom pulled up to the Granger House Bed and Breakfast a few minutes later. He noticed Maggie walking towards the back of the house hand in hand with the man he had met yesterday. Tom tried to remember his name. "Oh yes, Jack Callahan," he said to himself.

Maggie and Jack looked over to the patrol car, and Tom got a glimpse of their expressions as they changed from animated to wary. They waited as Tom walked towards them, then they all walked in the back door together.

Griff and Rolly were at the kitchen table playing cards and Joe was at the sink filling up a scrub bucket with soapy water. All three men glanced up at Tom and then past him to Maggie and Jack. Tom took off his hat and said, "Hi, all. I told you yesterday I would be back with some more questions."

Everyone in the room gave a slight nod and Tom proceeded. "You might all want to sit down a minute. I have some things to tell you."

Maggie, Jack, Joe and Tom joined Griff and Rolly at the long table. Tom cleared his throat and said, "I wanted to let you know that the lab did match the blood we found in the cracks of the hardwood floor to the DNA sample Maggie gave us. And as all your stories seemed consistent, the state police detective and myself feel that at this time we are going to proceed with the assumption you are telling the truth about what happened between you and Scott that night."

They all looked relieved, and Tom had to correct them. "This is *not* good news for any of you."

Maggie asked sharply, "What do you mean? You know what happened that night. It's not Scott's blood on the floor. He left here immediately after he attacked me, and no one in this house saw him again."

Tom took a deep breath, squared his shoulders and said, "Well Maggie, as I said, the evidence has given your version of what went on with Scott some credibility, but it also gives you, everyone here, and Greg Detrick a motive for murder. And not one of you has an alibi."

"Oh, my God," Maggie exclaimed, "So by telling you the truth, I actually just incriminated all of us."

Tom held her gaze and said in a low but deliberate tone, "If you were attacked and anyone here knew about it, they would have had motive to retaliate against Scott."

Griff said, "So what happens now, Tom? How do we prove to you we're innocent? Do you want lie detector tests, what do you want?"

Tom turned his attention to the older man. He felt a pang of regret as he looked into the wizened old eyes that had, up until today, always reflected kindness and good humor back to him, but showed only caution and uneasiness. "I would like each of you to come down to the station and give us handwriting samples."

"Why?"

Tom was slow to answer, so Maggie answered for him. "The letters. It's the letters Cynthia got, right?"

Tom nodded and Maggie continued, "The note Cynthia found that night and all the letters she said she received over the years, they must have been from Scott's murderer."

He let the silence speak for itself.

"Well, I'm going down there right now. If it will help clear our names we'll give you handwriting samples and whatever else you need," Griff said.

Maggie didn't look so sure. "I feel the same way, Gramps, but this is getting serious. I think we should talk to a lawyer."

"I wouldn't advise you against it, Maggie," Tom said, "but on this particular thing, there is enough circumstantial evidence to get a warrant if I have to, and a lawyer isn't going to be able to help you with that. Why don't you come down and we get this out of the way, and, as Griff says, if the analyst can't match any of your handwriting to those letters, you'll be in a better position."

Maggie looked around at the other men in the room. Rolly was the first to speak. "We'll just get our jackets, Tom, and go directly to the station. Let's get this over with."

CHAPTER EIGHTEEN

The evening meal that night was prepared in silence. Everyone went about their routine; Griff and Rolly set the table, Caleb put out the butter and condiments and Joe built a fire in the fireplace, but the mood was decidedly less jovial than usual.

Caleb looked at his mother with a question in his eyes, instead of saying anything, she turned away and started stirring the chowder. They had all gotten back from the police station before Caleb had returned home from school; he had no idea what was going on. Maggie knew she had to tell him soon, but not in the middle of getting dinner ready.

Jack had driven them all to the station in an old Buick sedan Griff kept in the barn. He had walked back to his own place after dropping them back at Granger House. Maggie had told him it had been a long day, she just wanted to get through this dinner and her talk with Caleb, and that she would call him in the morning. Jack had leaned down and kissed the side of her mouth, squeezed her hand, and then walked down the drive towards the cottage. Maggie had watched him go, part of her feeling scared and raw, wanting to shout out to Jack to stay and be with her, just to rest against him, just for a moment. But that didn't come naturally to the other part of her that had lived her life as a self-sufficient woman for too many years to let her ask for his help now. So, she had turned and walked back into the kitchen to start dinner.

When dinner was finished, Caleb went upstairs to do his homework, and Griff, Rolly and Joe walked out to their favorite spot on the dock to mull over the days events. Maggie was discussing some nice day trips with a guest in the living room when she heard the sound of gravel spraying as a car drove too fast down the driveway. She walked out on the porch just in time to see a black Cadillac come to a shuddering stop in front of the porch steps.

The large driver's-side door swung open and a high-heeled red leather pump appeared, then Cynthia Harding climbed out. She and Maggie stood fifty feet from each other, hatred emanating from each woman like heat off of pavement.

"What do you want?" Maggie asked.

Cynthia surveyed the house and some of the guests who were sitting in rocking chairs on the front porch with distaste. She looked back at Maggie and said, "I have some documents to give you from the town's zoning board."

"You could have mailed them," Maggie said shortly.

A cruel grin spread across Cynthia's face. In a calm even tone she said, "I could have, but I wanted to hear from your own lips what the hell you did to my boy, you lying whore."

Maggie felt the heat start to radiate from her neck, working its way up to her face. She moved rapidly off the porch towards the big black car, hoping to avoid having any of her guests overhear what was surely going to be a heated confrontation.

Maggie walked down the steps and stood on the other side of the car. In the same even tone Cynthia had used, Maggie said, "Why don't you ask Tom, you leather-faced shrew?" Maggie surprised herself, although she and Cynthia had always openly disliked each other, it was the first time she had actually been able to look her in the eye and give back as good as she got. It had been a long couple of days, and she was in no mood to be bulldozed by this woman.

Cynthia raised her eyebrows. "So, the *real* Margaret Granger comes out? Where are all your fans now, Maggie, to hear the way you really talk?"

"You're the only one I have ever needed to talk to like this, Cynthia."

Cynthia squinted her eyes and got a grim look on her face. "I mean it, I want to know what kind of bullshit story you told Tom Snyder about that prom night. What did you do to my precious boy? Or should I ask what did your grandfather, or one of the idiots that follow him around all day, do to him?"

Maggie was so angry she didn't even think about how loud her voice became when she said, "Your precious boy? Your precious boy, Cynthia, was a rapist and a coward."

Cynthia looked as if she had been slapped. She opened her mouth and shut it, no words came out. Maggie took advantage of her momentary shock to keep going. "That's right. I did tell Tom what happened that night. Your son raped me right here on my living room floor, how's that for a happy high school memory?"

Cynthia took a step towards Maggie and said in a dangerous low voice, "Is that what you told the police? Oh, God, that's what you told your grandfather that night, isn't it? That's why he killed my baby. What did your grandfather do, catch you with your pants down and that was your sorry-ass story, that Scott was raping you?"

Maggie's voice was a low growl as she tried to shield her guests from hearing what was being said, although she was sure they could tell whatever was going on was ugly. "No one here killed your 'baby,' Cynthia. He attacked me that night and then walked, or I should say ran, out of this house under his own power. I have no idea what happened to him after that."

The tendons in Cynthia's neck stood out like corded rope. She took another step closer to Maggie. "If you ever tell anyone else that story, I will ruin you. In fact, I'm going to ruin you anyway." She threw an envelope at Maggie, who caught it and opened it.

When Maggie was finished reading the first page, she looked up at Cynthia, her face pale. "You can't do this!"

"I'm not doing anything," she sneered. "The town's zoning board realized *all on its own* that you are operating a business in a residential area, and that is illegal."

"I got a variance when I opened the bed and breakfast twelve years ago."

"Really? They can't seem to find it? No one on the board remembers any variance. And even if there was one, even if somewhere there's a copy of it, the town has the right to review these things whenever they see fit. There has been a lot of development since you started this business. People paid a lot of money for some of these nice new homes here on the lake; they might not want a business in their backyard. Especially one that allows total strangers to stay right here amongst them."

Maggie was trembling with rage. "You can't do this, Cynthia, I applied for the variance and it was granted, you can't just come in here now and close us down."

Cynthia admired her perfectly polished nails and then looked back up at Maggie. "Oh, yes I can. I may never know what happened the night Scott was killed, but I sure as hell know you had something to do with it. After all this time has gone by the police may not be able to find enough evidence to pin this on you or one of your 'boys,' but I'll make sure you pay one way or the other."

Maggie had never wanted to hit another human being as much as she wanted to punch Cynthia in the face. She took a step closer to her and balled her fists. Cynthia didn't move, just stared back coldly. Maggie heard from behind her, "Mom? Mom, what's going on?"

She turned to see Caleb standing on the steps, clearly worried about his mother. Maggie lowered her voice and tried to sound normal. "It's alright, honey. Mrs. Harding is just delivering some papers to me. I'll be right in to check your homework."

Maggie turned back to Cynthia, who was studying Caleb with a lifted eyebrow. Maggie had tried to keep Caleb away from Cynthia as much as possible, hoping and praying he wouldn't look so much like his father that Cynthia would realize she had a grandson.

But Maggie could see it now, with Caleb standing there in the half-light, a baseball glove in one hand. He did look like Scott at that age, and she had a horrible feeling Cynthia was seeing it too.

To distract Cynthia from scrutinizing Caleb any longer, she said a little too loudly, "Alright, you've delivered your papers and said your piece, now get off my property."

Cynthia returned her attention to Maggie.

Maggie said, "I'll fight you every step of the way on this." She shook the envelope in her hand. "You may have this little town's board in your pocket, but I'll appeal to the state level if I have to, and your reach doesn't go any farther than the county line."

"And how long will that take, Maggie? Months? Years? We'll have you closed up as soon as the next meeting convenes on the fifteenth. How long can you and your decrepit old men survive here without paying customers? And put the lawyers fees on top of that." She made "tut tutting" sounds and shook her head with mock sympathy.

Maggie's heart grew cold; she knew Cynthia was right. Maggie had put away some savings and a nest egg for Caleb's college fund, but how long would they last without the income from the B&B? She wouldn't make it through the year if you added lawyer's fees on top of taxes and living expenses.

"Maybe you should just pack it up now and spare us all the trouble of a long drawn-out process. Send the old men to a nursing home, and you and the boy could finally go shack up with your faggot friend Greg Detrick."

Cynthia paused, "Of course, you all may be in jail soon anyway, and then I think the town will be able to repossess this place for back taxes in no time. Wouldn't that be a hoot? No more Maggie, no more bed and breakfast, and we'd get some prime land to build a town park on for free!" Cynthia clapped her hands together letting out a dry rasping laugh. "Oh, and your poor son. If everyone is in jail, who'll take care of him? I wonder who his next of kin is." Cynthia gave Maggie a cold and meaningful stare as she let her words trail off.

Maggie had never felt such rage swell and push inside her. She put a hand on the hood of the still warm car, leaned over and held up a finger in Cynthia's face. "First off, none of us killed your son and we're going to prove it." Maggie held up a second finger. "Second, it'll be a cold day in hell when I let you take one square inch of my family's land." She held up a third finger. "And thirdly, I figured out why Mr. Harding went out for a pack of cigarettes thirty years ago and never came back...you're a bigger bitch on wheels than even I thought humanly possible. Now, get your nasty bony self off my property before I put my boot up your ass."

Cynthia's grin slid off her face. She climbed slowly back into her car, started the engine with a roar and peeled out of the driveway. Maggie stood watching her; the anger and adrenalin in her stomach making her feel sick and shaky. What now? She wondered. What battle was she going to fight first?

Her head was spinning as Maggie walked back into the kitchen, she could feel the beginnings of a tension headache. As she was rubbing her temples, Griff shuffled in and asked, "Was that Cynthia Harding's car I saw out front?"

"Yes," Maggie said shortly. She was still holding the envelope with the notice from the town's zoning board folded inside it. She looked at her grandfather and motioned to the kitchen table. "Let's sit down, Gramps, we've got some things to talk about."

Griffin settled in his usual chair at the table and looked at his worried granddaughter. He noticed for the first time the strained look around her eyes and the way she was twisting her fingers together. "What is it, Mags? Is it the investigation? Don't worry about that, the police will look at all our handwriting and see none of us wrote those letters to Cynthia, and they'll go on and look somewhere else for the killer." He patted her hand.

"No, that's not what bothering me right now, or at least that's just part of it." She handed her grandfather the envelope and watched his face as he read it.

When he finished, he looked up at her with a puzzled expression. "I don't understand. We filed for a variance for a business in a residential area and it was granted. We have a copy of it around here somewhere."

"I know, Gramps, but Cynthia has stirred up the board enough that even if we found the copy, they would still review our right to run a business here, probably open it up for a vote, and you know Cynthia's got all those board members in her pocket. I think she gives them huge discounts on cars or something, hell, she could give them free cars for life for all I know. All I'm saying is, if it's put to a vote, we'll lose."

"I have some friends in this town myself, you know. She can't just run us out that easy. We are going to fight this, you'll see."

Maggie looked tired. Her grandfather knew she was feeling beaten at the moment, he also knew she'd eventually come around and get her fighting face on, but she needed a push. "I'm going to get Rolly and Joe in here and we'll figure this out."

Half an hour later Joe, Rolly, Griff and Maggie were still sitting around the kitchen table discussing what to do about the zoning board notice. None of them had come up with any constructive solutions, only fantasies of hanging Cynthia by her toes in the town square.

Joe hadn't said much of anything, and Maggie turned to him and asked, "So what do you think, Joe? Any ideas how to get ready for this town meeting on the fifteenth?"

Joe shook his head and stared at a spot on the wall. Then he turned and focused on Maggie. "Nope. But I know we survived the hurricane in '72 that wiped out all but ten acres of crops, the weevils that ate all the corn in '83 and that virus that hit the cows in '87, and if we can get through what Mother Nature has thrown at us, Cynthia Harding sure ain't gonna be what gets us."

All four were silent for a moment and then Rolly let out a raucous laugh and slapped his leg.

Griff chuckled too. "You're right, Joe. What the hell can Cynthia Harding do to us that we haven't already beaten, huh? We'll just face this one thing at a time and stick together. We'll come out on top. We always do."

Maggie had to smile at her mismatched family and felt a little better, but she still didn't feel as confident as they did. Only she had seen the pure hatred and determination in Cynthia's cold black eyes. They were facing a force of nature these men didn't understand — the wrath of a mother who sought revenge against the people she thought killed her son. They thought Mother Nature was difficult to face? They had no idea.

That night, after all the guests were accounted for, the house had been tidied up and the doors locked, Maggie climbed the stairs to her room, the old wood banister cool and solid as it slid under her hand. She stopped at Caleb's door and tapped on it. "Good night, honey," she said.

"Whatever," Caleb responded in a surly voice.

Surprised at his tone, Maggie opened the door and stuck her head in. She found Caleb sitting on the floor with his back against his bed. He was staring at the wall, his schoolbooks scattered around him on the floor. "What's the matter, hon?"

He didn't turn his head to look at his mother. "Why don't *you* tell *me?*"

Maggie's stomach sank. This was it, she thought, this was the moment she had been dreading. But she had to talk to him, tell him what was happening. Caleb was a smart and sensitive boy, he knew when something was wrong. She knew he had felt the tension in the air at their unusually quiet dinner that evening.

Maggie walked all the way into the room and shut the door quietly behind her. She sat down on the floor Indian-style next to her son. "You can tell something's going on, can't you?"

He still didn't look at his mother. "Duh."

Maggie sat for a bit trying to figure out where to start, and how much to tell. Caleb was twelve. He needed to know some things, but he didn't need to carry the weight of all of it either. Maggie took a deep breath. "Do you remember when I told you that your father and I had been very young when you were conceived, and that I had decided to raise you on my own?"

Caleb nodded. He had heard this before.

"Well, I think I need to tell you the rest."

Alert now, Caleb turned to his mother. He had wanted to know more about his father for so long, but whenever he had brought the subject up in the past, she had avoided his questions or told him she would tell him more when he was older. And now, here it was, he was going to learn about his father, he knew it. He felt a lot more nervous than he thought he would. "Are you going to tell me who my father is?"

Maggie slowly nodded. She put her arm around her son and pulled him to her, crushing him in her arms, and then putting him away from her so she could look into his face. "The most important thing to remember is that I love you. I love you more than I could ever say."

Caleb searched his mother's eyes. He was scared now, he didn't know why, but he knew what his mother had to say wasn't going to be easy to hear. "What is it, Mom?"

"You know the body they found in the lake this week?"

"Yeah, I heard it was some guy who used to live around here. He was some big-shot football player in high school."

Maggie nodded and kept her eyes on her son. "Yes, he was Cynthia Harding's son."

"The woman who was here today? The one that owns the car dealership in town?"

"Yes." Maggie paused. "I knew him in high school. In fact, I dated him for quite awhile."

Maggie took a deep breath to say more, but a light came on in Caleb's eyes and he jumped up off the floor. "Oh, my God. *He* was your boyfriend when you were young? He's the one? He was my father?"

Maggie couldn't get the words out. She just nodded her head as she felt the tears slide down her cheeks. She watched as several emotions flitted across her son's face. Surprise, anger, confusion, they were all there. He sat down again with a thump next to her. He let her put her arm around him, but his muscles were rigid and he sat very straight. "What was his name?"

"Scott. Scott Harding."

He rolled the name around on his tongue, "Harding, Scott Harding...Caleb Harding."

"No." Maggie said a little too quickly. "Caleb *Granger*."

Her son turned an angry face to her. "So why didn't you tell me before? All along I figured it was someone you met at college, not someone right from here. I have a grandmother in town."

Maggie's tears were flowing freely now. "Your father never knew about you, and I especially didn't want his mother to either."

Caleb's voice had grown loud and angry. "Why not? Why wouldn't you want me to know *all* my family? You're always talking about how important family is, but you've kept me from half of mine all my life!"

Maggie shook her head and tried to figure out how to say the next words, how to find them, and then she realized she couldn't. She'd rather Caleb be angry with her than have him know he was the product of his father raping her. He was so raw right now; she didn't know what that information would do to him. All she said was, "I never saw your father again after the night you were conceived. Your father and I didn't leave things on good terms. I just wanted to raise you on my own."

Caleb glared at his mother. "You didn't even try to find him to tell him he had a son?"

"No."

"You didn't even tell his mother I was her grandson?"

"No."

"I don't understand, Mom. I just don't get it."

"They were *not* nice people, Caleb." Maggie's voice grew loud and defensive. "I'm not sure how else to put it, but I honestly believed, *still* believe, you are better off without Cynthia Harding in your life." More gently she said, "And now it turns out your father couldn't have been in your life anyway."

"But you didn't know that until this week?"

"No."

"When were you going to tell me about him? I mean, if they hadn't found him *dead*?" He screamed out the word with a wounded voice. "Would you have *ever* told me?"

She tried to put her arms around him, but he pulled away. "Yes, I was going to tell you, but when you were a little older."

"Right."

"I *was*, Caleb. I just thought…"

"What? That I wouldn't want to know who my father was?"

"No. I just…nothing. What can I do, Caleb? What can I do to help you feel better?"

Caleb stared down at his hands without replying, then looked up into his mother's anguished eyes and said, "Introduce me to my grandmother and tell her who I am. I want to know my whole family. Even if I can't know my father, I can know her."

Maggie felt bile rise in her throat. "No. Not now. Cynthia Harding is *very* angry right now. She just found out her son was murdered almost thirteen years ago, and she thinks…she thinks…"

"What, Mom?"

"She thinks that I, or your grandfather, had something to do with his death. The farm is the last place anyone knows that Scott was alive."

Shocked, Caleb said, "She can't think that. No one would think that."

He let Maggie put her arms around him then. She wasn't sure if she had told him too much, but she knew the other kids at school were probably talking about all this, and she would rather he hear it from her first. "It's alright, honey. Tom Snyder is looking into it. He's going to find out what really happened to Scott, and then we'll all be cleared. Griff, Joe, Rolly and I went down to the station today and they took some handwriting samples. They're going to help show that we had nothing to do with his death."

Caleb stared up in disbelief at his mother. "You were at the station today? All of you? Were you ever going to tell me that either?"

"We hoped this would all be cleared up pretty quickly so we could tell you when it was less scary."

"Less scary? Mom, I swear you treat me like I'm two!"

Maggie contemplated her son and realized he was the same age she was when her grandmother had died and Maggie had taken on most of her duties around the house. Maggie hadn't felt like a child then either. She was going to have to reassess how she viewed and treated her son. "OK. From now on we'll let you know what's happening. I just don't want to worry you. This is all stuff for the grown-ups to worry about, not you."

Caleb went back to staring at the wall. "I'm tired. I'm going to bed," he said in a flat voice.

Maggie tried to kiss his head, but he pulled away. She got up to leave and said, "I love you, Caleb. You know that don't you?"

"Whatever."

CHAPTER NINETEEN

Tom had gathered all the evidence he could from the bottom of the lake where Scott's remains had been found. The remains themselves were being analyzed by the county coroner and Granger House had been thoroughly searched, and still he didn't have enough to piece together what happened to Scott Harding. He decided to go back to the Harding's neighborhood and ask anyone that had lived there back then if they remembered anything at all about that night.

It was a long shot that the closest neighbors still lived in the same houses they had thirteen years ago and that they would have any clear recollection of that night, but it was all Tom had left and it was worth a try.

He assigned one of the deputies to start knocking on doors at the far end of Cynthia's block, while Tom did the same at the other end, going back and forth across the street. A young couple lived in the third house Tom approached, they had recently moved into the neighborhood from Baltimore. They didn't even know who Cynthia Harding was, but told him to talk to the people across the street. They had lived in their house "forever."

Tom strolled across the street and knocked on the newly painted red front door of the brick ranch-style house the young couple had indicated. A few moments later a middle-aged woman opened the door. Her hair was mostly gray with brown streaks from a home hair-color kit that was growing out. "Hello. Can I help you, officer?"

Tom touched his cap and said, "Hello, ma'am. I'm Sheriff Snyder and I was wondering how long you've lived here in this house?"

The woman took a long look at the badge on Tom's chest. With an expression of annoyance that seemed comfortable on her face, she glanced from the badge to Tom and back again. Deciding he was legitimate, she answered, "We've lived here for almost thirty years."

"Great."

"I don't know what's so great about it. The house is the size of a shoe box and people come down this street doing forty miles an hour. Lucky any of my kids survived growing up riding their bikes and walking to school on this street."

Tom cleared his throat. "Well, ma'am, that's kind of what I wanted to talk to you about?"

She tilted her head and asked, "How fast people drive on this street?"

"No, ma'am. About how one of your neighbor's kids didn't survive growing up here."

Her mouth and eyes both opened up wide. "Who are we talking about, Sheriff?"

"Mrs. Harding, across the street, her son Scott."

"But I thought Scott left town ages ago. Didn't he leave when he found his high school girlfriend sleeping with his best friend, or something like that? Cynthia's always yammering on about it, I just tune her out half the time to tell you the truth."

"It appears that her son didn't leave town after the prom but was actually killed that night. We are asking all the neighbors if they remember anything unusual that happened around that time."

Her hand flew up to her bony chest. "Oh, goodness! That's horrible." As shocked and dismayed as she appeared, Tom suspected that as soon as he left she would immediately be calling all her friends, excited to tell them about how she had been questioned by a police officer about a murder, embellishing the interview into a full-blown interrogation.

"I know it's a long time ago, but is it possible you remember anything, ma'am? That would have been prom night thirteen years ago."

She thought for a moment and then shook her head. "Well, our daughter Sharon would have been a junior in high school that year — I remember because she had a little crush on Scott Harding, he was such a good looking boy, and she was always one year behind him in school — but another senior boy did ask her to the prom. We didn't know the boy she went with that well, so my husband and I were up waiting for her to get home until very late. I don't remember anything unusual happening in the neighborhood that night."

Tom was disappointed, but not surprised, he knew it was a long shot. He was about to thank her and turn to leave when a burly man in a tank top and sweat pants walked up behind the woman. "What's going on, Charlene?" he asked in a raspy voice.

"This is Sheriff Snyder, hon. It turns out Scott Harding didn't leave town after all." She paused dramatically and turned to her husband and said with relish, "He was murdered! The sheriff here is asking if we saw anything that night."

The man's eyes grew a bit larger, but that was all he conceded to appearing surprised. "I heard there was a lot of police over at the lake, is that where you found him?"

"Yes, sir. Your wife says your daughter also went to the prom that night and you were up late waiting for her to come home. Did you notice anything unusual?"

"Besides the hicky the size of a baseball on Sharon's neck?"

The woman hit her husband in the chest. "This is serious, Clyde."

Clyde scratched his ample belly and looked thoughtful for a moment, then his expression changed, and he looked as if he remembered something. "You know, there was something that night, but it's a little thing. I'm sure it doesn't have anything to do with Scott."

Tom felt the hair on the back of his neck rise; somehow he knew it *was* going to have to do with Scott. "What is it, sir?"

"Well, my wife never lets me smoke in the house."

"Of course not, it's disgusting."

"So I was on the front porch a lot, smoking and waiting for Sharon to get home. We didn't know the boy she went with real well, and it was her first formal dance. I guess I was a little worried about her, and so I was watching every car that came down the street, hoping it was this guy bringing her home.

"I was standing out there for about a half an hour before Sharon got home, so that would have made it about 11:30 'cause she had a midnight curfew and she just made it by the skin of her teeth, and I saw that old Dodge pick-up a guy in town had restored and kept in mint condition. I'm telling you, that truck looked like it did the day it rolled off the assembly line fifty years ago."

The man was wistful for a moment and then continued, "Anyway, I always loved that truck, he had it painted a forest green and it had all the original hardware on it. I asked that guy to sell me that truck a hundred times, but he wouldn't."

Tom asked, "Do you remember who it was that owned the truck?"

"Oh, yeah, I have breakfast with him all the time at the diner. It was

Joe Tripp's truck, from the Granger's place. I guess I remember him passing not only 'cause of the truck, but 'cause it seemed unusual for him to be out so late away from the farm. That guy never seemed the partying type, always stuck close to the farm, ya know? And I thought it was weird to see him out so late on a Friday night."

Tom kept his expression bland as he asked, "You're sure it was Joe Tripp driving, not just his truck with someone else at the wheel?"

"No, sir, I was admiring the truck and definitely noticed it was Joe driving and wondering what an old homebody like him was doing out on the other side of town so late."

Tom made a note on the pad he was carrying as the man continued, "And you know, not long after that he got rid of that truck. Sent it over to some antique car museum in Pennsylvania. I was so disappointed. Man, I wanted that truck."

His wife said, "Oh, will you let it go already, Clyde. You've been talking about that truck for twenty years! It's just a damn truck!"

As the couple began to argue, Tom said, "Thank you both. You've been a big help."

CHAPTER TWENTY

Jack felt his pocket vibrate.

"Hey, Kath."

"So what's going on? You haven't called me for two days, the last time I talked to you the police had just been to the Granger's to question everybody. What's going on?"

Jack was sitting at his kitchen table leaning back on the chair legs and tracing his finger over the yellow pattern on the old Formica tabletop. He told his sister about the results from the blood tests and that Maggie, Griff, Joe and Rolly had to go down to the police station and give handwriting samples.

"Oh, man! I can't believe the police are actually considering those guys as suspects."

"I get the feeling the sheriff doesn't think they had anything to do with Scott Harding's death, or maybe he just hopes like hell they didn't, but he doesn't think he has the whole story either, and the Granger farm was the last place anyone knows he was alive. And you know if any of those guys knew Scott had attacked Maggie..."

"They would have had a motive."

"Yeah."

The phone line was quiet for a moment while Kathy digested this new information and Jack continued to run his finger over the table. He found a deep scratch in the tabletop. He remembered his father putting it there when he was cutting fishing line with his Swiss Army Knife. His mother had given his father hell for that.

"So what happens now? Do they need a lawyer?" Kathy asked.

"I think we'll wait until the sheriff has something conclusive about the handwriting and see what happens next. I do know if there is anymore questioning or testing or whatever, they need to get a lawyer. I thought I might call a friend of mine I went to college with. He's an attorney in D.C., maybe he knows someone around here we can call if we need to."

"We?"

Jack stopped rubbing his finger over the groove. "What?"

"You keep saying 'we' need to do this or 'we' need to do that. What's with the 'we,' Jack? Is that a 'we' like 'Maggie and me,' or just a universal 'we'?"

Jack hesitated before answering and Kathy pounced on the momentary silence. "It *is* a Maggie and me 'we,' isn't it? Did something happen? I'm getting the feeling you are more involved in this than I thought. Is something going on?"

There was part of Jack that actually wanted to confide in his sister, tell her about the feelings he had thought were long dead, or maybe even imagined, that were coming back to him so strongly now. But confiding in someone, even his sister, was unfamiliar to him. It felt unnatural to try to put all he was feeling into words.

So he just said, "I have always cared about Maggie, you know that. We were good friends for a long time, and Griff was close to Mom and Dad. I think I should help them if I can."

"Alright, I buy that, but I still think you feel a lot more for Maggie than friendship and family obligation."

"Maybe," Jack conceded.

"What did you say? I *knew* it! Jack, what's going on? Did something happen with Maggie? Tell me."

Beep.

The next day was Saturday, and Jack realized with a start that his first week back in Lake Meade was almost over. He also realized he hadn't called into work to see if anyone needed him — in fact he hadn't even thought about the office the entire time.

Jack thought to himself, *I have barely been away from that office for more than a day or two at a time in eight years, and now I'm gone a week and don't even think about it once?* He contemplated this development while he pulled on a pair of faded blue jeans and buttoned a flannel shirt.

Jack searched around the kitchen and found a jar of instant coffee in the cabinet and thought longingly of the freshly ground coffee he knew would be brewing at the Granger's. Taking down a mug out of the cabinet, he told himself to stop coveting his neighbor's coffee and put the kettle on to boil. Next, he put two slices of white bread he had bought at the local market in the oven and turned the dial to broil. He hadn't thought to buy butter or jam and he wrinkled his nose at the thought of dry toast for breakfast.

A few minutes later Jack sat down at the table, two slices of toast burnt on one side and completely untouched on the other were laid out on a paper towel in front of him, along with a mug of brownish instant coffee. It took him only another minute to wad the toast up in the paper towel, throw it in the garbage and pour the coffee down the sink.

Grabbing his jacket hanging on a coat rack by the door, he headed down the front porch steps, got to the end of his driveway and contemplated which way to go. He knew he could turn right and walk down the lane towards the diner and get a short stack and hash brown potatoes. His other option was to walk across the lane to the Granger's where he was sure he would also find an excellent breakfast and even better company. He kept walking straight.

Halfway down the Granger's drive, he heard a rustling sound coming from the woods to his left. Caleb was walking towards him with a fishing pole in his hand. The boy's face looked solemn. Jack stopped and waved. Caleb looked up and waved back, his expression didn't change. When he was standing next to him Jack commented, "You were out early fishing."

"Yeah, couldn't sleep."

Jack hadn't dealt much with twelve-year-old boys. His only contact with children was his nieces and nephews, and the oldest was only in second grade, and they mostly talked about Spongebob Squarepants and were happy if he threw them up in the air a few times for a giggle. He wasn't sure what to say next to this sullen pre-teen, so they both walked towards the house not saying much.

"Didn't catch anything, huh?" Jack motioned his head toward the fishing pole Caleb was holding.

"Nah, I have a good spot just past the dock, but nothing was biting this morning. Just my luck I guess."

Jack struggled again for something to say. The boy looked so low Jack figured Maggie must have told him some of what was going on, maybe all of it. He wanted to steer the conversation onto safer ground so he said, "Your Mom and I had a sure fire fishing spot out in the eastern part of the lake. It was out by the Johnson's place, but I don't know if it's still the Johnson's now."

"Yeah, I know where you mean," Caleb said. "The Johnson's don't live there anymore, but that's what Gramps always calls it. Did you guys catch a lot of fish there?"

Jack was happy to be onto a lighter subject he could handle. "Oh, yeah. Your mom actually caught a five-pound bass out there once, I thought we were going to turn the boat over trying to get it in the net."

Jack shook his head at the memory and Caleb gave him a half smile back. "Do you think you could show me where?" he asked.

"Sure. I'll make you a deal, you tell your mother you invited me over for breakfast when you just *happened* to run into me on the lane heading for the diner, and I'll take you out to our favorite fishing spot afterwards."

Caleb laughed then. "OK, it's a deal, even if you were already on your way to the house when I saw you."

"No reason that can't be our little secret, is there?"

The two walked companionably to the back door and into the kitchen. Jack smelled the coffee and saw a platter on the table with three different kinds of quiches laid out on it. Maggie burst through the kitchen door, grabbed the platter and backed out again, disappearing into the dining room. She hadn't even noticed Jack or Caleb standing in the doorway.

Griff and Rolly were sitting at the table sipping coffee. Joe was cutting into another quiche, he looked over at Caleb, who grabbed some plates off the kitchen counter and brought them to him. Griff looked up at Jack and said, "Grab a mug, son, and come sit down for some breakfast."

Maggie walked back in the kitchen wiping her hands on a dish towel and finally saw Jack.

Caleb said to her as if reading from a script, "Oh, yeah. I met Mr. Callahan when I was coming back from fishing. He was heading for the diner, but I told him to come over here for breakfast instead."

"That's fine, Caleb."

Jack noticed the boy didn't respond to his mother. The sullen look was back on his face. He sat down at the far end of the table next to Rolly, not next to Maggie as he had last time Jack had been over for a meal.

"I didn't know you were going fishing this morning," Maggie said to him.

"Just felt like it," Caleb mumbled then took a sip of juice.

Maggie looked vaguely uncomfortable, and Jack thought he had a pretty good idea how her conversation with Caleb had gone the night before. In fact, the whole group seemed quiet and downcast, not the usual boisterous kitchen noises he had come to expect at the Granger's.

When breakfast was over, Jack brought his plate to the sink and rinsed it off, then put it in the commercial-size dishwasher. He heard Caleb say in his mother's general direction, "Mr. Callahan said he would take me out fishing after breakfast, that OK?"

Maggie looked over at her son. "Yes, that would be fine. You can do your chores later, it's a nice day to be outside fishing."

"Why don't you come with us?" Jack asked. "I'm going to try and find our old fishing spot and you might be able to find it better than I can."

"Oh! That would be fun. Can you give me a few minutes to clean up from breakfast?"

Rolly said, "You three go on now, we can handle a few pie pans and some plates, for goodness' sake. Go on and catch us some fish for dinner."

The mood lightened in the bright airy kitchen, only Caleb still looked unhappy. Jack could tell he wasn't thrilled at the prospect of his mother joining them on their fishing trip.

Half an hour later Caleb, Maggie and Jack had gathered their fishing gear and headed to the Granger's dock with a cooler of drinks and sandwiches. Maggie stopped in front of a fifteen-foot metal fishing boat with a small outboard engine. Caleb climbed down into the boat and put his fishing pole in a holder, then turned back to help his mother lower down the cooler.

Jack noticed that even though there was palpable tension between the two, they loaded the boat and cast off without having to say a word to each other. He knew they were going through a rough patch, but they were obviously very connected and he doubted they could stay distant from each other for too long.

He remembered having that kind of relationship with his father and felt a sharp moment of grief for its loss. The feeling was intense, but passed quickly. He was thankful he had been so close to his father. Caleb had never had that, and had just found out he never would.

Maggie pulled at the cord to start the little engine. It turned over easily and she pointed the boat towards the eastern end of the lake. No one spoke for a while as the early spring air rushed over their faces, each one letting the calming breeze blow away their troubled thoughts.

About fifteen minutes later, Maggie slowed the boat and let it drift near a rock jutting out from the shore. "Didn't we usually fish right past that rock?"

Jack looked to where she was pointing. "I think you're right. Isn't there a little shaded area right around the other side?"

Maggie smiled. "Oh, yeah. There it is."

She turned off the engine and let the boat coast to a stop. She and Jack were both remembering all the happy hours they had spent on that patch of water.

Caleb looked from one to the other and rolled his eyes. "Is this it? Is this the *great* fishing spot?"

Maggie turned towards her son. "Yes, this is the *great* fishing spot. I caught a seven-pound bass here once."

Caleb studied at her skeptically, "Mr. Callahan said…"

"Jack," Jack said to the boy.

Caleb continued, "Jack said you caught a *five-pound* bass here once, not seven."

Maggie looked shocked and held her hand up to her heart. "I am sure it was *at least* seven pounds, maybe eight even."

"Oh, Mom, there is no way you caught an eight-pound fish in this lake. I have never caught more than little one or two pounders in here."

"That's because you were never at this particular spot before."

"Yeah, right." Caleb took out some bait from his tackle box and cast his line. Maggie and Jack did the same.

Throughout the morning, Maggie and Jack reminisced about past fishing experiences and Caleb periodically said, "Shh, you're going to scare the fish away!" They'd apologized and talked more softy.

When the sun was high in the sky Maggie said, "Why don't we bring the boat onto shore over there? I don't think the people that bought the Johnson's place will mind if we have a little picnic."

Maggie steered the front of the boat right up onto the muddy shore and the three climbed out. Jack carried the cooler up to the edge of the woods. The spot was cool and shaded by old oak trees that swayed gently in the spring breeze, patches of soft grass and moss wound around them.

All three sat down on a blanket Maggie had brought. She handed around roast beef sandwiches, apples and sodas. They ate in silence, watching the squirrels and chipmunks run up and down the tree branches in a perpetually hurried and busy state that reminded Jack of New York. He wondered what Linda was doing right now at the office. Probably labeling more piles of documents for him to read when he got back. The thought made him feel less than thrilled, so he turned his attention back to the wildlife around him.

After they were done eating Maggie said, "I have to use the little girl's room."

Caleb said, "Aw, Mom, that's gross!"

She tussled his hair as she walked past him into the woods. He pulled his head away and looked out towards the water.

Caleb and Jack sat in silence for a while, then Caleb asked him tentatively, "I heard you and Mom talking about all the stuff you did here when you were kids."

"Yeah?"

"Well, if you had such a great time here, why didn't you come back? Until now I mean."

Putting down the soda he was about to take a drink of, Jack said, "When I was just about sixteen, my father had a heart attack on our front porch here at the lake house." Jack paused; he had never really talked about that day before with anyone. "I guess I decided I didn't like it here anymore after that, and my mother thought it would be too painful to bring me back."

Caleb's eyes got bigger. "Wow, sorry. I didn't know."

Jack said, "That's OK. You can ask me anything."

Caleb looked down at his hands and then back up at Jack. "Were you really sad when your dad died?"

"Oh, yeah. I was pretty upset for along time after he died."

Caleb fiddled with the top of his soda can. "My dad died here too. I just found out yesterday."

Jack said quietly, "I know. I'm sorry."

Caleb looked back at Jack with tortured eyes. "But I don't feel anything! I didn't know him. I don't feel sad or anything. I'm never gonna know him now." Caleb got quiet and rubbed at his eyes with the back of his hand. "I always thought someday I would find him, you know? Mom would tell me when I was older who he was, and then I'd go find him and meet him. Maybe even meet that whole side of my family."

Caleb's face was red and his hands were balled up on his lap. Jack felt his heart constrict for the boy's pain. He put his hand over Caleb's tight little fists and said, "I am so sorry for that, Caleb. I can't imagine what that must be like for you."

Jack wanted to say more, to make everything better, but he knew he couldn't. He rubbed his hand over Caleb's one more time then sat back and rested against a rock. They heard Maggie come back through the woods and say, "Alright guys, lets get back out there and catch us some dinner!"

After another hour on the lake, all three had caught a decent-size fish and Caleb was smiling again. They put the fish in the empty cooler and headed for the Granger's dock.

Caleb and Jack were each carrying one side of the cooler handle. Maggie was walking behind them carrying the fishing poles and blanket. They were each teasing the other about who had caught the biggest fish when they all noticed the police car pulling out of the driveway.

Maggie turned towards the house and saw Griff open the back door.

The look on his face had Maggie dropping everything in her arms as she ran to the screen door. When she got to him, Griff's face was pale and he was leaning heavily on the doorframe. Rolly was hovering behind him trying to pull at his arm, telling him to come back into the kitchen and sit down. Maggie noticed a tremor in the hand that was resting on Griff's arm.

"What is it, Gramps? Rolly, what's the matter?" Maggie asked as she steered the two men back into the kitchen and into two chairs.

Griff was shaking his head and moving his mouth, but seemed to be having trouble gathering his thoughts. Rolly answered for them, "It's Joe. Tom Snyder just came and picked him up in the squad car. He said he's taking him to the station for more questions. The state police detective was here too."

Rolly looked into Maggie's eyes. "Tom looked real serious this time, like he knew something, something bad. What are we going to do, Maggie?"

Maggie looked from Griff to Rolly and back again, then she straightened and said, "OK, the first thing we're going to do is get Gramps upstairs. I am sure his blood pressure is through the roof, and I'm going to ask Doctor Jurvis to stop by on his way home to take a look at him." She turned to Jack to explain. "The Jurvises bought the property next door, the big brick house with the pillars, and he is nice enough to stop by occasionally when one of us is under the weather. He knows trying to get any one of these guys to the doctor's office would take an act of God."

Caleb was standing behind his great grandfather's chair shifting his weight from one foot to the other. His mother looked at him and asked, "Can you help Rolly get Gramps settled upstairs?"

Caleb's eyes were wide and scared, but he answered his mother in a clear voice, "Yes, ma'am." Then he turned to his great grandfather and helped him gently out of his chair.

Griff seemed to finally get some words organized and he asked Maggie, "What are you going to do?"

She took her grandfather's hand. "Don't worry, Gramps. I'm going to go down to the station and see what's going on. If Joe needs a lawyer, we'll get him one. Right now I really need you to go on upstairs and rest, Rolly too, I don't need to have either of you getting sick on me now."

Jack had been standing quietly behind Maggie and now said to the older man, "I can help her find a lawyer if we need to, Griff. Everything's going to be OK."

Griff looked a little relieved, nodded towards Jack and then he and Rolly started shuffling their way towards the back stairs that lead to the family's bedrooms, Caleb right behind them, ready to help if either needed it.

All three looked back at Maggie as she gave them a thumbs-up sign.

"It's going to be fine guys, you just go on up and rest a bit. I'll have Joe home with us in no time."

They all looked heartened and turned to make their way up the steps. When they were out of sight, Maggie's face showed the stress she was feeling as she ran to the phone and dialed the number for Doctor Jurvis's office. "Hello, this is Maggie Granger, the doctor's neighbor. I was wondering if he had a moment, I need to talk to him about my grandfather...thanks."

While Maggie spoke with the doctor and got his assurance he would stop by on his way home, Jack dialed his old college friend's number on his cell phone. He was a corporate attorney in Washington, D.C. and Jack hoped he would have the name of a good criminal defense attorney in the area.

Ten minutes later, Jack had a name and number of a criminal defense attorney in Chestertown written on a piece of paper in his wallet. He hoped to hell he wasn't going to have to use it.

CHAPTER TWENTY-ONE

"Joe," Tom said, "You understand this is part of the official investigation into the death of Scott Harding thirteen years ago?"

Joe nodded. Tom said, "I need you to answer verbally so it can be recorded."

"Yes," the older man replied. He sat ramrod straight in the uncomfortable metal chair across a table from Tom and the detective. A small black tape recorder was running a few feet away from him.

Joe was a man of routine. He rarely went anyplace outside of the farm except for the diner, the hardware store and the church for bingo night. He was not comfortable here in this back room of the police station. In all the years he had lived in Lake Meade, he had only been to the front counter in the police station's lobby to pay a parking ticket. All he wanted to do was go home.

"Joe," Tom said, "I need you to tell me where you were the night of Maggie's prom."

"Told you. Went to bingo then came home. Greg told us Maggie and Scott had a fight and broken up and she was in bed, then I went on to my cabin and went to bed. That's it."

Tom leaned forward in his chair and got closer to Joe. "What if I told you, Joe, that in the course of this investigation we interviewed a lot of people, Scott's friends and neighbors, and during one of those interviews one of the Harding's neighbors says he saw you drive by in your truck about 11:30 that night. What would you say to that, Joe?"

Joe looked down at his weathered hands and grew considerably paler. "I don't know nothing about that."

Tom's voice rose, "Joe, do you understand what I'm saying to you? When I asked one of Scott's neighbors if he remembered anything from that night, he told me that he did notice you drove by in your old green Dodge truck.

"This man had been standing on his front porch taking a smoke and waiting for his only daughter to get home from the prom. He specifically saw you drive by in your old Dodge pickup. He remembered because he had always admired that old truck and what great shape you kept it in. He thought it was unusual to see you out so late in that part of town. He remembered that after all these years, Joe. So what do you say to that?"

Joe shrugged and said, "Must have got it wrong."

"Him or you, Joe? Which one of you is wrong? 'Cause you can't both be right. Either you were home tucked in bed or you were driving past Scott Harding's house at exactly the time the person who murdered him would have been leaving a note for his mother. So which is it, Joe?"

Joe was visibly upset now. Rocking slightly back and forth in his chair, he was rubbing his hands together under the table and looking up at the ceiling, anything to avoid looking at Tom. "Don't remember, it was a long time ago, maybe I did go out for a ride before I went to bed."

"So *now* you might have gone out for a ride?" Tom stood up and leaned over the table until Joe met his eyes. "Tell me what happened that night, Joe. Did you go after Scott Harding when you found out he had raped Maggie?"

Joe visibly winced as Tom said the word "rape." He answered, "No. Just found that out yesterday."

"And what did you do with the truck, Joe? Why'd you get rid of it? Was there blood on it you couldn't get out? Or just bad memories?"

"What? No! It just blew a rod, and I didn't want to replace the whole motor, so I gave it to a antique car and truck museum outside of Pittsburgh that had put an ad in the Lancaster paper about wanting donations, said I could write it off on my taxes."

Tom sat back down in his chair. He was staring intently at the older man and rapping his knuckles rhythmically on the desktop. "Alright, let's leave that for now." Tom shifted in his chair then continued, "Joe, did you do most of the mechanical work on the tractors at the Granger farm."

"Yep."

"Some of those old tractors used big metal gears in the engine works didn't they."

Joe's expression didn't change as he answered, "Yep."

"Did you ever have occasion to take apart some of those tractors, maybe have some of those gears around the barn?"

"Yep, but not anymore. Just have the one tractor for mowing now. It don't have any big metal gears though, it's a new one."

Tom wasn't sure how much more he wanted to reveal, so he looked over at the detective who took over the questioning.

"Mr. Tripp," he said, "it is difficult to determine what the murder weapon was, the bones of Mr. Harding having been in the lake such a long time, but with technology today, a computer can look at the imprint made to his skull and give us some idea of what the object that made the dent in the skull looked like. The lake washed away any trace evidence we might have found, but the indent in Scott's skull was deep. Someone hit him very hard, Joe. Someone that was extremely angry with him, someone strong."

Joe was looking at the detective with an unblinking stare. He didn't know this man, he didn't know what he was talking about, and he wanted to go home.

The detective tried again for a reaction. "We have a good idea what the murder weapon looked like, or at least the part of it that came in contact with Scott Harding's head." He kept his gaze on Joe; Joe continued to stare back at him. "Do you know what the weapon that killed Scott Harding looked like, Mr. Tripp?"

Joe didn't bother to answer so the detective continued, "It looked just like a gear, Joe, just like a big gear that would have been part of the mechanics of a farm tractor." He pulled a white plaster mold out of a box and placed it on the table in front of Joe. It was about five inches across, curved, with three pronounced bumps.

Joe continued to stare at the detective.

The detective's voice raised as his frustration with Joe's non-responsiveness increased. He ticked off his points with his fingers as he said, "Scott Harding was last known to be alive at the Granger farm, he was wrapped in a burlap feed bag, it looks like he was killed with something shaped like a large gear, his body was found in the lake that borders the Granger farm, *and now* we have a witness that puts you near the victim's house around the time he is suspected to have been murdered!"

Joe cocked his head a bit to one side and turned with a questioning look at Tom, who said, "Joe, it doesn't look good. This adds up to all arrows pointing to the Granger farm and specifically you. You were the one that handled the mechanical stuff the most, and you were the one spotted near Scott's house that night."

Tom's gut was doing flip-flops. No matter what the evidence said, it was hard to look at the older man in front of him dressed in a dark brown work shirt, jeans, a Carhartt jacket and mud caked work boots as a murderer. Over the last hour of questioning, he had watched Joe's ruddy complexion turn pale and the creases in his face become more pronounced. Joe Tripp had aged ten years in that little room. Tom knew he was questioning his prime suspect in Scott Harding's murder, but he wasn't happy about it.

"The evidence right now is circumstantial, Joe," Tom said, "but there's a lot of it. We're going to have to bring Griff and Rolly down here for more questioning too. If you weren't tucked into your bed that night, nothing to say those two didn't lie to me either."

Joe shifted in his chair, his brows furrowed. "You don't want to bring Griff or Rolly down here, they're old now, this wouldn't be good for them. Griff has high blood pressure, and Rolly gets light headed now sometimes. He don't want anyone to know, but I know."

"What else do you know?" Tom leaned forward in his chair and picked up the plaster mold. "I don't want to bring anyone else in here either, Joe, but we need to know what happened that night. I know you three stick together, but this is serious. I need you to tell me what happened that night, all of it. What happened when you found out what Scott had done to your girl?"

Joe looked like a caged animal, he wanted out of that room. "I told you already, Tom, over and over again. I don't know why you won't believe me, but that's it. None of us knew nothing about what Scott did to her until Maggie told us just yesterday."

Tom and the detective sat back in their chairs and started consulting their notes, getting ready to try another round of questions when there was pounding on the door. Tom stood up and opened it to find Maggie Granger looking like she was going to spit bullets. "What the hell's going on here, Tom?"

Tom walked Maggie and Jack back to his office, leaving the detective and Joe in the interrogation room. Tom realized he still had the little white mold in his hand from the indent in Scott Harding's skull. He put it down on his desk and turned to face Maggie.

Her face was red with anger. She had only seen Joe for a moment, but he had looked worn and terrified. "What? You can't find Scott's real murderer so you're going to drag an innocent old man from his home to try and brow beat a confession out of him?"

Tom sat down in the creaky leather chair behind his desk and folded his hands together over his ample belly. He motioned Maggie and Jack to sit down too. "Maggie, this is not a witch hunt. So far all the evidence is pointing right to your farm, and this morning I talked to one of Scott's neighbors who remembers seeing Joe that night. Joe lied to me, Maggie, he didn't go right to bed after they got back from bingo."

Jack turned to Tom to ask, "Isn't it unusual that someone would remember after all these years something so trivial as Joe driving by their house? It was thirteen years ago, how could they remember specifically that it was 11:30 at night?"

"It was prom night, and he was standing on his porch having a smoke, checking his watch every five minutes until his only daughter got home from the dance at midnight, and he saw the 1964 mint-condition forest green Dodge truck he had been lusting after for years drive by, and he knew the guy driving it wasn't the type you normally see out late on a Friday night. This surprised him and he took note.

"And for this guy, the neighbor, it wasn't just some random night thirteen years ago. It wasn't even so much that it was his daughter's prom night either. It was the night his neighbor's kid, the star quarterback at the high school, a kid he'd known all his life, up and ran away. This guy remembered that night, all of it."

Jack wasn't sure what else to say. His eyes drifted to the white mold on the table. He asked Tom what it was.

Tom hesitated and then decided he wasn't revealing anything that Joe wasn't going to tell them himself when they released him, and he knew he was probably going to have to release him unless they got some more substantial evidence…or a confession. "That is a mold generated by a fancy computer over in Annapolis at the state police lab. They took a scan of the indentation in Scott Harding's skull and the computer created that model of what the murder weapon most likely looked like, or at least the part of it that came into contact with his head."

Jack stared at it intently, something about it was stirring a memory, but he couldn't quite bring it to the surface. "It kind of looks like a gear, doesn't it?"

"Yes, that's what we're thinking too." Tom looked right at Maggie. "Like a gear on a tractor or piece of farm equipment."

Maggie's head was spinning; she didn't know what to say or do anymore. She felt like she was standing on quicksand, she was out of her depth and she knew it. She said to Tom, "We're going to get Joe a lawyer. I don't want you to question him anymore until we have someone here that knows what they're doing to help us defend him."

"That's for Joe to decide. I haven't placed him under arrest officially yet, but I won't lie to you, the ADA is reviewing the evidence we've got and she may call any minute to say go ahead. We're allowed to keep him for questioning at least twenty-four hours, and that's what we're going to do."

"You're going to keep him here overnight?"

Tom nodded his head. He watched as Maggie tried to process everything he had just told her. She was scared to death for Joe, but she was trying to think clearly and remain calm for his sake.

"Well, I guess there's nothing we can do about that, but I would like to tell Joe we're going to get him a lawyer."

Tom nodded and got up out of his chair and motioned for them to follow him back down the hall to the interrogation room. Tom opened the door and Maggie walked straight to Joe and put her arms around him. The older man stayed stiff in his chair looking blankly back at her.

"Joe? Joe, I want you to know we're going to get you a lawyer now," Maggie said, "I don't think you should answer anymore questions till we get someone here, OK?"

Joe nodded, but didn't say a word.

Maggie tried to look hopeful for him. "Jack has the name of a good defense attorney and we'll get him here right away. Tom says he can keep you here overnight, but don't worry, we'll be back in the morning and we'll get this straightened out. You just keep quiet now. I think we need a professional in here to help us before you say anything else."

Joe just nodded again. Maggie was struck by the irony of her having to tell Joe not to talk.

Maggie didn't let her emotions show until she and Jack drove out of the police station parking lot. "What are we going to do? Did you see Joe? He can't stand being locked in that place one night, what if they arrest him and keep him there until they have a trial? He won't even make it that long let alone…"

She let the sentence go unfinished. Jack concentrated on driving. He knew there was nothing he could really say to ease her mind. She would gather her strength in a minute and be back in fighting mode, then they could talk strategy.

By the time they hit Granger Lane, Maggie had wiped her face and blown her nose and was asking Jack about the attorney in Chestertown. "We're going to get Joe out of that place by tomorrow or I'm going to go there myself with a sledge hammer and break him out!"

Jack smiled. She was back in fighting mode.

They returned to the farm just as the doctor was leaving. He was a neat little man who wore a well-tailored dove-gray suit and red striped tie, but he was quick to smile and had a calming way about him. He and Maggie talked on the front porch steps.

"Doctor Jurvis, thanks so much for stopping by. How are Griff and Rolly?"

Doctor Jurvis pushed his glasses up on his nose and sat down on the step. Maggie sat down next to him. Jack stood a few steps below them looking up.

The doctor said, "Your grandfather's blood pressure is dangerously high. I was worried that he may have suffered a mini-stroke, but after examining him closely, I don't think that's the case. I think he's just flustered over Joe's situation, but if he remains under this kind of stress a stroke is a very likely possibility."

"What can we do?"

"I convinced him to take an anti-anxiety pill, and I have prescribed some medication to help get his blood pressure under control." He handed Maggie a page from his prescription pad. "I'll stop by again on my way home tomorrow and see how he's doing."

Maggie twisted a tissue through her fingers and asked the doctor about Rolly.

"I would actually like to examine him further at my office, maybe run a few tests."

"What do you think is wrong? I have noticed he's been having more than his usual trouble walking lately, and he's been more forgetful than he was. I just put it down to age, do you think there could be something more?"

"I think it's possible he may be suffering from what is called loosely in my business a 'dry brain,' that is, calcification can form at the base of the skull and prevent fluid from circulating properly around the brain. This can cause confusion, tremors and dizziness. It is not uncommon in older people."

Maggie looked worried and asked the doctor, "Is there anything that can be done?"

"Yes, actually. It does involve surgery to remove some of that calcification, but it has become a fairly routine operation and has an excellent recovery rate. And the good news is that patients usually recover a considerable amount of memory and stability that they had assumed was lost forever to the process of aging."

"Oh!" Maggie looked hopefully at the doctor. "Now I just have to convince him to go to your office, which is not going to be easy."

He laughed. "Just tell him you're taking him to bingo night or the fire hall for a pancake breakfast. His eye sight has gotten bad enough he may not notice he's not in the church or fire hall until it's too late."

He and Maggie shook hands, she thanked him again and the doctor drove off in his white Volvo station wagon. Jack sat down in a rocking chair and pulled out his cell phone and the little piece of paper he had written the defense attorney's information on. "I'm going to call this guy and see how quickly he can get over here in the morning," he said.

Maggie kissed him on the cheek. "Thank you. I had better go see what the heck I'm going to serve everyone for dinner." She walked into the house and was met by the smell of spaghetti sauce and garlic. Maggie opened the kitchen door to find Candy bustling around the kitchen.

"Candy? What are you doing?"

The older woman brushed some errant gray and black hair away from her face and tucked it behind her ear. "Oh, Maggie, how is Joe?"

"We're going to get him a lawyer, but they're keeping him at the police station over night. What are you cooking?"

Candy looked toward the two bubbling pots on the stove. "I hope you don't mind, I was finishing up a load of wash when Caleb came into the laundry room and told me about Joe. I got so upset I just had to do something with myself. I figured it was getting close to dinner and you were still at the police station, so I put an Italian dinner together for everyone. Is that OK?"

She looked hopefully at Maggie who walked across the room and put her arms around her. "Candy, you are a life saver, you always have been. What would we do without you?"

She pushed Maggie away and picked up a big wooden spoon. "Stop it now. I just put some sauce on for goodness sake. I know it's not fancy, but I think the guests will enjoy it. Now tell me what's happening with Joe. Why'd they come and take him to the station?"

Maggie walked to the freezer and pulled out two loaves of frozen homemade garlic bread and put them in the oven. "Tom spoke with the Harding's neighbor this morning who says he saw Joe drive by their house that prom night between the time Scott left here and when Cynthia went home to find the note."

Maggie heard a crash and turned to see Candy, eyes wide and mouth open, a broken glass bowl on the floor by her feet. Maggie ran over to her and said, "Are you alright, Candy? Did you hurt yourself?"

The bowl split in half. Maggie gently picked up the jagged pieces and put them sharp side down in the trashcan. She turned back to see Candy fumbling for a seat at the kitchen table. Maggie guided her into a chair and sat down next to her.

Maggie studied Candy's face and asked, "What is it? It's going to be all right you know. I'm sure they can't hold him on a thirteen-year-old memory from the neighbor. I mean, how can he be sure after all these years that it was really Joe he saw and at that specific night and time."

Candy's eyes were starting to brim over with tears. She turned to Maggie and said, "It's all my fault. He's in jail, and it's all my fault."

Candy's hands were shaking. "Hold on, Candy, let me get you a glass of water, then you can tell me what's the matter. I can't see how any of this is your fault."

Maggie got up and took a glass out of the cupboard then went to the sink. As she was filling the glass with water she heard the bang of the screen door and turned just in time to see Candy running down the path toward her car. Maggie stood there looking out the back door, the glass of water still in her hand. She watched gravel fly as Candy spun out of the driveway.

"Well, I'll be damned."

Maggie had barely put the glass down on the counter when Greg came bursting through the door leading from the dining room. "Claire just told me about Joe! What's happening?"

Maggie was still shaking her head over Candy's reaction, but she tried to focus on what Greg was asking her. She told him about the new evidence that had prompted the sheriff to take Joe down to the police station.

"And, you know Joe," Maggie said, "he doesn't like to leave this farm if he doesn't have to, and he really doesn't like being closed in, so he is not doing very well at the moment. Jack is on the phone right now with an attorney from Baltimore. We're going to try and get him out of there first thing in the morning."

Greg gave her a hug and then they both sat down at the table. Maggie poured them some coffee and asked, "I haven't talked to you since Cynthia Harding came by, have I?"

"She came here? What did she want?" Greg blew on the hot coffee and then took a sip, watching Maggie over the top of his mug. He knew anything having to do with Cynthia Harding wasn't going to be good news for the Grangers.

Maggie told Greg about the zoning board meeting and that they could lose their right to have the bed and breakfast. "With everything else going on, I almost forgot about it for a minute."

Greg reached over and took her hand. "Don't worry about that now. Let's focus on Joe first. I really don't think they can retract your variance without your neighbors saying that it is causing them problems having the B&B here. I don't think they would do that."

Maggie let out a deep breath and looked at Greg. He could always make her feel better. In the darkest moments of her life, he had been a steady hand.

Greg smiled back at her. Maggie asked, "What are you grinning at?"

"I just wish I could have been here to watch you two go at it!"

Maggie chuckled. "Oh, you do, do you? Well, it wasn't pretty, but I did get to call her a few nasty things, and I have to say, it felt good." They clinked their mugs together. Then Maggie's brow furrowed as she remembered one of the things Cynthia had said to her during their fight, the memory clicking in. "Oh, my God, Greg. She knows!"

His smile faded at the worried expression on Maggie's face. "She knows what?"

"About you."

"What do you mean?"

Maggie looked to make sure no one else had come into the kitchen and then leaned closer to him. "I just remembered that she called you a 'faggot,' Greg, during our fight. She knows! My God, she could go to the school board or just start rumors or…"

Greg was looking contemplative, but not upset. Maggie said, "Aren't you worried?"

"Not really. I told you before, I think it's time I came out. I don't want to lie by omission anymore. And now that it's not really a secret who Caleb's father was, no need to let people wonder if he might be mine."

Greg leaned back in his chair. "I think this could be a good thing, Mags. I'm going to meet Monday morning with the school superintendent and tell him myself. I'm not going to wait around for Cynthia Harding to decide when she's going to tell them. I'm not giving that bitch that kind of power over my life."

Maggie leaned over and rested her forehead on his. "Thank you for letting people think we were a couple for so long. You have been such a good friend to me."

She sat back in her chair and Greg patted her hand absently. His expression had changed. He looked puzzled. "Wait a minute," he said, "I don't know how or when she figured it out, but if Cynthia knows I'm gay…"

Maggie suddenly understood where his thoughts were going. "Then why would she believe a note that said Scott had found us together having sex?"

"…And that was suppose to be the whole reason he left town."

Maggie tapped her fingers on her chin. "And all the letters Cynthia got," she said, "weren't they suppose to say Scott was staying away because he didn't want to see us together? Wouldn't Cynthia have realized the letters were suspicious long before now if she knew you and I would never have been together, that Scott would never have found us like that?"

"And if she hated me so much, why wouldn't she have spread the juicy bit of gossip around long before now. You know spreading rumors is her favorite thing to do. Unless she didn't want people to know I'm gay, she wanted people to think Scott had found us together that night and run off."

Greg and Maggie stood up from the table at the same time and said, "Oh, my God," simultaneously.

Jack called the defense attorney from his cell phone while sitting in a rocking chair on the front porch of Granger House. Occasionally, a guest walked by but no one lingered. Jack explained to the lawyer everything that had happened in Lake Meade since Scott Harding's remains were found and how Joe Tripp was being detained for questioning.

After listening to Jack's story the attorney said to him, "Well, I think they have enough to hold him for questioning, but it's borderline that they can arrest him. There is only circumstantial evidence, and I can make a pretty convincing argument that a witness's thirteen-year-old memory of someone driving by his house, let alone remembering the exact time he drove by, is pretty flimsy."

"So you'll come tomorrow?"

"I'll see what I can do. I understand you want your friend out of jail immediately, but they are allowed to hold him for seventy-two hours, and there's not much I can do about that. Just tell him not to say *anything* else. I'll get there as soon as I can."

Jack sighed, he had hoped to be able to tell Maggie they would be able to go back to the police station first thing in the morning with an attorney in tow. "How soon do you think you can get here?"

Jack heard the pages flipping on what he assumed was the man's day planner. "I have a Rotary Club meeting tomorrow afternoon…I guess I can miss that." There was more flipping and then, "I could be there by eleven or twelve tomorrow afternoon."

Something in Jack's memory clicked. The Rotary Club. The gear shaped emblem. Jack jumped out of the rocking chair and said, "Oh my God!"

Jack, Greg and Maggie ran into the living room at the same time and almost collided. They all started talking at once. Finally, Maggie whistled and everyone stopped talking. She said, "Wait a minute, what did you say, Jack?"

Excited, Jack repeated, "I just remembered what reminded me of that model the police made of the murder weapon, it was on Cynthia's desk at Harding Prestige Motors. Wait, what did *you* say?"

"Cynthia knows Greg is gay, so she must have known all along that Scott didn't find Greg and I that night having sex. That was the whole premise of why she would believe Scott left town and why he would have stayed away all these years, it doesn't make any sense, unless…"

"Unless she knew he never left town," Jack said.

Maggie sucked in her breath. "Do you really think…Cynthia?"

From behind her she heard, "What about her?"

Maggie turned to see Caleb coming through the door from the kitchen. She changed the subject. "Caleb, honey,were you just with Gramps? How's he doing?"

"He's OK. He says he feels a little better since the doctor gave him something. He and Rolly are going to come down in a minute to help with dinner. Why were you talking about Cynthia Harding?"

Maggie took a step towards her son. She had told herself she was going to treat him more as an adult than a child, but right now her mind was reeling. She knew he was still coming to terms with the idea that Cynthia was his grandmother. How did she say to him now that they suspected she was the one who murdered his father?

She just couldn't figure out the right words at that moment. "Greg, Jack and I have to go back to the police station for a little while. Do you think you could help Gramps and Rolly get dinner out? Candy made a beautiful spaghetti dinner. Everything's all ready."

Caleb looked at her, an unasked question hanging on his lips. He seemed to change his mind about something. "OK," he answered slowly, "I'll make sure dinner gets on the table, but what were you saying about Cynthia Harding? And when is Joe coming home?"

Without a backward glance, Jack and Greg were talking low with their heads together and heading out the door to Jack's car. Maggie gave Caleb a quick kiss on his head and turned to go after them. "I can't talk right now, honey. I promise when I get back I'll tell you more," she yelled over her shoulder as she ran down the steps and slid into the car next to Jack.

As the car sped down the driveway Caleb mumbled to himself, "Fine, if you're not going to tell me anything, I'll just go see my grandmother and ask her myself."

CHAPTER TWENTY-TWO

It took Caleb about thirty minutes to ride his bike from Granger House to Harding Prestige Motors. It was dusk. He had remembered to wear the bright orange jacket his mother had bought him for when he rode his bike in the dark. His hands felt clammy on the handlebars and his heart was beating faster than normal.

What am I going to say to her? Hi, Mrs. Harding...Grandma...your son was my Dad... so what's new? I heard you think my mom or Gramps might have killed your son...my father. That's just crazy, they would never kill anyone.

"Ahh! That sounds so dumb!" Caleb muttered to himself. He shook his head and tried to sort out what he wanted to say and how he wanted to say it. Once he got into town, he stood holding his bike on the sidewalk across from the dealership staring into the plate glass window with the fancy gold lettering that spelled out Harding Prestige Motors.

Trying to calm himself he pulled a stick of gum out of his jacket pocket and slowly chomped on it as he contemplated the sign. Harding Prestige Motors, he thought, *I'm* a Harding.

Startled from his thoughts, he watched as a car pulled out of the dealership's driveway just a few feet from him. Taking a deep breath he walked the bike to the front door and leaned it against the side of the building, he took off his orange jacket and draped it over the bike seat, and then pushed open the door.

There was no one in the large open showroom, but he could see several office doors open. He walked past them until he came to a door with a gold plate that read, "Cynthia Harding, Owner." Caleb could hear a woman talking on the phone. He stuck his head in the office and saw Cynthia twirling a phone cord around her manicured finger and leaning back in her chair. When she turned her head and saw Caleb, she immediately stopped talking and sat upright.

"I'll call you back," she said abruptly into the phone and hung up, turning her full attention to the boy standing awkwardly in front of her. Her elbows rested on her desk, hands entwined.

Caleb summoned his courage, lifted his chin and took a step farther into the office. He stammered a little as he said, "Hello, Mrs. Harding, my name is Caleb Granger."

Cynthia didn't move. There was a stillness about her that made Caleb even more uneasy than he already was. "I know who you are," she said.

"I, um, I just wanted to come here and meet you, I guess." Caleb's voice trailed off. Nothing was going as he had planned it in his mind.

Cynthia's eyes were calculating, wondering what this child wanted with her. She had to assume his mother had told him who his father was and he was here trying to stake his claim as a Harding. He was so young to be that arrogant. But then, he was Maggie's son, she thought.

Cynthia decided to play along and see what Caleb wanted. With a slow smile spreading across her lips she said, "Caleb, why don't you just sit down and we can have some hot chocolate and talk."

Caleb relaxed a little. It must have been his imagination, but he thought at first she had been looking at him funny, like she didn't like him, even though they hadn't even really met yet. His mother's words, "They are not nice people," came back to him. But now she looked OK, he thought. She was smiling at him and searching for a mug for the hot chocolate.

Cynthia found the mug and got up from behind her desk. She said, "I'll be back in a minute, the hot chocolate is in the break room." She winked at him and walked out of the room.

As soon as she was outside of the doorway Cynthia's smile faded, and the hate she felt for Maggie intensified. Here was Maggie's son, a healthy active boy sitting right in her office, while her own son was nothing but a bundle of bones on a morgue slab. Her hand curled tightly around the ceramic mug. She walked into the break room and filled the mug with powdered hot chocolate mix, careful to mix the little extra ingredient in well so he wouldn't taste it.

Meanwhile, Caleb looked around the office at all the pictures of Cynthia with different people, smiling and shaking hands, usually with a car in the background or some kind of trophy or certificate in her hand. Then he noticed the picture sitting on her desk of a young man in a football uniform. He recognized the eyes. They were his eyes.

Cynthia walked back in the room and found Caleb holding the picture of Scott. She wanted to snatch it out of his hand. How dare he touch it? But instead she controlled herself and said in an even tone, "That's my son Scott."

Caleb put the picture back down and took the mug Cynthia held out for him. "Yeah, I guessed that." Caleb wanted to say more, to ask more, but he couldn't seem to make his tongue work.

Cynthia sat back down in her seat across from him. She tried to make herself appear sympathetic to his nervousness. She reached over and patted his hand quickly and said, "You know who he is, don't you?"

Caleb looked down into his mug and nodded.

"And you know we just found out he's dead?"

Caleb nodded again. Not able to make eye contact.

Cynthia continued to hide the repulsion she felt toward this boy who was half her grandson and half of Maggie Granger. He was a bastard and she had never had any intention of recognizing him as any blood of hers, but now here he was, right in her face, looking so much like his father. She had to handle this carefully.

Caleb was absently drawing circles with his finger on the wooden base of an award with a glass gear mounted on it.

Cynthia tried not to visibly cringe as she watched Caleb's fingers rub the polished wood and leave smudgy little marks. She moved the award out of his reach and said in a carefully pleasant voice, "Do you know what this is?"

"Is it a trophy?"

"It's like that. It's called an award. I got it for being an exceptionally active member of our local Rotary Club."

Caleb seemed surprised. "Hey, that's what Jack and Mom were talking about."

Cynthia looked sharply at Caleb, but kept her voice even when she said, "What were they talking about?"

"They said your name, and then Jack said something about the Rotary Club Award." Caleb shifted in his seat some more and continued, "Mom said you think she or Gramps had something to do with my...with your son being killed. You don't really think that, do you?"

Cynthia ignored his question and instead asked in careful and clear tones, "What did Mommy and Jack do after they were talking about me and the Rotary Club Award?"

"They got in the car and drove off in a hurry. I think they were going back to the police station. I'm hoping it was to bring Joe back home."

Ignoring Caleb now, Cynthia began tapping her red fingernails on the desktop. Caleb could sense that he had said something of importance to her. "So you don't really think my mom, or anyone at my house, had anything to do with your son getting murdered, do ya, Mrs. Harding?"

Cynthia returned her full attention to the boy and gave him a toothy grin. "Of course not, Caleb. Now finish all your hot chocolate, and call me...Grandma."

CHAPTER TWENTY-THREE

The door to the police station burst open just as Tom Snyder was about to take Joe back to a holding cell where he would spend the night, a woman's voice demanding to see him "right now!" Before Tom could make his way to the front of the station, Candy Stokes came charging down the hall towards him.

A deputy was jumping along behind her saying, "Mrs. Stokes, you have to wait out here." He saw Tom and said, "I'm sorry, Sheriff, she just came right on through."

Tom nodded. "It's alright, Kyle. I'll take care of it." He turned to Candy, who was clutching her big black leather purse in her callused hands and shifting from foot to foot. Tom motioned her back to his office, but she stopped when they passed the interrogation room door and Candy looked in to see Joe sitting at a table. Candy and Joe's eyes met.

At the sight of her, Joe flew out of his seat, the state police detective sitting across from him jumped up too. "Hold on, Joe."

"Candy," Joe said, "what are you doing here?"

She walked over to him and without warning reached up and pushed him hard square in the chest. So hard he fell backwards into the chair. "You dumb bastard! What the hell do you think you're doing?"

Not expecting this outburst from the usually pleasant mannered cleaning woman, it took Tom a moment to realize what was happening. He took Candy by the arm and guided her to a seat at the other side of the table. The detective and the sheriff looked at each other quickly. They didn't know what her outburst was about, but they both had a feeling they were finally going to find out more about quiet Joe Tripp.

Candy leaned forward and looked straight into Joe's eyes. "Why didn't you just tell them, Joe? It doesn't matter anymore."

Joe looked down at his hands and mumbled, "Matters to me."

Candy reached across the table and put her hand over his. "Joe, whatever we did we will answer for it when our time comes, but this is not about you and me. This is serious, Joe. This is a murder investigation, do you understand? They could send you to trial and...for crying out loud, Joe, they could send you to jail for the rest of your life!"

Joe's head, which had been hanging low over the table, came up to look at her as if he finally understood what was happening to him. "But I didn't do it."

Tears welled up in her eyes and spilled over to run down Candy's round cheeks. "I know that, hon, but we have to make sure Tom here knows it too."

Joe looked tentatively over at Tom, his eyes full of conflict.

Tom decided to address Candy instead of Joe, as she obviously knew something and was willing to talk. "Do you know more about what happened the night Scott Harding was killed, Candy?"

Candy never took her eyes off Joe, tears streaming down her face. She nodded and said in whispered tones, "Yes."

Tom waited.

Finally releasing Joe's hand, Candy opened her oversized purse and searched for a tissue. She wiped the tears away from her eyes, blew her nose, straightened up in her seat and turned to face Tom. "Joe was with me that night. After the bingo game, after he went home and talked to Greg, he didn't go back to his cabin to bed, he came straight to my house. I only live two streets away from the Harding's, that's why their neighbor saw Joe drive by."

Tom looked back at Joe, "Why wouldn't you just tell us that?"

Joe continued to look down at his hands as Candy continued, "Because my husband was still alive then. I was a married woman, and Joe and I were having an affair. Joe was protecting me, he doesn't want anyone to know about that."

Tom shook his head in disbelief. He had known both of these people his whole life. His mother and Candy Stokes had belonged to the same quilting circle for twenty years, and yet, he had had no idea there was anything between Joe and Candy other than a common employer. Tom asked

Joe, "Is this true? Were you driving to Candy's that night when Cynthia's neighbor saw you?"

Joe nodded his head and gave a forlorn look to Candy. He reached out then to reclaim the hand she had been twisting her tissue around in and held it. Candy forced a smile and said, "It's just silly, Joe. Johnny's been gone now for over a year, we don't have to keep pretending."

She turned to address Tom. "My husband and I, well, I think you know, Tom, he was a drinker."

Tom nodded. He had to bring Johnny Stokes in to the station to dry out on several occasions.

Candy said, "For the last half of our marriage there wasn't much between us but a shared address. He dove in the bottle the minute he got home from work, or he'd stop at a bar after work and sometimes not even make it home. And on Friday nights he *always* went out and usually didn't show up again till Saturday afternoon. Joe always came over on Friday nights after he got home from bingo with Griff and Rolly.

"Joe came over that night too, that prom night, and he told me about Greg being at the house and telling them all that Maggie and Scott had broken up. He felt bad because it was supposed to be such a special night for her and it turned out to be such a poor evening."

Tears welled up again in her eyes as she said, "And we really had no idea how bad an evening it was until just the other day." Her voice became a whisper. "I went with Maggie over to Dover Mall to pick out that prom dress, and look what happened in it, just look…" Candy pulled her hand out of Joe's and held the tissue up to her eyes. Joe moved his chair closer to hers, leaned over and put his arm around her.

After a few moments Candy stopped crying and dabbed at her eyes. She smoothed her hair away from her face and patted Joe's arm. "I'm OK now. It's just been one shock after another this week, I'm just a little overwhelmed."

Tom asked Joe, "So is this your official statement? You were with Mrs. Stokes right after you left the farm until…

"Five o'clock in the morning," Candy answered.

Tom looked at Joe who nodded. Tom motioned to the running tape recorder and Joe said out loud, "I was with Candy Stokes from about eleven-thirty Friday night to five o'clock Saturday morning."

"*What?*" They all turned to see Maggie standing in the doorway.

Maggie walked wide-eyed into the little room, followed closely by Jack and Greg. Tom sighed; the room was getting mighty crowded.

"It appears that Mrs. Stokes here is supplying Joe with an alibi for the evening in question," Tom said to the room at large.

Maggie blinked and looked from Candy to Joe. Joe's face had turned scarlet and Candy was trying to hide a smile. Then she gave up, threw her hands in the air and said, "Joe and I have been seeing each other for the better part of fifteen years."

Maggie was speechless. Greg made a whooping sound and Joe, if possible, got even redder.

Tom asked Maggie, "And what are you and your entourage doing back here already? I told you we weren't going to release Joe tonight."

Maggie was having trouble turning her attention from Joe and Candy, who were now openly holding each other's hand. Greg decided to talk first, as part of the explanation was his alone to tell.

"Maggie and I were talking about an argument she had with Cynthia the other day, and in that heated exchange Cynthia revealed that she knew I was gay." Greg paused and looked intently at Tom. Tom didn't register surprise or offer a comment so Greg continued. "We realized that if Cynthia knew that, the whole premise of why Scott left and why he wouldn't come back…"

Tom sat up straighter in his chair. "Doesn't hold water."

Tom took an assessment of all the people crowded in the tiny room. He had lost control of this situation and he had to get some order. "Alright, hold on. You and you," he pointed to Joe and Candy, "will stay here with the detective and finish giving your statements." He turned to Maggie, Greg and Jack. "And you three will come with me into my office and I will listen to what you have to say."

Once they were all crowded in Tom's office, Jack told Tom about the mold of the murder weapon reminding him of the glass gear on Cynthia's award. Tom got out the mold from his filing cabinet and set it on the table, squinting at it and rubbing his chin. The he looked up at his wall where he had his own Rotary Club award with the gear shaped trademark emblem embossed on the front. Tom looked from it to the mold and back again without saying a word. Then Tom got up and left the room. He told everyone to remain in the small room until he returned.

About fifteen minutes later, Tom came back and told them, "The detective and I reviewed all of your statements, and we think there is at least enough suspicion here to warrant looking into Cynthia Harding's movements that night."

Everyone looked hopeful, but Tom held up his hand. "However, neither the detective or myself can see any motive for Mrs. Harding to hurt her own son. And quite frankly, we find it difficult to imagine a woman of her size having had the physical capability of striking a lethal blow to a boy the size of Scott Harding, let alone move him from one location to another."

Jack asked him, "So what are you going to do?"

The sheriff raised his eyebrows at him. "That's not really your concern, Mr. Callahan. What I will tell you is that we are still going to keep Mr. Tripp here as our guest this evening. Hopefully, we'll have some more answers tomorrow, and we'll go from there."

What he didn't tell them was that the state police detective was faxing a copy of the handwritten invoice Cynthia had left for the new police cruiser to the handwriting specialist in Annapolis. They would find out in the morning if Cynthia could have written the notes she had claimed were from Scott.

Jack drove Maggie and Greg back to the farm. They had tried to convince Candy to leave with them, but she had insisted on sitting in the lobby of the police station until Joe was released. She thought it might help Joe get through the night if he knew she was in the building as well. No one spoke in the car on the way back to Granger House.

The three clambered up the back porch steps to find the bed and breakfast winding down for the night. Griff and Rolly were sitting in front of the dying fire in the living room, and a few guests were scattered around reading books or chatting quietly. Greg and Jack both sat down on the sofa with a sigh, while Maggie walked over and sat down on the hearth next to Griff.

Griff put his arm around his granddaughter and kissed the top of her head. "So what's been going on, my dear?"

Maggie looked up at him and assessed his coloring and demeanor. He had his ruddy complexion back, and both he and Rolly seemed much heartier than they had that afternoon. Maggie looked around and thought the other guests were far enough out of ear shot that she could quietly tell them what she, Greg and Jack had all concluded about Cynthia Harding and what they had told Tom Snyder.

Rolly's dark eyebrows rose up on his head. "Cynthia? You think Cynthia killed her own son?"

Maggie nodded and said, "I know it sounds crazy, but the more I think about it the more sense it makes. I mean, I don't know *why* she would have done it, but it would explain why she didn't go and try to find him in all these years. And she did travel at least once a year for business, she could have sent those letters to herself."

Griff poked at the fire some more. "But why do that? She was sending the letters to herself for goodness' sake."

"So she would have an excuse if anyone asked where he was. She could provide some kind of proof to back up her story. And if the worse case scenario happened, like it did, and his body was found, she'd have plausible deniability."

"I don't know," Rolly said, "I can't say I think too much of Cynthia Harding, but to murder your own son? I just can't imagine that."

"Maybe it was an accident," Maggie said.

Griff asked, "What about Joe? Did Tom take anything you told him seriously? Is he going to look into Cynthia as a suspect and let Joe go?"

Maggie shrugged. "He listened to us, but he's still keeping Joe overnight. My guess is we gave him enough to think about so that he'll look closer at Cynthia and where she was that night, but I don't know what he's going to find or if it'll be enough for him to stop investigating Joe."

They sat in silence for a few moments, all thinking their separate thoughts, when Maggie asked, "Did you two know about Joe and Candy?"

"What about them?" Griff asked.

Maggie told them about meeting Candy at the police station and her alibi for Joe. A grin split Rolly's face and he slapped his knee. "That old dog!"

Both Greg and Jack laid their heads against the back of the sofa and closed their eyes. It had been a stressful day and the warmth of the fire and sounds of the room were lulling them to sleep. Maggie looked over at them and smiled, then she turned back to her grandfather and asked, "Is Caleb up in his room? I had to run out before and I was a little short with him, I want to let him know what's going on with Joe. I promised him I would try to treat him a little more grown up than I have been."

Both men looked at each other, their brows wrinkling. "You know," Griff said, "I haven't seen him since dinner. I assumed he went out to practice hitting the ball, but he should have been back by now."

A cold shiver went through Maggie. Her mother's intuition suddenly kicked in and was sending off loud clanging bells in her head. She stood up and hurried into the kitchen then up the backstairs to Caleb's room. He wasn't there. She ran back down the stairs and out the kitchen door. She called his name and ran towards the dock. He wasn't there either. On her way back to the house she ran into the Walters returning from their evening walk.

Mrs. Walters asked, "Did I hear you calling for your son, Maggie?"

"Yes. Yes, I was. Have you seen him?" Maggie said, a moment of relief sweeping through her.

"When we first started our walk we saw him ride his bike down the lane. We thought it was a little odd he would start out so late in the day. We thought maybe he had a friend close by he was going to see. Are you all right, dear? You look pale."

Maggie had gone white and the moment of relief abruptly changed to an icy feeling in her chest. Jack and Greg had come running out of the house when they heard Maggie yelling for Caleb. Jack ran up to her and put his hand on her arm."Is everything all right? We heard you calling for Caleb."

Maggie whispered, "He's gone."

CHAPTER TWENTY-THREE

Greg agreed to stay at Granger House with Griff and Rolly while Maggie and Jack went out to search for Caleb. They jumped into the cab of the truck with "Granger House Bed and Breakfast" painted on the side and tore down the drive.

Maggie was intent on studying the edges of the road as they rode slowly down Granger Lane in the direction of Main Street. They didn't see any signs of Caleb on the lane and decided to turn left onto Main Street and head downtown.

Neither one spoke as they each searched for any sign of Caleb. Maggie asked Jack to pull over in front of the bike shop where Caleb liked to go, but the doors were closed and the lights were off. Then further down the street she saw a few of his friends coming out of the ice cream parlor on the corner. She asked Jack to pull over again. Maggie rolled down her window and asked the boys if they had seen Caleb at all that evening. They all shook their heads. Maggie thanked them, trying to hide her acute disappointment, and Jack pulled away from the curb, continuing their slow drive down the Main Street of Lake Meade.

A few minutes later, they were in front of Harding Prestige Motors and that's when Jack saw it. He turned sharply into the parking lot; Maggie bounced around in her seat and said, "What is it?"

Jack pointed toward the front door and Maggie saw it too, Caleb's bike with his florescent jacket hanging off the seat. She jumped out of the truck and ran over to it. Maggie was sure it was Caleb's bike and jacket. She tried to open the door to the dealership, but it was locked. Jack had gotten out of the truck too, and he and Maggie were looking through the front window for any sign of Caleb, or anyone else, inside. The showroom was dark and deserted.

Maggie started to walk around the building. "Where are you going?" Jack asked.

"To see if Cynthia's car is still here."

Jack followed Maggie around the back of the shop and saw a light on in the service garage at the back of the dealership. She and Jack walked in as Maggie yelled, "Hello! Hey, is anyone here? Caleb?"

A short round balding man wearing grease stained work overalls waddled out from a backroom. "C-c-can I h-h-help you?" he stuttered.

"Have you seen a little boy here? He's twelve, blond hair?"

The man looked curiously at Maggie. He could see she was shaking slightly and her eyes were unusually bright. "A-a-actually, y-y-yes," he answered.

With some relief Jack and Maggie looked quickly at each other and then Maggie turned back to the portly man. She had to stop herself from pouncing on him. Taking a breath she asked, "Is he still here?"

"N-no, ma'am. I s-s-saw him earlier w-w-with Cyn-Cyn-Cyn," he gave up on saying her name, "the b-b-boss lady. She c-c-closed up the front a little early today, and I s-s-saw her walking to her car. She h-h-had a little boy with her. He was kind of leaning on her, looked like he was s-s-sick or something."

Maggie felt her face go numb and before she could ask anything else the man said, "I asked h-h-her if anything w-w-was wrong. Wanted to know if I c-c-could help her at all, but she said n-n-no, that the boy wasn't feeling too well and she was g-g-going to bring him home."

Maggie was having trouble gathering her words, so Jack asked, "Did she say anything else?"

The man just shook his head and looked at Maggie. "Are y-y-you the boy's mother?" he asked.

Maggie nodded, trying to hold back the tears that were burning in her eyes.

"Maybe y-y-you should ch-ch-check at the hospital. She might have tried to g-g-get to you, but if the boy was real s-s-sick, maybe she just decided to get him to a d-d-doctor."

"Maybe," Maggie croaked.

"Did you happen to notice which way Cynthia turned out of the parking lot?" Jack asked.

The man thought for a moment and said, "I think she t-t-turned left out of the parking lot, the way sh-sh-she always does to go home." His face lit up like he had thought of something helpful, "Hey! Maybe she t-t-took him back to her place, why don't you t-t-try there?"

Jack thanked the man and turned to see Maggie was already running back to the truck. Jack got in on the driver's side and asked, "Where to first? Cynthia's?"

"Yes, she turned the opposite direction from our house, so she wasn't bringing Caleb home. I'm going to call Greg and ask him to check with the local hospitals and make sure Caleb's not there."

While Maggie spoke to Greg on the cell phone, she pointed to the two turns they had to make to arrive at Cynthia's house. Maggie clicked off the cell phone just as Jack pulled the truck up in front of an ornate mailbox with the name "Harding" embossed on it in gold lettering. Jack stared up the driveway of the white brick colonial home and searched for Cynthia's car.

"The house looks dark," Maggie said, "and I don't see Cynthia's car, maybe it's in the garage."

Before Jack had turned off the ignition, Maggie jumped out of the truck. Jack followed her up the driveway and peered in the garage window while Maggie cupped her hands over her eyes and stared in a picture window at the front of the house. They both met on the front walk and shook their heads at each other. There was no sign of the car or anyone at home.

Maggie wasn't sure where else to look and was just about to ask Jack for any ideas when two sets of headlights and blaring sirens came barreling up the driveway at them. Maggie and Jack stood frozen to the spot, shielding their eyes from the glare of the lights on top of two police cars.

Grunting a little as he hauled himself out of his squad car, Tom Snyder walked over to Maggie and Jack and asked, "Do you two ever go home? This is the third time I've seen you today. What the hell are you doing now snooping around Cynthia's house?"

Maggie said to him, "Caleb's missing, Tom, and Cynthia has him!"

Tom registered the panic rising in Maggie's voice and that her eyes were darting all around the property, searching for a sign of her son. "Hold on, Maggie, what do you mean 'Cynthia's got him?'"

Maggie told him about finding Caleb's bike at the dealership and what the mechanic had told them. Before Tom could say anything, one of his deputies walked up to him and said, "Nothing seems damaged, Sheriff. I think they just set off one of the outside sensors on the windows."

To the younger man Tom said, "Thanks, Hank, I can handle it from here. Why don't you go back out on patrol? Keep your eyes out for Cynthia

Harding's Cadillac and a little boy, twelve years old and blonde."

The deputy nodded at Tom and got back in his police cruiser. Tom explained to Maggie and Jack that Cynthia's alarm system sends a signal directly to the police station. He had been on his way home when the alarm went off at the station and the dispatcher radioed to let him know. He had detoured to Cynthia's house to assist the deputy in responding to the alarm.

Scratching his chin Tom said, "I'll radio in to have someone back at the station double check all the hospitals and make sure there were no accidents."

Maggie's voice was desperate. "We have to find him, Tom, and we have to find him now. Honestly, I believe Cynthia killed her own son, a son she claimed to love. Now she has *my* son, Tom. If she would murder someone she actually claimed to care about, what the hell would she do to the son of someone she hates?"

Tom said in a soothing voice, "I'm going to put out an APB on Cynthia's car. I'll make sure it goes out for the whole state. We'll find her, Maggie, and we'll find Caleb."

Maggie couldn't hold back the tears any longer, they ran freely down her face. Her mind was racing. Where else could she look? There had to be another place to look. She couldn't just go home, not without Caleb.

Tom said to Jack, "Why don't you take Maggie home and let us handle this. I'll call you as soon as I hear anything." Tom got back into his cruiser and headed towards the police station.

Opening the door of the truck for Maggie, Jack asked her, "So where to now?" Maggie looked at him gratefully. He knew she wasn't going to be able to go home and wait by the phone.

"Let's drive back to the dealership, it's the last place we know Caleb was, it's a starting place anyway."

Jack drove back to Harding Prestige Motors and pulled over on the street opposite the parking lot, the dealership looked empty and foreboding in the dim glow of the streetlights. Maggie stared into the distance in the direction the mechanic told them Cynthia had driven as if waiting for a sign telling her where to go next.

After a few moments, Jack noticed a light go on in Maggie's eyes. "What is it? What did you think of?" he asked.

Maggie motioned to the road ahead of them and said, "If you go that direction for another block and then turn left, there is an access road about a quarter mile down. It's an old dirt road that runs around the lake, mostly fishermen use it, it takes you very close to the spot where they found Scott's body."

Before Maggie had finished her sentence, Jack pulled away from the

166 ~ Heather Mosko

curb and drove in the direction she was pointing.

Jack and Maggie bounced around in the cab of the truck as they bumped along the rutted dirt road that ran parallel to the lake. Maggie said quietly as if to herself, "She wants an eye for an eye, a son for a son."

Jack turned to look at her quickly and then back to the dark dirt road in front of him. "But you didn't kill her son, Maggie. Why would she want to take yours?"

"Because somewhere in her twisted mind, she believes I had something to do with Scott's death. Maybe I didn't kill him. But she believes he's dead because of me."

CHAPTER TWENTY-FOUR

Slowly they drove down the dirt road, Jack trying to avoid hitting any major potholes while helping Maggie scan the woods for any sign of Cynthia or Caleb. They had been on the dirt lane about ten minutes when Jack saw a flash out of the corner of his eye. It was gone so quickly he thought he might have imagined it. He slammed on the brakes and threw the truck in reverse.

Maggie asked, "What is it? Did you see something?"

Jack continued to reverse and watch the direction he had seen the brief flash of light, until he saw it again. He stopped the truck with a jerk and Maggie handed him a flashlight she had taken out of the glove compartment. Jack pointed the light into the woods towards the lake. He saw the flash again. It was the flashlight beam reflecting off a taillight, the taillight of a Cadillac.

"There it is!" Maggie jumped out of the truck and started to run towards the car.

Jack jumped out of the truck and grabbed Maggie's arm. He whispered, "Wait a minute. Hold on. You don't know which way they went or if she's armed. Just stop a minute and let me call Tom and let him know where we are."

Jack tried the phone, but couldn't get a signal. "I can't get a signal way out here. Let's drive back out to the road until we can use the phone and call Tom."

Maggie looked at him like he had lost his mind. "Caleb's probably only a few feet from me with a homicidal maniac and you think I'm going to get in the truck and drive in the opposite direction? Are you crazy?"

By the look on her face, Jack knew it was no use arguing. "OK, why don't you go and call Tom and I'll stay here and see if I can find Caleb."

Maggie didn't change her expression. "Jack, *I* know these woods like they were my backyard, and up until this week, *you* barely stepped off of Manhattan for sixteen years. And you want *me* to go make a phone call while *you* to go off tramping through the woods? I don't think so."

"Then what do you want to do?"

"I think it's obvious. You go back and call Tom, you'll probably get a signal about halfway back to the road, and I'm going to see if I can find Caleb."

"I don't like it."

Maggie gave Jack's arm a reassuring squeeze. "Go on. Get going. You'll be back in ten minutes or so. I'm going to head in that direction." Maggie pointed to the right of the car. "That's towards the Olson's dock."

Maggie started to walk off when Jack grabbed her, pulled her to him and gave her a fierce but brief hug, then he pushed her away and jumped in the truck heading back to the main road.

The flashlight gave her a small beam of light she shined on the path just in front of her, but without the truck's headlights, Maggie couldn't see more than a few feet. The moon was only a sliver, so it wasn't much help. She had a moment of apprehension as she took her first step into the woods. She hadn't been lying to Jack, she did know these woods like the back of her hand, but usually she was walking through them in daylight, and not panic stricken chasing after someone who wanted to harm her son.

As soon as the thought of Caleb entered her mind, all fear was pushed out and she focused on the ball of illumination in front of her. Maggie cleared her mind and let her feet take her in the direction of the Olson's dock. She tried to walk quietly so not to alert Cynthia and hopefully gain some advantage by surprising her.

After she walked for a few minutes the trees began to thin out and Maggie could see the rippling water of the lake in the distance. She stopped for a moment to try and hear something, anything. Then there was a faint scrapping sound. Maggie started to walk faster towards the water and the direction of the noise.

About twenty yards later she saw the dock clearly, and in the faint moonlight, the outline of someone lumbering towards the end of the dock. Maggie quickly turned off the flashlight and crouched down behind a tree.

There's Cynthia, Maggie thought, *but where is Caleb?* Then she realized the dark figure was dragging something, something heavy. Her son.

Maggie tried to control the urge to run screaming at Cynthia. There had to be a way to surprise her without scarring her so much she dropped Caleb over the edge of the thin rickety dock. But Cynthia was already halfway to the end, only twenty feet from the water, there was no way to approach her from the side unless you were actually in the water.

Without making a sound, Maggie took off her shoes and put them on the edge of the lake. Then she unzipped her jeans and laid them next to her shoes. Maggie walked into the water and stifled a scream as the coldness of the lake enveloped her. The water was dark and murky, her feet sunk into the mud on the bottom. Maggie took a deep breath and started to swim under water towards the ladder that hung off the end of the dock.

Maggie had to leave the flashlight with her shoes and jeans at the edge of the lake, so she had difficulty finding the old metal ladder. It took her several tries, but she finally caught hold of it. Maggie lifted herself out of the water as quietly as she could and began to climb up the rusted rungs.

The cold chilling breeze touched her wet skin and Maggie began to shake. She was close enough to Cynthia now that she could clearly hear the scrapping noise as she dragged Caleb across the old wooden surface of the dock. Maggie could even hear Cynthia's labored breath as she stopped and started every few seconds, dragging Caleb closer and closer to the end of the dock where Maggie hung onto the top rung of the rusted metal ladder.

Maggie peaked over the top of the dock and saw Cynthia's back hunched over the limp body of her son. Caleb was lying on some kind of plastic tarp, and Cynthia was pulling on a corner of it to drag him along. It took all of Maggie's will power not to jump up right then and throw herself on her son, but she was heartened by the even rise and fall of Caleb's chest. He was probably drugged, but he wasn't dead.

Watching Cynthia's back and legs as they got closer and closer, Maggie calculated her next move, wanting to spring on Cynthia and grab her son, but knowing she had to wait for just the right moment. Maggie could see the faint light in the distance of the Olson's cabin, but the Olson's were an elderly couple and the dock was too far away from the house for them to hear if she screamed for help. The Olson's had no idea what was happening only a few hundred yards from their back door.

Maggie tried to gauge when Cynthia would be within arm's reach. Even though her hands itched to reach out and grab the woman, she decided to wait until Cynthia's leg was within reach and try to catch her by surprise, grab her ankle, and tip her over into the water. Maggie still had no idea if Cynthia was armed or not, so she didn't want to risk confronting her head-on if she didn't have to. She would get her into the water, grab Caleb, and get the hell out of there.

Cynthia was barely four feet away from Maggie. Maggie braced herself as best she could on the old metal rungs of the ladder and got ready to reach out for Cynthia's bony ankle. Just as Maggie shifted her weight to reach out, there was a loud screeching sound and the metal rung Maggie's right foot was resting on came apart from the ladder. Maggie slipped but caught herself and put her right foot on the next rung up.

Maggie looked up to see Cynthia staring down at her. There was deadness in her eyes that made Maggie's blood run cold. "Well, well, what have we here? I didn't know this lake had slut fish."

Maggie tried to lunge up and grab Cynthia's leg, but Cynthia was too fast. The pointed toe of a black leather boot shot out and caught Maggie square on the chin. Maggie's head snapped back, and she felt a searing pain radiate through her face, but her fingers held on to the ladder as if by a will of their own. Maggie shook her head to try and to shake off the pain, then found her footing and started to climb up the ladder again.

As she reached the top of the rung, again a black leather boot shot out and kicked Maggie on the side of the head. This time Maggie saw stars and both her feet and one hand slipped off the railings, but she still held on to the top rung of the ladder with the other. She wouldn't let Caleb out of her sight. Maggie felt dizzy and there was a sharp pain that had embedded itself in her temple. She saw Cynthia's leg go back, ready to give her another blow to the head, but this time Maggie was ready for her.

Cynthia's leg swung at Maggie's head. Maggie let go of the ladder and grabbed onto Cynthia's boot. She heard Cynthia yell and watched her arms swing around to gain some balance. Cynthia learched forward then threw her weight backwards to correct herself, but moved too quickly and fell down flat on her back onto the dock. Maggie kept hold of Cynthia's leg and used it to climb all the way up onto the dock. Her head was spinning, and she couldn't get her legs steady enough to stand up, so she crouched on all fours and crawled over to Caleb.

Maggie rested her head on Caleb's chest and felt the reassuring warmth of his breath against her face. She was so happy he was alive that she hadn't noticed Cynthia had stood up and was towering over them. Maggie looked up and watched as Cynthia straightened her jacket and brushed off her sleeves.

She looked down at Maggie and a cold smile spread across her lips. "And I thought it was divine providence your son was delivered right to my doorstep tonight, but now I have been smiled on once again. *You* have been delivered to me as well."

Maggie tried to sit up higher, but the pain in her head made her wince and her stomach churn. She looked up at Cynthia. "I know you are one crazy bitch," she said trying to catch her breath, "but if you think I'm going to let you kill my son and then me, you really are nuts."

Cynthia laughed, a rasping unpleasant sound. "Do you think this is all just an accident, Margaret? This is a miracle! A divine intervention!"

Maggie watched in horror as Cynthia's face almost glowed with self-righteousness. "You took my son away from me thirteen years ago, and I have waited patiently, bided my time, because I have faith, Margaret. I may not have my son anymore, but I have a strong faith, and I *knew* that someday you would get yours, and with any luck *I* would get to be the one to give it to you."

Cynthia contemplated Maggie with a puzzled expression. "You don't see it do you? Can't you see the wonderful symmetry of it all? You cost me my son's life, and now here you lie at my feet, both you and *your* son's lives literally laid out before me to seek vengeance on. It's beautiful, really, when you think about it."

Maggie had always known Cynthia was coldhearted, but she had never had any idea the depth of her bitterness had warped her mind so completely. "But, Cynthia, *I* didn't kill your son. I didn't kill Scott. And neither did anyone at the farm."

Cynthia's expression was almost bland. "Oh, you mean the actual blow that killed him, that ended his life?" Her eyes filled with madness and hate as she spat out, "The life that was so full of potential, the life that had a golden future before you came along. Before Maggie Granger came along and fucked it all up!"

Cynthia screamed the last words so loudly Maggie prayed someone might have heard her. She wanted to keep her talking, hopefully keep her yelling to let Jack and Tom know where they were. "Cynthia, *you* killed your son, not me."

"I *had* to! Don't you understand that? You *made* me kill my own child! There are actually people in this town that think you are so nice, so sweet," Cynthia spat out the words, "but I know what you really are, Margaret. I've always known. Can you imagine someone that *forces* another person to kill their own son as being thought of as *nice*? I've had to choke on that for thirteen years!"

Maggie moved her body so that it was over Caleb's, trying to sheild him from the ominous boots that were coming closer every moment that Cynthia ranted. "How did I *make* you murder Scott, Cynthia? I never told you to kill your son."

Cynthia's mouth opened in disbelief, then she said, "My son came home from prom night covered in blood, telling me he had just done something bad, something horrible. I asked him what he had done, and he just kept saying your name. Then he started saying your grandfather's name. I had to slap him so he could get some control, and finally he told me he had attacked you, raped you."

Cynthia took a shuttering breath and Maggie said, "That's something *he* did to *me,* Cynthia. I never did anything to him, or you for that matter, you stupid self-righteous bitch."

Maggie mumbled the last words and was rewarded with another blinding blow to the side of the head. Her head was pounding now, and she could feel the side of her eye swelling shut. She wanted to keep Cynthia ranting as loud as possible until Jack got back. She tried to find her breath to talk more.

"So he admitted to you what he did to me?" she asked.

Cynthia gave short harsh laugh. "He was a baby. He had no idea that you had manipulated him into thinking he raped you. You and I are both women, Maggie. We know how women manipulate men with sex. I have always known you were a little slut, flaunting yourself in front of my boy, making him want you and then teasing him until he couldn't control himself. Then he thought he had done something wrong. He was just being an eighteen-year-old boy with eighteen-year-old boy urges."

"What? I've got a newsflash for you, Cynthia, but most eighteen-year-old boys don't have the urge to rape someone."

Cynthia went on as if she hadn't heard her. "I was so angry, so angry with him for being so fucking stupid to fall into your trap. I knew he had ruined his life. I knew you would tell everyone he had raped you, and he would lose his scholarship to college, lose the respect of the people in the community, and maybe even go to jail, for God's sake. All our plans, all our beautiful plans ruined in one night because of a…a farm girl."

Cynthia paused and stared out into the distance, her mind going back thirteen years. "I was so mad at him that before I even knew what I was doing, I had grabbed the glass Rotary Club award off my desk and hit him on the side of the head with it. I didn't even realize it was in my hand until he fell to the ground and I looked over and saw it there. Saw his blood on it."

"How did you move him, Cynthia? How did you get him to the lake? He was so much bigger than you?"

"We had an ambulance in the garage. I had ordered it for the town's rescue squad, and it was going to be picked up the next day. I took the gurney out, rolled Scott on it, loaded him back in the ambulance and drove to the lake." Cynthia paused for breath, her eyes looking hollow at the memory.

"I drove past your farm first, I wanted to put him in the lake, not far from you. If my son was ever found, I wanted to make sure the police knew where to look. I found those burlap feed bags in your garbage can and used them to wrap him up. I left all the clues the police would need if they ever found my baby, but they still couldn't put it all together. Idiots."

"But if you wanted them to find him, why didn't you report him missing. Why did you send the letters?"

Cynthia looked at Maggie like she was a half-wit. "I didn't *want* them to find him. I said *if* they found him, I wanted them to look at you as the one who murdered him. But it was best if everyone just thought my handsome boy went away. Went to find his fortune, away from this small inane town." Cynthia continued almost wistfully, "That's how I wanted people to think of him, as a young man out conquering the world, just like he would have if he had lived."

Maggie was feeling nauseous from the blows to her head. She rested her forehead on Caleb's arm and tried to concentrate on breathing and trying to keep Cynthia talking instead of kicking. She said, "And you know what, Cynthia? You did it all for nothing, you killed your own son for nothing, because I would have *never* told anyone what happened. I would have never risked Griff, Rolly or Joe going to jail because they hurt or killed your son on my behalf. Scott could have gone on as if nothing had happened."

Maggie felt a sharp pain in her side and realized Cynthia had now moved on to kicking her in the side. The point of her boot had hit squarely on a rib and Maggie felt a "pop." She moved herself farther over onto Caleb, hoping she could keep him from receiving any of the blows.

Cynthia crouched down a few inches from Maggie's face and said, "That *is* ironic, isn't it? But at least I got the satisfaction of watching people whisper and wonder whenever they saw you and Greg together. Some people may think light shines out your ass, Maggie, but no one in this town has ever forgotten you were the girl who cheated on her boyfriend prom night with his best friend and then turned up pregnant and unwed a few months later."

Maggie turned her head to look into Cynthia's eyes. "And you knew all along that Greg was gay? That he and I would never have cheated on Scott."

Cynthia sneered, "Of course I did. Scott told me his junior year that he thought Greg was gay. I don't know how he knew. Maybe because you and Greg had always been so close but never dated, or maybe he just saw him in the locker room after gym staring at the other guys like *normal* men stare at other women. I don't know and couldn't care less. I just knew that if your best friend was a fag, it was more confirmation that you were not the right girl for my Scott.

"Scott needed a good girl, a girl that could stand by him while he ran for elections at the local, and someday, state or national level, someone who could throw dinner parties and mix with the right people. Not a hick that lived with three old men and wouldn't know an elegant dinner party from a hoedown."

Cynthia stood up and loomed over Maggie. Maggie tried to prop herself up on her elbow so she could watch her. "So what are you going to do now, Cynthia? You really think you can kill me and Caleb and no one will know?"

Cynthia laughed again, sounding more maniacal by the minute. "What I think is that I am now going to kick you so hard in the head that you'll black out, and then I will roll you into the water to finish the job. I am then going to roll your son in after you. I have given him enough Valium so he will peacefully sleep through his drowning, something you should thank me for incidentally. Then I'll be off."

"Tom is going to know you did it, Cynthia."

"As soon as I'm done with you I'm going to hop in my Cadillac and head west. I am sick to death of this backwards ass little town anyway. I have plenty of money stashed in bank accounts no one has any idea about, I could be in Mexico in a week and live like a queen the rest of my life."

Cynthia looked at her watch and then back at Maggie. "Well," she said, "time's a wastin', and I've got a margarita and a pool boy named Juan waiting for me south of the border. Finally, I can put you and your son where you belong, at the bottom of this lake, where you made me put my Scott."

Cynthia pulled her leg back and aimed for the side of Maggie's head. When the point of her shoe was only inches from Maggie's temple, Maggie's hand shot out and grabbed the heel of Cynthia's shoe.

Maggie gave the heel of the boot a hard quick jerk up and watched Cynthia lose her footing and tumble backwards. As Cynthia lay stunned on the dock, Maggie crawled over to her. She reached down to get a hold of Cynthia's arms, trying to pin her down on her back, but the older woman was too quick, and she grabbed Maggie's arms at the same time. The two women began struggling, rolling back and forth across the splintering wooden surface of the dock.

Somehow they both struggled to their feet and continued pushing and pulling at each other. Maggie gathered all her strength and gave Cynthia a hard push towards the water. Cynthia flew against the brittle wood of the old dock's railing, it made a loud splintering sound and gave way when Cynthia's weight was thrown against it. She fell head first off the dock into the blackness. There was a splash and then silence.

Maggie turned back to Caleb, crouched down next to him, and rested her head on his chest to check that he was still breathing. After a moment she pushed herself up, steadied herself on piece of railing that was still intact and looked over into the water to see if she could find where Cynthia had fallen.

All at once the little dock started shaking with the sounds of feet running down it. Bright lights from several police cars were shining in Maggie's face. Before she even saw him through the glare from the police spotlights, Maggie was in Jack's arms.

His arms felt good wrapped around her, warm and secure, but all she wanted to do was get Caleb to the hospital. She had no idea how much Valium Cynthia had given him. Tom Snyder and two of his deputies ran up behind Jack. Maggie pushed away from him and grabbed onto the front of Tom's shirt, not caring that she was shaking with cold and spent adrenalin, dripping wet and in nothing but a soaked shirt and her underwear. "Is there an ambulance here?"

"Yes, they're right behind me. Where's Cynthia?"

Maggie gestured to the lake. "We struggled and I pushed her up against the railing, it gave way and she went over the side."

Tom ran over to the edge of the dock where the railing had fallen away and shone a large hand held spotlight into the water. One of his deputies asked, "Should I get some divers in there?"

Tom turned back around and said, "Don't bother, just get a boat out there with a hook to pull her body in. It looks like she fell and hit that rock ledge we found her son's body on. I can see her from here, her eyes are open, and she's not coming up for air."

CHAPTER TWENTY-FIVE

"Get out!" Kathy said.

"I'm telling you the truth," Jack assured his sister. "It all happened last night."

"Is Caleb alright?"

"Yes, he's fine. The doctor said he wasn't given a lethal dose of Valium, but it was a lot for a twelve-year-old boy, so they kept him in for observation last night. He can come home this afternoon. I'm going over to pick Maggie up after I get off the phone with you and we'll go get him."

"And what about Maggie?"

"She's just so happy to have Caleb back in one piece she doesn't even seem to notice she has a black eye, a swollen jaw, and a cracked rib. I had to drag her out of the hospital last night, but I convinced her she wasn't going to be any good to Caleb today if she didn't get some rest, and he's going to need his mom today more than ever."

"And I assume they released Joe?"

"Yeah, they released him this morning. Tom got more confirmation, as if he needed any, that Cynthia was the murderer when the report came back from the handwriting expert that Cynthia was the one who wrote all those letters that were supposedly from Scott."

"Joe must be thrilled to be back at the Granger's."

"Well..."

"What?"

"He didn't go back to Granger house. He went home with Candy."

"Oh!" Kathy exclaimed. "Who knew Joe Tripp was capable of having a hot and heavy affair all these years!"

"Still waters run deep."

"You could apply that saying to yourself you know."

"But I'm not having an affair," Jack said.

"Oh, really? Are you going to tell me you don't feel anything for Maggie?"

"I didn't say that. I said I wasn't having an affair."

"Then what are you having?"

Jack paused and took a deep breath. He was too tired after the last few days to try and play games either with Kathy or himself. "I'm in love, Kath, that's what I am. I have been since I was fifteen years old. I love Maggie Granger and I'm not letting her go again."

Kathy was completely silent for a while and then said, "Holy shit. I've been waiting for you to say those words for so long, and now that you have, I've got nothing to say."

Jack was quiet too. He had a lot to think about. "I'll see you, Kath."

"See you soon, Jack, and good luck."

"Thanks."

CHAPTER TWENTY-SIX

Jack, Maggie and Caleb stood on the dock at Jack's cottage staring at his old rowboat.

Maggie said to Caleb, "You've only been home from the hospital for three days, Caleb, I don't think you should be doing so much."

"Aw, Mom! You promised me you weren't going to treat me like a baby anymore."

"I'm not treating you like a baby, you were in the hospital." Maggie turned to Jack for support.

He gave her a half smile and held his hand up with his thumb and pointer finger close together. "Maybe just a little bit," he said.

Maggie punched him in the arm and Caleb said, "See. I told you."

Jack rubbed his arm. "The doctor did say he was fine and he could go back to normal activities today."

"But..." Maggie looked from Caleb to Jack and back again. "But... "

"Face it, Mom, I'm fine and you have no reason why I can't take Jack's rowboat out on the lake."

"All by yourself?"

Caleb scowled at her. "Jack told me he got this boat for his birthday, his *eleventh* birthday, and I'm twelve! Plus, I won't be alone for long. I'm going to row over to Eli's and we're going fishing."

Maggie looked at her handsome son and knew he was right; she had no rational reason why he couldn't go out in the boat and enjoy the day fishing with his friend. Unfortunately, since the night Cynthia had taken him, Maggie couldn't stand for Caleb to be out of her sight. But, she took a deep breath and shoved her overprotective instincts aside. "OK. You've got me. Go have fun with Eli, but be home by 4:00, and keep your cell phone on so I can check in on you."

Caleb practically jumped off the dock into the water he was so excited. "Thanks, Mom! I'm going to take him to that fishing spot you guys showed me, maybe I'll bring home a seven pounder too!"

Maggie couldn't help but give him one last hug before he left. As she put her arms around him, she said, "And it was at *least* eight pounds."

Jack got out his digital camera he had bought for the trip and forgotten to use until then. "Hold it! Just stay like that, guys. Awesome."

After Jack had taken the picture, Caleb squirmed out of his mother's embrace and climbed down the ladder into the little rowboat. He looked at it and said, "Jack, I think we need to paint this boat. It's pink."

"It's red. Just a little faded that's all. You can help me paint it. Maybe we'll paint a name on it too, how about 'The Maggie.'" And he reached out and pulled Maggie to him and gave her a smacking kiss on her lips.

Caleb looked appalled. "Gross!" he said and started rowing out into the lake.

Maggie and Jack stood at the end of the dock watching him until he was out of sight. Maggie sighed and Jack rubbed her shoulders. "He'll be fine you know. We used to row out to that spot all the time when we were his age."

"I know, but ever since Cynthia…"

Turning her towards the house, Jack said, "It's all over. All of it. He was unconcious through the whole thing, he doesn't even remember what happened. Now there're no more secrets, no more skeletons hiding in the closet." Jack winced at his choice of words. "So to speak."

He and Maggie walked up the porch steps into the house. Jack started to walk towards the kitchen and asked Maggie, "Do you want some tea?"

Maggie was standing on the stair landing and answered, "Maybe later." Her eyes were still puffy and tinged with purple bruising where Cynthia had kicked her in the face, but still she waggled her eyebrows at Jack seductively, pointed to him then herself and then to the bedroom upstairs.

Jack stood at the bottom of the stairs looking up at her, a goofy grin spreading across his face. "Really?"

"Come on, Callahan," Maggie said as she continued to walk upstairs. "Why don't you come up here and show me what I've been missing all these years."

She laughed as Jack chased her into the bedroom that had once been his parents, caught her around the waist and swung her in a circle. He set her on her feet and turned her to him, cupping her face in his hands and gently leaning in to kiss her.

She responded to his touch instictively, opening her mouth and letting his tongue explore her. She moaned as he released her mouth and began kissing her neck as he unbuttoned her blouse. She reached behind his back, grabbed hold of his shirt and pulled it over his head. They both fell back on the bed, half laughing and half frantic to get the rest of their clothes off.

Goose bumps came out on every surface of skin Jack ran his hand over, his mouth tasting the sweet flesh that vibrated under his touch. Their love making was like an ancient dance, rolling on top of each other, sweaty and full of joy. They didn't take their eyes or hands off one another until they were too spent to move.

Watching the sun grow lower in the sky through the billowing sheer curtains of the bedroom window, Maggie lay in Jack's arms, sated and content. She felt as if all her muscles had turned to jelly and her bones were nothing but rubber. Jack's eyes were closed and he was running his fingers gently up and down her arm.

He opened his eyes and turned to her, about to ask if she were alright, when he saw a cat-like smile spread across her lips. He had his answer.

A crease formed in her brow as she asked, "You have to leave tomorrow, don't you?"

Jack kept stroking her arm and looking into her eyes. "Just until Friday, I'll drive down right after work." Jack shifted so he was up on one elbow looking down at Maggie. He loved the way her hair fanned out around her, framing her face in strawberry blond curls.

"Get ready because I'm going to `court' you, Margaret Granger," he said.

"Court me?"

Jack brushed some hair away from her forehead and his expression turned serious. "I want to see you, date you, court you, whatever, as much as I can, but I can't just walk away from my job, I made a commitment. I have an apartment, I have..."

"Shhh." Maggie held up her finger to his lips. "You don't have to make excuses to me. We haven't seen each other in sixteen years, Jack, I didn't expect you to just drop your life and stay here with me, with us, after just two weeks." She traced her finger over his mouth and down his chin.

"Just tell me you'll be back, tell me this can be the beginning of something for us."

"I'm not sure if this is the beginning or just the continuation for us, but I can guarantee you one thing, it's not the end. I'm in love with you, Maggie, and I may not know exactly what's going to happen next, but I know whatever it is, I want you and Caleb to be part of my life, my future."

Her eyes sparkled. "Who knew you'd grow up to be such a sweet talker, Callahan."

They both laughed and Jack bent down to kiss her. The kiss deepened, and Jack rolled Maggie on top of him. They kissed until they were breathless, both struggling to move the tangled sheets out of their way.

CHAPTER TWENTY-SEVEN

Sunday night and Jack had hated saying good-bye to Maggie. They had stood on his front porch for a long time, holding hands and watching the sun set over the lake. He had left after dinner, waiting as long as he could before starting on the drive back to New York.

After two weeks in the small Maryland town, never seeing more than a half dozen cars at any given time on the street, Jack found it difficult to get used to the traffic on the city streets again. He counted the blocks to the parking garage where he kept his Audi convertible.

You'd think I'd been gone a year. Suck it up, Callahan, you've lived here for nine years. Two weeks in the country can't make you that soft.

When Jack finally opened the door to his apartment, there was a faint stale smell of a space that had not been lived in for awhile. The message light was blinking on his answering machine, but he didn't feel like checking his messages at the moment. Instead, he picked up the phone and called Maggie to say goodnight.

The next morning Jack went through his routine halfheartedly, going to the gym and then to the office by 7:30. He wondered if Maggie and Joe were at the diner having pancakes and sausage while he drank his mocha latte from Starbucks.

"Good morning." Linda greeted him with a smile and followed him into his office. "Did you have a good time in Maryland?"

Jack put his briefcase down on the desk and looked over at his assistant. She was the first person he had been genuinely happy to see since he got back. "Yes, I did." Jack gave her a cockeyed grin. "It was different than I expected, but turned out to be very good."

Linda looked at him appraisingly. There was something about him, something...happier. She pointed at him and said, "Oh my God, you met someone! You met someone while you were away." She leered at him knowingly. "Jack Callahan, the first time you leave this office in eight years and you go and fall in love."

Jack grinned back at her. "Go figure."

The day progressed as usual. Linda left several stacks of legal documents and contracts for Jack to review, all with little yellow sticky notes giving him further directions to sign, initial or change.

At lunchtime Jack brought a sandwich back to his desk from the office cafeteria. He sat down in front of his computer and tried to figure out how to download the pictures from his digital camera. While the camera was loading the pictures onto his computer, Jack flipped through an architectural magazine that had come while he was away. He read an article on new environmentally friendly building materials being used to construct homes, then another on an office building in Virginia that had been converted from an old sewing factory and another on innovative ways for new residential developments that used common green space.

As Jack read the articles, a familiar excitement stirred in him. The same feeling he had when he was in college studying architecture, dreaming of the homes and buildings he would create. He looked over at the pile of neat white pages stacked on his desk and sighed. He had almost forgotten how much he loved creating instead of managing.

There was a beep on Jack's computer, and he turned to find a message telling him all the pictures had been successfully downloaded from his camera. He clicked on the "start slide show" button, and the picture he had taken of Maggie and Caleb that day by the lake filled his screen. He stared at the picture for a long time.

That evening Maggie was standing on her front porch talking to Doctor Jurvis. He had stopped by on his way home from his office to check on Griff and Rolly.

"Your grandfather's blood pressure is back to normal, and I don't see any need for further medication."

"Great. And did you talk to Rolly about coming in for those tests?"

With a grin the doctor said, "Yes I did, and I tell you what, the man surprised me. I explained what I thought the problem was and that I'd like to find out if we could help him with the operation I told you about. I thought for sure he would tell me to go scratch."

"He didn't?" Maggie asked.

"No. In fact he said he'd be in first thing tomorrow. He told me if I knew something that could make him feel younger, he was all for it, and an operation 'sure as hell', I'm quoting now, mind you, 'didn't scare him none.'"

Maggie laughed and said, "Thank you so much. I can't tell you how much I appreciate you stopping in like this."

The doctor waved his hand at her and started down the stairs. "Nonsense, that's what neighbors are for. How many times has Joe plowed us out in the winter, and how many dinners did you bring over when my wife was ill last year?"

Maggie's smile faded, "I hope after the town meeting on the fifteenth we'll still be neighbors."

The doctor stopped at the bottom step and looked back up at Maggie. "You mean the zoning thing, about the bed and breakfast's variance being reviewed?"

"Yes," Maggie answered, her anxiety over the upcoming meeting showing in her voice.

"Oh, don't worry about that, Maggie, all the neighbors got a notice and everyone I talked to is going to vote that the variance stand. The bed and breakfast doesn't bother anyone here on Granger Lane, and it's good for the town. The antique shops, the diner, even the gas station would sure hate to lose your customers. Your business is an important part of keeping this town viable, no one wants to lose that."

Maggie couldn't believe what she was hearing. She had tried not to dwell on it, but the upcoming meeting had been weighing heavy on her mind. Now she felt as if a great burden was sliding off her shoulders. "You mean you're going to vote that we can keep the bed and breakfast?"

"Me and everyone else on the street." Without another word he gave her a wave and got in his car. Maggie felt so light she wanted to float right off the porch. Before she could turn and run into the house to tell everyone the good news, she saw a Jeep Cherokee pull in the space the doctor's car had just pulled out of.

"Who's this now?" Maggie said to herself.

The door opened and Jack stepped out of the car. He grinned up at Maggie's stunned expression and made a sweeping gesture to the car. "I thought I'd need something more rugged than the convertible if I was going to live out here in the country."

Maggie's hand flew to her mouth.

Jack walked around the car to the bottom of the porch. "I thought Lake Meade was in need of a local architect. You know, a nice little office in town, Callahan and Associates, although I don't have any associates yet, but I'm a pretty smart guy. I bet in no time I'll have..."

While Jack was talking, Maggie ran down the stairs, jumped into his arms, and was covering his face with kisses.

Griff, Rolly, Joe and Caleb walked out on the porch and stared down at the two. Griff and Rolly started laughing, Caleb looked surprised and then a grin bloomed on his face, while Joe said quietly, "'Bout time."

About the Author

Heather Mosko grew up in New Jersey and has a degree in Communications/Journalism from Shippensburg University. She lives with her husband, two sons and a crazy black lab named Buddy in southeast Pennsylvania where she is hard at work on her next mystery-romance. *Lake Meade* is her first novel.

Printed in the United States
204804BV00003B/28-39/P

9 781892 343314